FREE STORMS INVASION!

The earth was burning. Black smoke poured out of a hole in the ground, defying a heavy rain. Out of the smoke climbed a woman, her clothes and long black hair smoking. She stumbled, got to her feet, and began to flee. From behind her came a snarl of full-automatic gunfire. The woman pitched forward into the lush prairie grass, unmoving.

It was a bad omen for the brothers and sisters of the High Free Life.

A platoon of Mobile Forces troopers dismounted from their canvasback trucks and began to advance in a slow line, M52 storm carbines at the ready, faces depersonalized behind black shades. The rest of the company was deployed along a line four hundred meters to the west, supported by four Marauder armored cars armed with automatic 20-mm cannon. Another figure burst out of the blazing underground dwelling, a man on fire. He dropped to the wet ground, moaning, trying to roll the flames out. One of the semi-faceless troopers briefly straightened to fire a single shot into the back of the moaning man's neck. The troops marched on . . .

STORM RIDER

LORD OF
THE PLAINS

ROBERT BARON

JOVE BOOKS, NEW YORK

The section titles for this book are songs from Cinderella's Long Cold Winter album, all well-beloved of the High Free Folk.
This song's for
Tracy & Scott
'n'
Pat & Scott
righteous bros and sisters all,
Thanks for yer support
Ride free!
—RB

STORMRIDER 3: LORD OF THE PLAINS

A Jove Book / published by arrangement with the author

PRINTING HISTORY
Jove edition / May 1993

ISBN: 0-515-11101-5

Jove Books are published by The Berkley Publishing Group, 200 Madison Avenue, New York, New York 10016. The name "JOVE" and the "J" logo are trademarks belonging to Jove Publications, Inc.

PRINTED IN THE UNITED STATES OF AMERICA

10 9 8 7 6 5 4 3 2 1

PART ONE

BAD SEAMSTRESS BLUES

1

The night was black as a City lawman's soul. Though it was summer, the wind that blew through the Flint Hills, bearing occasional raindrops that stung like thrown pebbles, was bone-chill. The three nomads huddled close around their little gasoline-primed driftwood fire, clutching mugs of coffee spiked with Taos Lightning to fight the cold. Two of them wore colors bearing the legend CHOSEN FEW on the backs of their leather jackets, and had the clan's characteristic silver chains hung round their shoulders and the insteps of their boots. The third, a small, nervous man with thin hair and protruding eyes, sported no colors at all. He sat apart from the rest.

A fourth man, tall and spare with a long face shaved clean—unusual for a motorcycle nomad of the Plains—and a bandanna wrapped round his skull, swaggered back from the little sad pile of firewood heaped by the parked bikes, holding a forked gray branch before him like dung-beetle antennas, prodding at the air.

"I wonder if the Catheads've finished wiping John Hammerhand's sorry ass for him," he said. "Damn atmospherics don't let us hear nothin'."

He tittered and poked the leather-covered arm of the bearded, acne-scarred man who sat staring moodily into the fire.

"Jesus fucking Christ!" The pit-faced man jumped and twisted around on his haunches. He held a Shawk & McLanahan double-action revolver with a bore you could stick your arm down.

"Ozone, you silly son of a bitch," he raved, "you stick me in the other arm with that motherfucker, you'll have a third asshole

3

smack between the one under your nose and the one behind your pencil dick!"

Ozone only laughed. It was his solution to most stressful situations. The other ones he usually solved with violence. Of course, he laughed even louder then.

"Don't get your underwear all bunched, Ernie," he said, "I'm just funnin'." He tossed his forked branch, shot through with holes from long immersion in water, onto the fire. Sparks flew up and vanished.

Ernie made a rumbling sound in his throat. He glared at Ozone a moment longer under bushy brows, then put the big .60-caliber Shocker back in its shoulder holster. Unconsciously he reached to gently feel his left biceps, which was wrapped in a bulky bandage.

"I'm just gettin' bored," Ozone said, hunkering down on the fire's far side from Ernie. "When can we get our money for wastin' that pukebag Burningskull?"

Ernie pressed fleshy lips to an invisible line beneath his mustache. The man they had risked their asses tracking into the Shaking Lands to grease had not gone down easy, even outnumbered five to one. He had punctured Ernie's arm for him, and laid their brother Aardvark in the dirt to stay.

"I'm about done telling you," he said. "We been out a moon since we did the dirty. Got two more weeks for things to settle down, then we meet the man on the Neosho for what you call the final installment."

The man who wore no colors was squatting with his arms around his knees. His pop eyes reflected the firelight dance. "If we live to get our money."

The third Chosen Few rider was a mass of hair and scar tissue. He slapped the pop-eyed man on the arm. "What you 'fraid of, bro?" he asked in a high voice. "Burningskull's ghost?"

"He had friends."

"He had enemies too," Ernie said. "And right now they got one thing in common. They're either dead, wishing they were, or digging holes in the dirt and tryin' to pull it in on top of them. No way they're gonna stop the Catheads hanging 'em all on a wire."

The crazy-man grin slipped off Ozone's face. "What're *we* gonna do about the Cats, Ernie? Huh? Huh?"

Ernie took a deep breath and sighed it all out. "Stay out of their way. Or, who knows . . ." He shrugged. "Maybeso we should make palaver with them. We done 'em a pretty good turn, laying out their blood enemy and the man who was prophesied to put 'em all down for good. Ain't that so, Judas Junior?"

The last was addressed to the man with no colors. He pulled his head farther into his collar and said nothing.

"You used to be a Cat," Ernie said nastily, "till you turned your coat on them. Then you got to be a pal of Burningskull, and look where that got *him*. You got no little notions of turning *us* over now, do you?"

The bulge-eyed man shook his head. He wouldn't meet Ernie's gaze.

"That's good," the Chosen Few leader said. "Real good. You cross us, you cross damnation."

The hairy one stood up. "What's in your pants, Mad Dog?" Ernie demanded. "You're fucking with my serenity. Settle down."

"I heard something," Mad Dog said.

"Just the damned wind. You assholes are getting on my nerves—"

A roar broke the night in pieces. A hurtling mass of golden gleaming metal followed it, out of the night and into the light. Mad Dog had time to reach for his piece and scream. Then the big outlaw bike reared up in a wheelie, tore his face off the front of his skull with its spinning front tire, and smashed him into the campfire with all its seven hundred pounds of weight.

For a moment the intruder poised there, a terrible black figure wreathed in smoke and frenzied flames. Ozone stood gaping. Two shots cracked and he fell, gagging and choking as his lungs filled with blood from the holes through his chest.

The motorcycle's engine bellowed. The bike blasted forward, casting a wake of sparks and burning brands into the face of the night. Ernie said, "Fuck!" and hauled his Shocker from its holster.

The figure fired again, across its body. The bullet smashed the joint of Ernie's shoulder and sent chunks of meat and cartilage and bone spraying out through the seam of the jacket. Ernie dropped the huge-bored handgun and ran for his life.

Through all this the man without colors continued to sit and hug his knees. His eyes were huge and resigned. The figure on the golden bike paused, shot him through the right shin, and howled on in pursuit of Ernie.

The Chosen Few leader was staggering and weeping along the

flank of the hill they'd used to shield their campfire from passing eyes. The pain was terrible, much worse than the pain from the wound their prey had given him in the Shaking Hills. That had been a clean wound, passing quickly through meat without touching the bone. This wound was nasty, the sort that could cripple a man up for good even if he got to care.

The tingle along the underside of Ernie's nut-sac told him he wasn't going to be getting much quality medical help way out here. That was worse than the pain: the grim certainty of being fucked. He heard the engine sound at his back, dying away to a husky growl. Death was choosing to overtake him slow.

Whoever it was had to have pushed the big sled a good quarter mile to prevent their hearing its engine. Even with the wind. Ernie would not try to bargain and plead with such a creature. He would save his strength for one last trick . . .

A mechanical snarl as a throttle was pumped, right behind him. He spun and dropped to his knees, both hands hanging by his boots in the wet grass.

"Who are you?" he screamed. *"What do you want?"*

"I'm the man you thought you killed," the rider said. "I want to teach you a little lesson about being sloppy."

Ernie felt his mouth fill with sour vomit. "Burningskull?" Puke and the name slopped out over his scarred underlip simultaneously.

"Yes."

The word hit Ernie like a bullet. He could make out the rider now, dimly through the blackness. Tall, lean as a strop, black hair cut short on top and flowing long over the shoulders in back, bandit mustache over a wide and wicked white grin. Impossibly, it was the man he had murdered.

It was Tristan Burningskull.

"But you can call me Death," the apparition added.

The hole Burningskull's bullet had punched in Ernie's left biceps had had a month to heal. It still hurt like the devil, but the arm was usable. His left hand hiked up the grease-soaked leg of his jeans, snatched a tiny auto-pistol from the top of his boot, and whipped it up in front of his face.

"Die, damn you! *Die!*" he screamed.

His answer was a savage ripping stutter of light and noise. He felt the spray of full-auto fire hit him like the fierce-driven Plains hail. Oddly, it didn't hurt, didn't even sting.

He tried to hold the little pistol on-line, take this bastard to

Hell with him—if even Hell would hold him. But the weapon was too heavy, it weighed more than the world. Gravity bore it inexorably down. He squeezed the trigger once, twice, three times. The shots came like firecrackers at a midsummer shivaree, faint with distance.

Ernie fell. He never felt himself hit the ground.

Tristan, last of the Hardriders, first of the Burningskulls, sat forking the legendary sled WildFyre with his Bolo in his hand. Deliberately he popped the mostly spent magazine from the well into the palm of his gloved left hand, slipped it into a pocket of his vest, replaced it with a fresh box.

"Good move, Ernie," he murmured to the body cooling quickly in the wind. "You saved yourself a world of hurt." He had also saved Tristan a dilemma, sprung him from between the horns of his burning desire for revenge and his own personal abhorrence of torture.

He holstered his Bolo and turned his ride around. It was time to confront a much stronger temptation to compromise.

The colorless man was lying on his side beside a fire that had mostly guttered out beneath the bulk of the late Mad Dog, who was starting to stink from all that smoldering hair. He clutched his ruined leg, weeping like a baby. His eyes were popped more than usual.

Ignoring him, Tristan dropped WildFyre's stand and dismounted to rummage among the sewn-hide possibles bags stowed by the fire. His own panniers were there, and his trusty Saskatoon Scout carbine with the ultra-fast Enfield bolt-action, the excellent swept-hilt broadsword he'd bought on the road to the war with the Cats, and most important . . .

"There you are, little fellow." He scooped up the stuffed toy shaped like a miniature grizzly, brushed grit from its soft brown fur, and held it briefly to his cheek. He felt complete again. The grizz had been his saddlemate longer than anybody.

"People will just have to learn," he murmured, stuffing the bear in his panniers. "You mess with the bear, you die."

He hung the bags over WildFyre's rear fender. Then he turned to the injured man. He had left him alive for a purpose.

"Well, Pud, old man," he said. He hunkered down next to the sobbing man, grabbed a handful of pale hair, and hauled his head up. "It's time you and me had a little talk."

"T-Tristan," Pud squeezed through pain-clenched teeth. "I . . . had to go with them. They would've waxed you . . . sure if I didn't."

"You led the pack on my trail. You did your damnedest to gun me down yourself."

Pud shook his head, endangering the roots of his already sparse hair. "No. Th-*think*. They knew the same songs you did; they'da tracked you anyway."

Tristan's lips compressed beneath his mustache. That was a true saying, no question. He let go of Pud's hair.

"All right, you've earned yourself some air time," he said. "Use it well."

Pud nodded, fresh tears of gratitude flowing in the tracks of the tears of pain. "What—what happened when Ernie drew down on you?"

"He busted my rib cage with that damned Shocker."

"No . . . after. You dropped the fat boy, Aardvark. But the others had you . . . dead to rights. I jumped in the way."

"Then you cut loose on me with that damned Dallas Micro."

"Missed . . . didn't I?"

Tristan made a face. It wasn't merely possible to miss with a spray from a machine pistol at just past sword range, it was all too easy. He'd seen it happen before. Still he felt little mice of doubt beginning to gnaw away at his angry certainty.

"Who kept getting in their way?" Pud asked, voice growing stronger as he focused more on the urgent need to persuade his nemesis and less on the pain. "Who stuck his fingers in the bullet hole in Ernie's arm? Who kept remindin' 'em they was right in the kobolds' backyard, an' if they fucked around too much they'd find themselves gittin' barbecued slow, without sauce?"

Tristan gazed down on him. He sighed, then straightened.

For four weeks the need for retribution had burned like a red ember in his gut. There were times when he was less aware of it—dodging the six-inch teeth in the jaws of a cloned *Tyrannosaurus rex* in the caverns beneath the Shaking Lands, getting made into a Tristan sandwich by the gorgeous eight-foot-tall Power-Lifting Daughters of the Kobold King—but it was always there, always griping him like a canker on the lip.

But his Jones for justice was greater than his need for revenge. He had known too much injustice in his life to be able to bear the thought of dishing it out himself. Pud's story rang true, too true.

Still, there was one barrier to buying it all with pretty paper and string.

"How do you expect me to believe you, Pud," he asked softly, "when you're riding a hit trail for your old pals the Catheads? You never really came over, did you? It was all a setup."

Pud was shaking his head in denial. "No . . . no. You gotta . . . believe me. It was never the Cats took out the contract on you."

"Bullshit." Then: "Who?"

"It was . . . the Brit. Redcoat captain from the Honourable Company. Al-Allanby."

"What?" It was so wildly improbable Tristan had trouble buying it as a lie. Surely a man pleading for his life would make up better. Perhaps the pain and fear had driven Pud mad?

He had met the elegant Brit officer at Rendezvous, along with his diminutive, waspish superior, Major FitzRoy, and their enormous Sergeant Major "Ginger" Mattock. Beneath that highly polished exterior Tristan had perceived Allanby as a hard man, no question there. A man who could clasp hands with a man and then turn away to write his death warrant if he thought it needed done; no question there either, Tristan realized. But *why*? What motive could an Honourable Company rep possibly have for wanting Tristan's skinny outlaw ass wasted?

He shook his head. "You've been out in the sun too long, cousin."

"No! W-wait! Check—check Ernie's body. He has a letter."

Moving with dreamlike slowness, like a man suspecting he's being had, Tristan walked to where he had left the Chosen Few leader. He knelt down beside the body. It lay as if crucified on its back, eyes and arms wide.

Tristan had given him the better part of a twenty-round magazine. He was a hell of a mess. Tristan searched gingerly through blood-soggy pockets, came up with a folded piece of paper.

It was sticky-wet and glued to itself with the nomad's bodily fluids. Tristan held up a penlight that Stormy, the King's Power-Lifting Daughter with the engineering bent, had given him as a parting present to show there were no hard feelings. It had been a bit of innocent two-way deception, of him and of herself; King Jubal's chocolate daughter had taken Tristan's decision to remain among his surface-dwelling kind—and by implication, with his current squeeze Jovanne, Prez of the Jokers MC—harder than her vanilla twin.

By the tiny flash's light he could make out part of a line written in an excruciatingly correct copperplate hand: "*. . . you have brought matters to a satisfactory conclusion, and waited the agreed-upon period, then meet me in the valley of the Neosho, above . . .*"

The letter was signed *Maj. Chas. Allanby.*

Thoughtfully Tristan carried it back to the scattered expiring fire in his fingertips. He stood looking down at Pud, who refused to meet his eyes, preferring to concentrate on clutching himself and weeping with gulping sobs. At last he let the paper flutter down on top of the injured man.

"All right, cousin," he said softly. "I can't say as I buy your story whole. But I've lost my taste for vengeance; there's blood enough spilled this night.

"I leave you with your partners' bikes and possibles, and your life. What you do with all those things is up to you. But one last thing: Don't hurry to set your wheels on a Road that intersects with mine."

And he turned and walked away, leaving Pud alone with the pain and the wind.

2

The King was a mighty man, a mountain of a man, some fat, some muscle, all mean and all wrapped up in black. A gold circlet gripped his balding head, pressing down greasy long black curls. He sat with elbow on knee and his magnificent tangle of beard propped in his left palm. The throne he sat on was made from the bones of bikes, frames and forks and pipes and handlebars, all chromed and gleaming in the watery shine that made it through the boiling clouds above. Surmounting it was the skull of a catamount.

Before him a square stretch of prairie was marked off by four parked ranks of motorcycles, all gleaming black, their riders likewise all in black. In the midst of the fifty-yard square two men fought, one with a pair of sai, one with a three-section staff.

A woman stood beside the throne. She was six feet tall. Her loose saffron robe could not disguise the athletic ranginess of her figure, nor the fine turning of hips and rump and lengthy legs. Her complexion was dark, the eyes slanted and cobalt blue, a blue such as the sky only rarely achieved these days, when the clouds briefly retreated. Her head was hairless save for black lashes and brows.

"What is it you do here, brother?" she asked in a voice like silk over steel. "You have lost most of your Nation to death. Why do you pit your followers one against the other? It seems a strange entertainment."

"It isn't entertainment," he rumbled. "It's revenge."

He raised his right hand to mop his brow. Despite the clouds it was a hot day as well as a humid one. His forehead was slick and shiny with sweat.

He cursed and dropped his right arm. He had forgotten again, that he *had* no right hand. What he had was a stump at the wrist, covered with a little lace cozy and surmounted by a rose the color of blood. He changed the rose every day to ensure its freshness. Appearance was everything, even to a soul as enlightened as his now was.

"Is it permitted?" he asked, giving her a defiant roll of his boar's eyes. The Acolyte was the ranking member of the Fusion missionaries left from their defeat at the Big Sandy. King Billy had subordinated himself and his proud Cathead Nation to the yellowrobes, a decision he had had several weeks to repent of. But he knew in the recesses of his capacious belly that it was too late to back out.

She had her head tilted slightly to the side, watching him with something like cool contempt. He longed to seize her and strip her, to bend her over his gleaming chrome throne and ramrod that icy aloofness right out of her. Hell, the bitch would probably enjoy it—for a while.

He felt sweat start afresh. A stinging rivulet ran into his right eye. *Mother Sky, I hope I didn't think that too loud!* He had not sold his people—and his soul—without receiving ample evidence that he'd surrendered to a Medicine neither he nor the Catheads could long resist. His Catheads had been crushed by the stinking Stormriders and their monster allies, but for the Fusion it had merely been a setback, an inconvenience. He had no doubt they would triumph.

Along the way they could do things to a body that made a man afraid to dream.

"If you surrender to the blandishments of Ego," she purred, "you impede your own progress toward that Oneness you have been allowed to perceive."

"I'll take that risk."

"What ritual is this, that you value it above your own Enlightenment?"

"The Twelve Apostles," he said.

She arched a fine-drawn brow. "I did not expect to find in you vestiges of an archaic City faith like Christianity."

"Not the Christ Road," he said irritably. "It's a Cathead thing."

"Enlighten me, please," she said, with the ghost of a smile.

"My people face the greatest enemy of their history," he said.

"The one the Prophecy of the Burned Witch foretold—this Burningskull, the bastard Hardrider. The get of old Anse the One-Eyed would finish the Catheads, the Prophecy says, and the son of a bitch has damn near delivered on the promise.

"But we ain't downed yet. We have enough spunk left for the Twelve Apostles."

He raised his rose and gestured with it. "I pick six of our finest fighters, and six mercenaries off the Plains—the finest mechanics and samurai, the greatest weapons-masters to be found. And I send them on the trail of Tristan motherfucking Burningskull.

"They may take him soon, they may take him late; an Apostle has been knowed to track his man twenty years and more before making his move. As long as he—or she—draws breath, an Apostle hunts."

"And how do you propose to attract these unaffiliated weapons-masters?"

"Gold," he said. "We have few enough riders left, but we've stashed away the Gods' own plenty of loot over the years. Half of it goes to the man or woman who downs Burningskull."

"Indeed? Did you not consecrate your wealth and that of your clan to the greater cause of Fusion?"

He glared at her beneath bushy beetling brows. She laughed, a wind-chime sound. "But do not fear, Brother Soul. This Tristan is a barrier to the True Light illuminating the Plains. His removal is a holy task."

King Billy let his breath out in a sigh. He was not eager to defy the Fusion. But he would not turn away from the Road he had chosen.

"But why not simply offer a reward for his removal?" she asked. "Why *this*?" A slender, elegant hand gestured to the sweating, half-naked combatants.

"It's more'n just the treasure," King Billy said. "Shit, anybody'd take the job for the money alone's too dumb to pull it off. Be better off tryin' to steal the loot—even from us—than go up against Burningskull.

"Twelve Apostles are only declared against the mightiest of foes—against Heroes. And make no mistake about it, Burningskull's a Hero, may his soul fry forever. Nothin' less than such would pose a threat to our tribe. There's a heap of glory to be gained here. The man or woman puts Burningskull in the dirt to stay, their name'll be sung till the mountains die."

"Should they survive the experience," the Acolyte murmured, "not to mention the wrath of their quarry's friends."

King Billy shrugged massively. "Even if they die, the song remains the same. That's the thing about glory, it's sometimes . . ." He held out a massive hairy-backed paw, palm up, and the rose-covered stump, as if balancing weights. "You know, *life—glory*, *life—glory*. For a real samurai it's not that hard of a choice."

"Indeed."

Out on the field of combat the sai-master dropped to one knee, ducking a whistling blow. He captured the center section of his opponent's staff between the forward-swept hilt and tapered steel rod of his left-hand weapon, drove the tip of the right through the man's eye into his brain. The man's limbs all flew out at once, tossing the staff away from him. Then he collapsed on the ground like a collection of old rags, raising a brief swirl of dust.

The assembled riders cheered. The sai-man thrust his hands in the air and turned, soaking up their plaudits. King Billy waved his one hand listlessly as attendants ran forward to carry off the body.

"Time was," he rumbled, "I'da been laughin' my ass off over this. Not no more."

He shook his head mournfully. "It's a terrible thing when all the laughter's killed out of a man's soul. Burningskull has a shitload to answer for."

"You are correct, Brother Soul," Acolyte said. She slipped around to stand before his throne. "I myself volunteer to run him to earth. I will become an Apostle."

King Billy rested his left arm on the arm of his throne, padded with a motorcycle seat, and rested his cheek in his hand. He held his right stump up to his face and sniffed it daintily, enjoying its subtle fragrance. He appreciated the finer things in life.

One of those was the decidedly exotic-foxy appearance of the Acolyte. A shame to waste such beauty, even if she was his nominal spiritual master and decidedly off-limits. On the other hand, there were always plenty of beautiful women to be found, especially if you were none too scrupulous as to how you acquired them.

The King pointed a blunt instrument of a finger at the victorious warrior, now performing an eye-blurring kata with his twin sai. "He didn't show me enough class to be an Apostle," he said, "and anyway, I don't want some squinty-eye little Jap puke vindicating the honor of the mighty Cathead Nation. We ain't *that* far reduced. Take him down, show me some class, and you got the job, sugar nip—I mean, Sister Soul."

She smiled and nodded, both slow. Then she glided forward, into the makeshift arena.

The sai-fighter finished his form, bowed, then heard the crowd's applause turn to catcalls. He turned, frowned.

"What's this?" he said with a sneer. "A *woman* comes to challenge me?" He looked toward King Billy. "Have I not won the honor of joining this Quest?"

"If you're worthy of the honor," the King said, "you won't balk at another go-round. What the hell—she's only a mouse."

The women of the Nation—who were anything but meek submissive house mice themselves—were hooting at the Acolyte now, screaming, "Take it off! Show us your tits!" She did not acknowledge them as she advanced.

The diminutive warrior considered, jutted his head, nodded. "Will it offend Your Majesty if I kill her?"

King Billy waved his good hand. He picked up his gilded wrench scepter and leaned back to enjoy the show.

The Acolyte flowed into a low stance and waited, one hand poised between her breasts, the other extended. A conventional enough posture for an unarmed fighter to assume. The sai-man raised his own weapons to the guard position and came forward with short steps, not permitting his legs to cross.

As he closed the master whipped the weapons about in his hands so that the heavy, pointed pommels faced forward, and the sharp spikelike shaft lay along his forearms. He obviously did not want to seem to be taking too much advantage of the additional reach the foot-long weapons gave him over the unarmed woman.

He came in with a high right thrust for the face. She slapped it away with her left hand. Instantly he thrust at her belly with the other hand. She slapped the wrist from the outside, guiding the weapon past her left hip, sliding forward into him, snapping the back of her right fist into his face. His head whipped back. He danced back several steps, blood streaming from his nose.

He stuck out his tongue, tasted the blood on his upper lip. He spat in the sand and twirled the sai in his hands so that the needle-sharp tips were pointing toward his enemy.

She smiled.

He began to circle clockwise around her, trying to come in outside her advanced left hand. She pivoted gracefully, continuing to face him. He took two quick steps forward, then launched a front kick for her knee. She skipped back, quick as a cat, out of harm's way.

The sai-master advanced. The Acolyte flowed to meet him, looking to cancel his reach advantage by closing to breathing range.

The crowd gasped. That kind of move was risky to put on somebody with a nasty sharp pointy weapon.

She got her forearms in between his steel spikes, wedged them apart, moved up in his face between them. He launched swinging strikes. She blocked them with rattlesnake-fast movements of hands and forearms. He tried to backpedal; she stuck with him as if they were tied together. He tried jabbing at her. The thrusts were deflected.

The sai-master began to sweat. The Acolyte looked cool. She continued to smile.

Finally she slid back half a step. He started to follow. She put a foot in his belly and thrust-kicked him away.

King Billy realized he was leaning forward, clutching his knee with his good hand. He was not simply a thug, a raping, pillaging murderer—though he was all of those things, of course. He had not won rulership of the largest, nastiest motorcycle clan on the Plains at Sunday night church bingo in Misery City. The Catheads were a fighting clan. Their King was a connoisseur of combat.

The six-foot-tall yellowrobe babe was good. There was no getting around the fact.

The sai-master was panting and rolling his eyes like a buffalo bull. He had a scarlet beard of blood. Since her riposte to his first attack the Acolyte had not made an offensive move against him. He lunged forward, hoping an all-out *banzai* attack would overpower her unbelievable defense, allow him to get through to that satin-skinned body . . .

Her deep blue eyes met his black ones. She uttered a piercing falcon scream. The sai-master froze.

She slid forward, slid her left leg past him. At the same time she dropped her body and drove a ferocious reverse punch into his sternum.

He dropped as if he'd been shot.

She straightened, pivoted to face King Billy, brought up a fist before her breasts, covered it with her other hand, and bowed.

"Aren't you getting a little cocky," he said, "turning your back on an opponent?"

"No, Brother Soul," she said. "He's dead."

A spatter of rain began to fall. The match attendants ran out to check the fallen contestant. One knelt, feeling for pulse with his fingertips. Then he held out a gauntleted hand and turned it thumb downward.

King Billy grunted and rubbed his chin. "I'm impressed," he admitted. "I got to admit you beat him square, even before you showed your funny stuff. How *did* you freeze him there, at the end?"

"*Qigong,*" the Acolyte said. She was not breathing hard. "The spirit power of the One, flowing through my limbs.

"Am I worthy to join the hunt?"

"Yeah. *Ohh*, yeah. But there's one thing you should keep in mind, sister. When you become an Apostle, you put your soul up for security. Every day you spend not working towards your goal shortens your life by one day. We Catheads don't have the strong Medicine your Fusion does, but we can muster a damn good curse when we need to."

She didn't bother hiding her smile at the notion that primitive Plains-barbarian magic could affect an adept of the Fusion, even a comparatively young and untried one.

"You need have no fear on that score, Brother Soul," she said. "Your goal is mine—is ours. Tristan Burningskull is a dead man."

She turned and walked away. King Billy watched her buttocks with undisguised interest.

"So are we all," he muttered into his beard. "The question is, *when*?

"And, *who first*?"

PART TWO

GYPSY ROAD

3

Two years later . . .

"Where are your bodyguards, Burningskull? You're the big man. Who you brought to protect you?"

The speaker was a big man himself, bare to the waist, head shaved to a long black topknot. His head looked as if it were balanced on a pyramid of rolling sweat-shiny muscle.

It was a sag-nuts little cluster of tents, some faded synthetic geodesics, some skin—and cured none too well, by the aroma. A few equally faded women watched, one blonde feeding a baby from breasts that sagged way beyond her apparent sixteen summers as she watched the confrontation. Chango was pretty much a solo; his sometimes accomplices were mostly in the dirt already, thanks to the Lord of the Plains and his picked hit squads.

Chango was a rapist, a robber, a razzer, and a murderer, who preyed on the High Free Folk as much as Diggers—sodbusters—and Citizens. He'd bragged that even the high-and-mighty Tristan Burningskull himself feared to face him.

It had not been a good call.

Tristan jerked a thumb over his shoulder at Jeremy, lounging with his back to the sled called Vengeance. Chango snorted derisive disbelief.

"Him? He's half your size—and you are nothing compared to me."

"He's one of the mightiest warriors I know, Chango. Don't let the size fool you. But he's only along for the conversation. I protect myself."

Chango laughed. He unwrapped a chain from around his waist—a narrow waist, but beginning to show a roll from easy living and easy pickings. The chain came free with a metal song.

The outlaw flexed his bare shoulders, which were as wide as the height of a short man, and tossed his long scalp lock to the back of what neck he had. He straightened the heavy chain before his face with a ringing snap.

"You grew up in a City, Burningskull," he sneered. "City life made you soft."

Tristan's arm whipped out. The Bolo cracked.

Chango swayed. His eyes had started from his head; a small blue hole had appeared in his sloping brow above them, forming a neat equilateral triangle.

He crashed forward with an avalanche sound. His long queue fell into the red morass where the back of his skull had been.

"Growing up on the Plains, on the other hand," Tristan said, stuffing the Lakota back in its holster, "didn't make *you* smart."

The women stood where they were, staring with wide dry eyes. The baby gave off nursing to scream at the high thin ringing in its ears that followed the shot.

"It's done," Tristan told the camp. "I'd suggest you hook up with a clan as soon as possible. There's a Blue Murder MC camp a few miles up Thunderhead Creek; might look 'em up."

He turned and strode back to WildFyre, mounted, and woke the engine with a sudden bellow. He cruised away into the rolling grasslands. Jeremy sat a moment on Vengeance, studying the camp with an impassive face. Then he turned his big black bike to follow Tristan's gold one.

"Small beer," Jeremy yelled into the wind of their passage.

"What?" Tristan called back. "I can't hear you." They were on the Hard Road again, heading for Tristan's permanent floating tent-city capital, currently set up in the lake district south of Niobrara. They weren't too far from Lakota country, pretty much due south of Lakota Forge, the Black Hills manufacturing center.

In normal circumstances this would have been a red zone; the Lakota were a belligerent bunch. While they did not exactly attack nomads on sight, they would see the nearness of a major High Free Folk concentration as a threat, if not a challenge. But they were undergoing another round of their sporadic border-war skirmishing with the Absaroka to their west, and were thus preoccupied.

Meanwhile, it was an opportunity for Tristan to demonstrate the principle that he and his people roved the Plains as they pleased. The suggestion had come from Jovanne, still Prez of the Jokers as well as one of his most important personal advisers. A shrewd one, Jovanne was.

"I said, I don't see why you're wasting your time fiddle-fucking around with small-timers like Chango," Jeremy yelled.

Tristan was sure that wasn't exactly what his friend had said the first time. He grinned and let it go. "It's a simple way to show class," he responded.

"What's the point?" Jeremy demanded.

Tristan sighed. Blue wildflowers lay like sheets of cloth on the earth left and right. The sky was mostly clear, and it was spring. It wasn't a time when he was eager to go explaining a point for the hundredth time.

But he loved Jeremy as his oldest friend—Jammer didn't count; he had been a mature adult when Tristan was captured at age eleven, had been more of an uncle than a friend. And Jeremy was useful to Tristan. Tristan accepted that he had to deal with him on his own terms.

"I'm not into conquest of the Folk," he said. "I don't want to put my boot on their necks, and I don't want the bros thinking I do. I want 'em to *want* to join me. Wasting an animal like Chango serves me well. Makes me look like a tough son of a bitch, lets the bros and sisters sleep a little better for not having to wonder when he's gonna drop by for a midnight visit, and helps the other detached assholes out there get their minds right."

Jeremy shook his head. "I still think you're acting like you're still a Striker, for Christ's sake."

Invoking Christ was a City-boy thing to do, but then Jeremy was a City boy—born as well as raised, unlike Tristan. That didn't stop him from being a nomad in good standing. The clans never dropped enough kids to replenish their numbers, so they were always looking for recruits. There was sometimes friction—as Chango's taunts to Tristan showed—but for most Stormriders, once you proved yourself, you were a bro for life.

"Old instincts die hard," Tristan admitted. "I'll keep playing the hands my way."

"You always do," Jeremy said.

The land was broken, pitched up in ridges perpendicular to the road. Lush knee-high grass covered the ground where the wild-flowers didn't predominate. At one time, Tristan knew—from his

long days browsing in Homeland's Library—back before
StarFall, this had been a virtual desert. Now the rains fell regu-
larly throughout the summer. Made a man appreciate a day like
this, though—riding slow, in the wind after a long cold winter,
with blue above and a hawk kiting on the thermals from the
roadway. A red-tail, he saw from the orange undersides—

"Tristan, look out!"

The shout came from just behind his left shoulder; he had
rolled out a little ways ahead of his friend. His eyes snapped
back to earth.

Low ridges closed in to either side of the road just ahead. His
mind registered two small and rusting metal poles, possible pre-
StarFall relics, flanking the highway left and right.

When Tristan rode in a possible red zone he wore the broadsword he had reclaimed from the Chosen Few over his back.
Now he whipped it from the scabbard, and held it upright before
his face edge forward.

A whisper of resistance, a tiny song of broken steel. Tristan
fancied he felt something brush his cheek. *Wired!*

He dropped a boot and sent WildFyre into the ditch, careless
of the legendary bike's immaculate finish. The almost mythic
Carondelet wrench Black Henry had built his masterpiece to be
ridden, not to sit under glass in a museum. As far as Tristan
could determine the paint was impossible to scratch.

He laid the big bike down, no easy feat holding on to a sword.
Fortunately he'd put in a lot of time practicing just that maneuver. Jeremy had ditched to the other side of the road. Tristan
transferred the blade to his left hand, and whipped out the Bolo.

Two figures had jumped up from behind a clump of brush and
were rabbiting up the ridge's flank. Tristan raised the Bolo and
stitched a line across the slope above them. They screamed,
curled into balls, and rolled back down to the ditch.

They were two of the washed-out young women from Chango's camp. Scouting around, Jeremy found a pair of scrambler
bikes hidden in a draw behind the ridge. The big outlaw sleds,
Vengeance and WildFyre, were not restricted to paved surfaces,
but handled much better on them than in the dirt. Tristan and his
friend had been making their leisurely way back along the ancient road grid. The women had obvious driven their machines
savagely cross-country to set up their ambush.

Tristan had one word for them: "Why?"

They looked at each other. Off-road dirt overlay the dug-in

grime of their faces; tears had eroded little arroyos down their cheeks. Tristan thanked Brother Wind and Mother Sky that neither was one he had seen nursing a baby.

"You killed our man," said the one on the left. Her ragged straggles of hair might at one time have been red. "Left us with nothing."

"Idiots," Jeremy spat. "Burningskull told you another clan would take you in."

The woman shook her hair back and held up her head. "They'd treat us like dirt. We were *Chango's* women. We don't crawl to no one."

Tristan shook his head. She hadn't gotten those dull-red marks on the places where the cheekbone neared the surface, at the outside of either eye, stumbling over a root and falling headlong while fetching water. Chango had no doubt kidnapped her, raped her—probably murdered her kin before her eyes, if he'd been acting true to pattern that day. He'd beat her and abused her.

And she had sacrificed her life for him.

He raised his Bolo, and killed each with a bullet through the forehead, the shots coming so quickly neither had much chance to fear. As he holstered his weapon he looked at the bodies lying sprawled and pathetic in the moist grass at his feet, and knew that most Stormriders would consider his act the highest mercy. Over-lenient, in fact.

There was no way he could have spared them, of course. Not and remain Lord of the Plains, Burningskull of the Burningskulls. Not and remain a bro.

What Chango's two women had done was the worst crime possible, in nomad eyes. To hang a man on a wire was obscene. Worse, it was sacrilege, because all roads were sacred, avatars of the One Big Road, and where would the High Free Life in the wind be if the bros and sisses couldn't ride the Road without fear of their heads suddenly parting company with their bodies as a result of a thin little wire stretched invisibly across the highway?

There were many ways for Death to overtake you on the Road. You could go over the high side, or be struck by lightning, or snatched up by a Stalking Wind. There were landslides, potholes unseen in twilight, trees fallen across the right-of-way. There was even the possibility of ambush, which in the curious structure of Plains morality was perfectly acceptable.

Of all the ways to get translated abruptly to Heroes' Holm—to give you the benefit of the doubt—the one the High Free Folk had nightmares about was the wire. Though of all deaths on the Road, it was perhaps consistently the quickest.

The penalty for stringing a wire was death by the most fiendish torture the fertile nomad imagination could concoct on the spot. Even those who hated torture, like Jovanne or Tristan's own mother Jen Morningstar, dead these many years, would turn their backs and permit it to happen without demur.

But part of the class which showed Tristan worthy of his power was going his own way. His quick execution of Chango's women would probably enhance his rep. People were a damn funny bunch.

"You've got a soft streak inside," Jeremy observed as they got their rides upright and rolled them back onto the old, oft-patched blacktop. Helping repair the Hard Roads was a religious duty for the Folk. It was one of the few forms of formal labor many of them would consent to.

The little man, whose artificial right foot gave him a limp but didn't slow him noticeably in a fight, spoke without heat or rancor. He spoke his mind, always; that was one of his primary values to Tristan.

"Don't like doing what I just did," the nomad chieftain said. "Never liked killing in cold blood."

"They were willing enough to do it to you."

Tristan shrugged, nodded. "Yeah. But women and children . . ."

"You've left plenty of widows and orphans along your back trail," Jeremy said, swinging his legs across Vengeance. "On razz, your battles with the Cats. Hell, back when you were a Striker—you still see a truckload more trouble from kinfolk of badasses you put in the dirt in those days than you have from these cockamamie Cathead Apostles."

Mounting his own iron, Tristan grimaced. In the last two years he had slain five of the fanatic assassins, three men and two women. Several of them had gotten mighty close.

"It's just—those women would have been taken in somewhere. Chango treated them worse than animals. It seems like such a Goddamned waste."

Jeremy's gaze was flat and dark as slate. "They tried to hang you on a wire. They deserved to die."

Tristan shrugged and kicked WildFyre alive. Her engine growled with instantaneous response. He never ceased to marvel at her.

"I guess. But I don't have to like it."

Jeremy showed sharp white teeth. "That's why it's better you're where you are, and I'm where I am," he said. "I don't know any restraint that's not tactical. But I wouldn't much want to turn into anything like Chango."

They hit the Road again and rolled.

The sun was sinking into the mountains at their backs, turning the domed tents of Tristan's nomad capital to various shades of flame. As Tristan and Jeremy approached, a knot of men and women on foot walked to meet them.

A great-shouldered red bear of a man walked before the group, holding a limp figure in his arms. Tristan let WildFyre coast to a stop before him.

"What's happening here, Redbeard, my friend?" Tristan called out.

A tear rolled down Redbeard's weathered cheek. He was President of the Seekers, a clan whose numbers had dwindled over the years.

It had dwindled by one more, Tristan saw with a twinge. Redbeard's burden was a young blond woman, who showed no sign of life in the dangle of her limbs.

"It's Sunny," Redbeard said. "Water party found her just after dawn, couple hundred yards outside camp."

"Gods." Tristan felt his lips peel back from his teeth. He traded grim glances with Jeremy. "I'm sorry. From the depths of my heart."

"Strangled?" Jeremy asked.

Redbeard nodded slowly. "Silk stocking, knotted around her poor little neck."

"The Strangler," Jeremy said, and spat into the yellow dirt.

"This is the fourth one he's taken," Redbeard said. Tears flooded from his eyes and matted his gray-shot red beard. "My one and only daughter, Laughing Girl accept her spirit. O Lord Burningskull, my clan rode often to war with yours when it was known as the Hardriders. Can you not give us justice?"

"Friend of my father," Tristan said slowly, "I feel the pain of your wound. But whom do I levy my justice against?"

"I don't know, Tristan. Brother Wind help me, I haven't a mortal clue."

He held his murdered daughter up before himself. "If I knew, I'd choke the life from the fuckard with these hands!"

"If you knew, I'd let you," Tristan said.

"He must be stopped."

"He will be." Tristan and Jeremy rolled on, leaving the silent Seekers to bury their dead.

"I just wish I knew how," Tristan added to Jeremy when they were out of earshot. "We're a lot closer to robbers than cops."

Jeremy nodded. His gray eyes were thoughtful, and his face was grim.

4

The big council tent was dark. So great was the weight of the nighttime blackness outside that it squeezed the yellow glow of two lanterns down to almost nothing. Or maybe it was the mood of the score of men and women crowded inside.

"It's Dallas," Jovanne said. She stood by Tristan, next to the head of the long table—actually two folding cafeteria tables erected end to end. The lanterns threw golden crescents across the lower halves of the tall woman's eyes. "Rangers're on the move, big time. Two thousand men, mechavalry and some armor."

She nodded to a small and bandy-legged rider, his leathers and the goggles pulled up on top of his head caked in mud, who stood off to one side. He produced a shy, weary smile and bobbed his head.

"Our brothers the Ghost Riders bumped into them on the Washita," Jovanne continued. "The atmospherics are tough right now, so Grimy Bill here rode all the way to tell us."

The assembly gave Bill a round of applause. *Maybe it's the smell that's getting to me,* reflected Tristan, who'd already been briefed. Even with the tent flaps rolled up to let the night breeze blow through, it was impossible to ignore the fact that nomad hygiene still wasn't up to where Tristan would like it to be. His mother's fastidiousness, which had so often exasperated his father Wyatt Hardrider, had rubbed off on him. His years of City life had lowered his odor tolerance further.

The Maximum Council of the High Free Folk was in boister-

ous, fragrant session. Twenty of the biggest and baddest motorcycle clans on the Plains were represented here. The Flaming
Arrows. The Sand Kings. Last Mile MC. The Enforcers. The
Predators. The Stray Satans. The Wayfarers. Night Riders, Diamondbacks, and Bandidos; Blue Murder and their archrival Marauders. The Jokers, of course, Jovanne's club and by adoption
Tristan's. The Outlaws, blood allies of the Jokers since the Cathead War. And others. There were plenty of big-name outfits not
represented, but that was mainly because they didn't happen to
be in the vicinity of Tristan's permanent floating capital. His pol-
icy of expansion-by-showing-class had worked well, despite
Jeremy's grumbles.

"The Washita?" repeated Tommy Hawk. As always the
Freebird war chief's handsome face was painted in fanciful geo-
metric patterns. "That's right between Water Horse and
Osagerie."

Tristan saw Jovanne's lips tighten. He knew she was biting
back a crack about the Freebird's quick grasp of the obvious.
Tommy Hawk was renowned for his courage and skill at war, not
his brains.

There was a time when Jovanne would have blurted out the re-
mark anyway, trusting her own rapid wits and reflexes to keep
her from harm. She was never going to be a diplomat, but that
was fine; she was on his staff for her strategic abilities. But she
had grown.

"That's a treaty violation," said Tramp, President of the Sand
Kings. "With both the Osage and Water Horse."

A round of laughter greeted that. The Council wasn't laughing
with him either. Tramp was known to be a bit naive.

"Dallas knows what treaties're good for," growled Enforcer
warlord Wolfman. "Wipin' your ass when they ain't soft green
leaves to be had." And he gave a nasty snaggle-toothed laugh.

Tramp snarled and tried to hurl himself across the table, grabbing for his Green River knife. Burly arms seized him and returned him to his seat none too gently.

Jeremy was seated across from Jovanne on a folding chair, his
legs folded, a scowl on his narrow features. Ignoring the horse-
play, he looked Tristan in the eye and said, "So much for your
big plan to take down Homeland."

Bitterness rippled through his words. His grudge against the
City of his birth was as big as Tristan's—almost. "They're getting too big for their britches too. We're going to have problems

with them soon. Those Purity assholes think it's their divine mission to cleanse the Plains of us scooter scum."

"Tell me something I don't know," Tristan said.

"How's this?" Jeremy said sourly. "You should have moved right after we trashed the Catheads."

There was a rumble of agreement from the assembled chiefs and warlords. Tristan's big shoulders rolled to a sigh. "We weren't strong enough then," he said. "We had just gotten our asses handed to us by the Catheads, you might recall. We were pretty well in the dirt."

"We were pumped from by beating the Cats," Jeremy said. "We were tired, yeah. But the boys and girls had tasted triumph. And they were seasoned."

"There've been more triumphs, Jeremy," Jovanne said. "We're more seasoned now."

"You sound like you're ready to roll against Homeland anyway," Jeremy said glumly.

She shrugged. "I'm assessing the situation. It's what I get paid for."

"What you get laid for, is more like it," came a voice from the far reaches of the table.

Jovanne's eyes narrowed. Then she relaxed. It was a process like a ripple running through tall Plains grass.

"Lonesome Dave," she said, drawing the name out. "Jealous?"

The Pistolero President just laughed.

"We have more riders now than Hammerhand ever had," said Tommy Hawk, who was not real swift at picking up on byplay.

"We will need them all if the Dallasites come trespassing on the Plains," said Hercules, warlord of the Dragon clan. Like all the Dragons he was black. He was bigger than most. He bore his colors on a red satin jacket.

Back in the Library, in those high school days when he had the whole vast place all to himself except for blind Mr. Bayliss, the Librarian, Tristan had read a lot of military history. He had early come to understand that he could not do everything by himself when it came to conquest. He would model himself on Temujin, the Mongol called Genghis Khan. He had been a mighty warrior and crafty leader, but his unparalleled conquests had depended as much on the heroes he had chosen for his marshals as on his own talent. Tristan reckoned that was a good way to go.

On the other hand, Genghis Khan had also thought nothing

about washing away the populations of entire cities. That wasn't a role Tristan fancied.

He was learning that finding the right heroes to be your right-hand men—and women—wasn't all that easy. Right now his staff consisted mainly of Jeremy and Jovanne and Jammer, when the Skald was around. What he currently had was the Council of the Folk, consisting of wheels from important clans and a lot of hot air.

"Are they really likely to come poaching on our grounds?" asked Lonesome Dave, leaning back in his chair. He was tall, if not so tall as Tristan, clean-shaven, with golden-blond hair and red eyebrows. He wore a leather jacket a size too large for him. "They have the Kiowas and Comanches to the left of them, the Osage to the right. They might not be in a hurry to stick it out too far, for fear of getting it pinched off."

"Kiowa and Comanch' are almost as tough as they talk," Hercules said.

"Not so tough as they used to be," Jovanne said. "With all due respect to our bros the Kwahadi MC, the last few years they've turned into not much more than running dogs for the tailheads."

"Can't exactly count the Osage out, though," remarked Rico, warload of *Los Tremendos Gavilanes*, a club out of northern Mexico. "Helped haul our butts out of the crack that *pendejo* Hammerhand got 'em into."

"We can't take for granted that those two thousand are all Dallas is going to send," Jeremy said. "If they want to push big, they can send two or three times that many and still have enough left over that the tailheads won't be too eager to rush off and leave their farms and factories unprotected."

"Dallas likes to do things big, that's for certain sure," Hercules said.

"So, Lord Burningskull," said Lonesome Dave in his smart and smarmy way, "what do we do now?"

Tristan grinned. "Invade Homeland."

It was as if he'd dropped a live grenade on the table. Everybody froze and stared as if they were getting ready to dive for cover.

The Pistolero chief shook his head. "Finally cracked under the strain," he said.

The suspended silence broke like water's surface tension. Babble spilled out.

"Much as I hate to agree with Goldilocks there," Jeremy said, his dry voice cutting through the noise like a band saw, "I think you've gone over the high side."

"No."

Heads turned. Silence fell. Jovanne stood straight. Her cheeks were flushed. She did not enjoy confrontation. It was one of the reasons she was Prez but not warlord, despite her strategic genius. Which no one had noticed until Tristan came along anyway.

"Whose side are on you on here, high-pockets?" Jeremy asked. The two weren't enemies by any means, but they were also not big mutual admirers.

"Look," she said, "it makes sense. Homeland is only going to keep getting stronger."

"Dallas is pressin' us now," pointed out Clutch, Prez of the Nightrangers.

"No. Dallas is waving its dick around so everybody can admire how big it is. If they try to hit us, we just pull a fade. Like smoke, babe; they'd think they're trying to punch smoke. It's what we do best."

"We can't run forever," Lonesome Dave said.

"No. We can't. But does anybody here think we're going to be able to take Dallas all the way down anytime soon?"

Lots of silence answered her. "No shit," she said. "So think about it. Dallas is crowding us. Homeland is crowding us. Pretty soon we could find ourselves crowded right out of existence."

"So you think we should bash our heads in against Homeland so Dallas can finish us off quick, and we don't have to suffer the suspense," Jeremy said.

"I think we need to put somebody down to stay. Homeland's cocky. They're also a lot smaller than Dallas. We can take 'em. But we can't wait forever."

She grinned. "Besides, if we win—at least we got a City to hide in."

That wasn't altogether popular, provoking growls of, "Long as we got wheels, what do we need walls for?" and, "Fuck a bunch of City noise! I was born in the wind, and that's where I'll die." But some of the assembly scratched their beards and looked thoughtful.

The High Free Folk were warriors. Wedded as they all were to the romance and glory of the balls-out motorcycle charge, brutal experience had taught them time and again the advantage enjoyed by the defensive in a time when automatic weapons were available and heavy artillery wasn't. Even though the nomads themselves, with their perpetual problems of supply, could seldom much use full-auto fire, a dismounted line of riflemen and women lying down in cover could break almost any charge.

So even though something there was in the nomad soul that didn't love a wall, not everybody failed to understand at the scrotum level how nice it would be to be *behind* the barbed wire and cement barriers for a change.

Tommy Hawk held up a clenched fist. "Freebirds are with you."

"The Pistoleros don't run from a fight," Lonesome Dave said, uncrossing his long legs, "but we like to be damned sure we're in the right one."

"The Marauders don't fear men, beast, nor Stalking Wind," announced their Prez, Liquid Louie. "But the thought of letting Dallas rampage around in our rear while we hammer at Homeland makes m'heart turn bad."

Moonhawk, war chief of Blue Murder, jumped straight to his feet and pounded a gauntleted fist on the table. "We're ready for Homeland!" he shouted. "Let's ride!"

"You didn't see these Dallas boys," said Grimy Bill quietly. His words hit a lull in the dispute, so every head turned to look at him. He shrank a little.

"Ghost Riders ain't 'feared of much either," he said, "but I'll allow as to how these're some pretty tough *hombres*. Looked like a lean, mean fighting machine."

"We need to know more 'bout what they intend," rumbled Hercules from the depths of his gigantic chest. "Ain't safe to move till we do."

"We need to take the initiative," Jovanne said, looking straight at Tristan. "We need to act, instead of just react."

Tristan jutted his jaw, rolled it all around. "I agree with you," he said. He looked around the table, and saw more concern than confidence on the bearded and painted faces.

"But I also agree the first thing we need is more information. So the action we'll take now is heavy scouting. Thanks to Brother Bill here, and his clan, for bringing us these tidings. You've served the brothers and sisters well."

He gripped Bill by the shoulder, and reflected that all that dirt had probably not resulted from the man's cross-country ride. He had a feeling he'd have to soak his fingers in turpentine to get them fully clean.

Oh, well. Worth the sacrifice, to end the meeting on a positive note. He didn't want the leaders to leave here bitching.

He caught Jovanne and Jeremy both looking darkly at him. *I suspect I'm going to get a plateful of bitching anyway, before too much more water flows downstream.*

Gee, it's fun being Lord of the Plains.

5

The man with the pale blond locks flowing over the epaulets of his dove-gray uniform rose. "Then it's a done deal," he declared in a ringing voice.

A gauntleted hand swept up a wineglass filled with champagne. "I therefore propose a toast, gentlemen: to the glorious sovreign Cities of Homeland and Dallas, and to order and purity being restored to this our turbulent land!"

"Hear, hear!" shouted Brigadier General Brace Webbert, shooting to his feet and hoisting his own glass so enthusiastically he endangered the chandelier hanging from the ceiling like a crystal wedding cake. He was six-four and strapping, a heroic figure in his white uniform with the gold trim. His own blond hair was shorn to a silvery plush. He commanded the elite Guards Brigade of the Mobile Force, formerly the Homeland Defense Force.

Dirk Posen, chairman of the Purity Democratic Union, raised his own glass and barely moistened his lips with the bubbly liquid. He allowed himself a thin smile. He was of medium height, with close-cropped brown hair and chiseled features, aerobics-fit and clad in a simple white jumpsuit. He was not a particularly handsome man, but the force of his personality beat off him like heat from a stove.

Colonel Sir Lane Selfridge of the First Mechavalry Regiment, Dallas Rangers, commander of the newly formed Dallas Expeditionary Force, tossed off his champagne with a flip of the wrist. "Mighty fine champagne," he said graciously, "though it does strike me an alliance so mighty and fateful should be sealed with something a mite stronger."

Posen's smile widened infinitesimally. "*This* is stronger than what is usually permitted in our City."

The colonel goggled. "You mean it's true what they say? Homeland is *dry*?"

Posen nodded. Brace chuckled. He was already pouring himself another glass from the heavy green bottle, one of several arranged like flowers in a silver bucket of ice.

"Officially," Brace said, and knocked back the second glass. "Of course, Staff hath its privileges." He burped slightly.

Posen fired a warning look at him. "The Clients—our Citizens—need to be protected from themselves," Posen said, in his best oh-so-reasonable voice. He could make his voice ring like a trumpet too, at need. "Those who have accepted the burden of administering the City are more responsible, of course. And given the stresses involved in caring for the welfare of tens of thousands . . ." A shrug: *We're all men of the world here.* "Our Staff requires outlets the Clients don't need."

"Hear, hear," Brace repeated, hoisting his third glass aloft.

Selfridge looked at Webbert with hooded eyes. They were blue, heavy-lidded, and somewhat slanted. The colonel himself was tall if not overly so, about five-ten, with broad shoulders and narrow hips. A handlebar mustache drooped to either side of his full mouth. Watching him watching Brace, Posen concluded he wasn't as young as he appeared.

Whether he was as empty-headed as he appeared was another issue.

"I understand perfectly, General," Selfridge said in his soft drawl. "We have our patricians, plebs, and peons ourselves. The higher must look out for the lower; *noblesse oblige*, and all."

He sipped his champagne. "How soon do you expect to move, General Webbert?" he asked.

Even with a load on, Brace had sense enough to glance at his Chairman before he responded. Brace Webbert had been Posen's henchman since the two were in high school. Posen had trained him well.

Posen nodded. "Soon," Brace admitted. "Real fucking soon."

Posen scowled. "Pardon my French," Brace added quickly. He drained his glass and swayed.

"Oh, don't mind me," Selfridge said affably. "I've been known to cuss a blue streak myself, as the occasion demanded."

The Dallasite colonel was too smooth by half, Posen decided. On the other hand, the man had been schooled from birth in the convolute graces of semi-feudal Dallas society; he was the son-in-law of the influential industrialist Count Omohundro himself. He could be highly skilled in the social graces without much concomitant skill at intrigue.

A child of privilege himself, if not as ostentatious as Selfridge's, Dirk Posen had begun life being groomed to rule. He had spent his young adult years as head of an underground—though never outlawed—political party, and as an eventually successful conspirator and rebel. For the last three years he had been the power behind the Homeland throne. If there was one thing experience had taught him, it was never to assume.

The colonel was looking at him, rolling his wine in the glass. "I understand you've been having trouble with more than these cycle scum of late, Mr. Chairman," he said.

There had been a damnable amount of Reconciliationist Party cell activity of late, and despite the promises of his secret police and the Mobile Force smuggling was on the rise. Posen doubted his guest referred to either of those.

"I'm not sure I get your drift," he said.

"These horse barbarians." Selfridge tossed off his champagne. "Merry Elves, or whatever they call themselves."

"Merry Pranksters," Posen corrected. *As if you didn't know,* he thought. *And now I call your bluff, you long-haired son of a bitch.* "Your intelligence service is as excellent as rumor makes it, Colonel."

Selfridge shrugged and laughed self-deprecatingly. "Aw, don't misunderstand, Mr. Chairman. I'm just repeatin' idle Plains gossip." The country in his voice grew thicker when he was trying to cover, Posen noted.

"Anarchist animals," Posen said. "We'll exterminate them in due course. We have more pressing priorities now—such as fulfilling the terms of our new alliance with you."

The colonel arched an eyebrow. "Still," he said, "I understand they've been quite a handful. Outta all proportion to their numbers, hm?"

Posen smiled. "As you say, Colonel," he said. "Idle gossip."

Selfridge eyed him a moment, then bobbed his head and laughed. "Well. Enough of business. It's got me plumb wore out, I do declare. All work and no play makes Jack a dull boy. I reckon it's time for a little *amusement.*"

"All work and no play makes Homeland productive," Posen said. "I believe there's a lecture on Civic Duty going on at Town Hall. Perhaps you could get there for the end of it—certainly in time to participate in the spirited discussions that always follow."

"Well, thank you kindly, Mr. Chairman," Selfridge said, "but I think I'll give it a pass."

He threw a wink to Webbert and slapped his arm around the taller man's shoulder. "But I think the general here'n I'll do the town. Got me a suspicion he knows where to find the kind of nightlife I'm hankering after."

Webbert smirked. "Reckon I do."

Frowning, Posen watched them go. Webbert had a taste for certain officially proscribed entertainments, some even foreclosed to Staff. Posen had judged it expedient to permit him to indulge those tastes. It was a little leverage on his old comrade in arms—just in case. Despite his personal distaste for such pursuits, Posen saw possible advantages to allowing Brace Webbert to guide the colonel on a tour of illicit pleasures. If nothing else it would buy some cheap goodwill.

There would come a time, of course, when they would close the doors of the last speakeasies and strip clubs for good. It was impossible now, but the time would come, and soon. Dirk Posen took the mission of Purity very seriously, and knew he would prevail.

The opened champagne bottle stood on the elegant hardwood table. Posen picked it up. He carried it to the French doors that gave onto the balcony and pushed through. The night was almost clear. The Front Range stars shone with uncompromising hardness, like a thousand tiny diamond drill-bits.

The bottle was half empty. Or perhaps, given the way he felt about its contents, half full. Posen held it out over the rough squared-beam railing and poured the champagne to the ground one story below. He hefted the bottle—now all empty—briefly, and considered throwing it after. But littering was as much a crime as drinking.

He turned and stepped back inside. A woman stood in the room. She wore a platinum evening gown, cut low front and back, shimmering clear to the parquetry floor. Her hair was ash blond, lent a certain silver sheen by the gown. Her face was perfect as sculpted ivory. Her eyes were ice.

"I thought waste was high on your official lexicon of sins," she said. The voice was dry and low.

"I was disposing"—he set the dead soldier down on the table with a click—"of poison."

"Then it's polluting the environment, is it not?" she asked.

He looked at her. His eyes burned like black coals. Her demeanor didn't soften.

"I'm the Chairman," he said levelly. "I can do no wrong by definition. Besides, I don't see why you say it's 'my' list. You were a loyal Purity Party member yourself, once upon a time."

"Yes," she said, with a smile that cut like a razor. "That was when we were illegal, and therefore interesting. Then came the revolution, and the magic went away. Nothing like legitimacy to take the spice out of life."

"I'm disappointed to hear you talk that way." He drummed fingers on the table. "It's totally inappropriate in one of your position. Perhaps a course in Rehabilitation would prove therapeutic—"

Her laugh cut him off. "Don't even think of it, Dirk. The Therapists don't like you to begin with. You'd never risk having them hear the things that would come out of my mouth once they started taking my head apart."

He turned away. She let her fingers trail across his shoulders as she walked past him to the open doors. They left a tingling line.

"You have no sense of humor, Dirk," she said. "That's your problem."

He turned to watch her as she passed. She was like an ice sculpture brought to life. The stuff of her gown clung to her buttocks and tapered legs like skin.

It was a wonder his gaze didn't make it burst into flame.

At the doorway she turned.

"I—I have no time for humor," he said.

"A lot of things you have no time for."

He dropped his eyes. She went out onto the balcony.

He pushed out to stand beside her. She was smoking a cigarette. God knows where it had come from. He pinched his nostrils shut.

"You shouldn't . . ."

"Save your breath, Dirk," she said without looking at him. "I'm long beyond redemption. Besides, Staff hath its privileges, as your wet-brained playmate said."

"You eavesdropped on us?"

She turned her back to the railing and leaned against it. "What else do I have to occupy my time? Behavior 'inappropriate to one in my position,' you said. Just what *is* my position?"

He took a deep breath. "My ... companion. My friend."

"Your kept woman. Your whore."

His hand came up as if to strike her. Her eyes transfixed it like steel skewers. It stopped. He looked at it with something like disbelieving horror, and dropped it back to his side.

Those who dealt out physical abuse were dealt with harshly in the Pure State. Unless, of course, they were officially empowered to do so. He felt as if he had opened a heavy metal door in his soul, seen yellow glow and smelled a rush of brimstone.

"You could make an honest woman of me," she said. "Or is traditional morality another one of those Purity platforms intended for Clients only?"

He moistened thin lips with the tip of his tongue. "But Elinor, it wouldn't work. It's politically impossible. I'm chief of the PDU; I was leader of the Restoration. You're the daughter of, of ..."

"The arch-traitor, I believe your—our—propaganda characterized him. Masefield the Mongrelizer. The man who built this house. The man ..."

She reached long fingernails to touch the underside of his chin. They dug in, almost to the point of blood.

"The man who was murdered on your orders."

"It was that mongrel Tristan who murdered him!" he blurted. "He was the last to see him ..."

He stopped. Her eyes were pale fire. *"Don't ever say that name to me,"* she hissed.

She turned and swayed several steps away from him. "Your bullyboys ambushed my father and Quanah," she said in a distant, remembering voice. "They were too incompetent to kill him, and too cowardly to go into that warehouse after him."

"Anyone would be reluctant to confront a cornered rat," he said.

She came around, slowly, and gave him a smile brittle as autumn leaves. "My, you have a way of sweet-talking a woman."

His cheeks grew hot. He wanted to rush to her, seize her. Take her. Yet he felt that if he did so she would turn her eyes on him full of contempt. And he would either burst into flame and melt, or freeze and then fracture, like an icicle falling to pavement. He didn't quite know which.

She was looking at him. Her eyes did not hold the killing

power, but for a tiny flicker in their blue ice-crystal depths to let him know it was there. Waiting. Restless.

She took a final drag on her cigarette and flicked it into the night. It described a red-glow arc, a brief meteor, and was gone.

"You have unfinished business, lover," she said, walking toward him. She seemed as unstoppable and insubstantial as the wind. He wanted to reach out and grab her, but he felt she'd pass through his hands like smoke.

She swept by. "Out on the Plains," she said. In the doorway she stopped and turned back. "Out there is what makes you so afraid, isn't it?"

Hardrider. Burningskull. The names beat in his brain like sledgehammer strokes. He felt the blood fall from his drawn face.

"I'm not afraid of anything! *Anything!*"

Her smile was sweet poison. "I can tell, lover."

She switched out the lights in leaving. Her laughter fell on him like razors as she walked off down the hall.

As it died, a different laughter pealed out behind him.

6

"Loved the decisive way you handled those yahoos," said Jovanne, walking beside him through the night.

He glanced at her. She had a leather jacket trimmed with wolf-skin on, the fur collar high around her chin, cradling her face. It made her look sexy as hell in the moon's fugitive light. Especially when she was being a bitch.

"I seem to remember somebody who looked a lot like you jumping from one side of the issue to the other," he said.

Her dark eyes narrowed. He wasn't entirely sure what she wanted from him.

Or maybe he was afraid he *did* know. In the two years they had been together—always comrades in arms, more often than not lovers—she had never entirely trusted him. She knew, now, that he posed no danger of taking her beloved Jokers from her—and, not without bitterness, the reason why: They were, in the end, small potatoes.

Now it seemed she *knew*—against the evidence of seven hundred days—that he would betray her another way. That he would strike her. It was not an uncommon response for a bro confronted by a mouthy bitch. Which in turn was one reason Tristan encouraged the sisters in all the clans to learn the use of weapons, instead of just certain clubs like the Jokers—or the Hardriders.

There were times, when things weren't rolling so smooth between them, that Jovanne seemed to try extra hard to get him to take a crack at her. As if she wanted to get it over with, end the suspense.

He wondered why she fought so hard not to understand him.

From across a mushroom huddle of dome tents music sounded, brash and electric. The bros and sisses were getting down around a bonfire, laughing, dancing, partying hearty. It pleased the Lord of the Plains to surround himself with life, with the sounds and bright lights and movements of nomad merriment. Even if he wasn't that often in a frame of mind to take part in them himself.

When he needed solitude and quiet, as he often did, there was WildFyre or a scrambler bike with panniers full, and the storm-whipped wilderness that had occupied most of the North American continent—most of everywhere, so far as the Library could tell him—since the Star had fallen. The open spaces were beginning to call to him, insistently, but he knew this was no time to seek refuge.

Like there'll ever be a good time, he thought with an insight that weighed on him like a rucksack filled with lead.

From around a tent ahead, shapes were coming, walking toward them abreast, dark and looming. Tristan felt Jovanne tense beside him, and his own hand drifted upward toward the round butt of his broomhandle Bolo, tucked in its break-open holster beneath his left arm. The Lord of the Plains was not universally loved, even among the High Free Folk.

The figures approached, tall, hair hanging to big shoulders. Armbands gripped each one's right biceps. The moon had been overtaken by racing cloud again, but light-spill from the party fire fell across their faces.

"Lord Tristan," they murmured respectfully.

Tristan relaxed. "Phantom, Slick," he said. "Good job."

The two swung respectfully wide and passed by. Dog Soldiers on patrol. The Soldiers were members of an exclusive Plains society, whose membership extended across clan lines and dedicated itself to keeping the peace at ritual gatherings such as Taos Rendezvous in the spring, the official beginning of the biker year. Originally, Dog Soldier duty was a sometime thing, the members resuming life in their respective clans between events. John Hammerhand had kept them on as military police in his ill-fated army. Tristan maintained a detachment to keep the peace of Chaos Central, his permanent floating capital.

The laws of Burningskull were few. But he was pretty damned strict about them.

Jovanne let out a breath. "You are supposed to be Maximum

Lord of the Plains," she said. "How long are you going to let those nitwits in the Council ride over you?"

"I'm not the Mayor of some City, or the Duke-President of Dallas. I'm only the Lord because people say I am. They follow because they believe in me, not because they have to."

"They sure weren't acting as if they believed in you."

He blew out a breath beneath his mustache. The real pisser was, he was going to get a virtually identical ass-chewing from his weapons-master, Jeremy. Jovanne had a natural grasp for strategy, probably a genius; as a fighter she was good but nothing extraordinary. Jeremy was a samurai supreme, a master of weapons and unarmed combat who disdained firearms. For years, in his stagy secret identity of the Black Avenger, he had been widely considered the definitive samurai of the Plains. He neither knew nor cared much about the movements of large bodies of troops, about the niceties of maintaining or interdicting supply, about the laying of traps weeks or months in advance.

That wasn't why he and the Joker Prez never really got along. The reason for that was that they were in most ways very similar.

"You have your Dog Soldiers and your Burningskulls," she pressed. "Not to mention me and Jeremy and Jesse and the rest of us poor devoted fools who'd follow you through Demon's Den. We could crack some heads."

"Is that how you run the Jokers?" he asked.

She walked a space in sulky silence. He grinned to himself. Around them the tents began to thin away as they reached the outskirts of Chaos Central. The light and commotion beat at their backs like the warmth of a distant fire. Tristan looked out over the dark and broken land and felt it drawing him. It would be so easy to just slip away—and never come back.

He thought of the dreams he had been having of late. *No. I can't blame my dreams. Or my destiny. The Road I follow is my own choice. When I was captive as a kid, that was one thing, that was truly beyond my power. But if I'm restrained now, it's by chains I've willingly assumed.*

Damn it all anyway.

"Why do you always have to do that?" she asked eventually in a quiet, sullen voice.

"Do what?"

"Get so damned reasonable—"

She might have said more, but a figure stepped out of shadow and struck her to the ground.

• • •

The short hair on the back of Dirk Posen's neck rose. Slowly he turned.

"The witch," he said through a tight, strange smile.

She came forth from the balcony. She was tall, a head taller than he. Outside the clouds were overwhelming the sky like a black invading army, but enough moonlight still shone to give a gleam to the curve of her shaven skull, and lend a ghostly life to the yellow billow of her robe.

Somehow the moonlight shone through the robe, to show the lithe, fine figure within. Dirk Posen felt his teeth grind together.

"I won't ask how you got to the balcony," he said. "I don't want to know."

Her laugh was musical, if not exactly music to his ears. It was a fuller, throatier laugh than Elinor's, without the ice-crystal edge. It was no more comforting. It produced a markedly different effect, though, in regions below the belted narrow waist of his jumpsuit.

"I thought the Chairman knew everything that went on within Homeland," she said. "Isn't that the point of Purity?"

"Yes," he said tautly. "But it's a goal. Not a reality. Yet. But it shall be."

She stood before him. Her smell was strong in his nostrils, and without his willing it they flared to drink it more. He showed teeth. *Nothing* was supposed to happen in the City without his will, and he could not master himself.

She smelled of clean, healthy female. There was a swirl of other scents, though, aromas he didn't recognize which swam in his head like exotic colorful clouds. Perfume had always been a forbidden luxury in Homeland, even before the Restoration, except for the brief permissive interval of Reconciliationist Rule— the Days of Darkness, officially now.

He longed to step back, so that their spaces did not overlap like the light-cones of too-close street lamps. He did not.

"You talk big, Little Brother," she said.

"Don't call me that!"

Laughter. Slim fingertips trailed across his drawn cheek.

"If you could command everything within your perimeter," she said in a husky voice, "you would. No sparrow would fall without your knowing. But you can't do it. And your police and spies and informers and Neighborhood Watch committees can't do it for you. Nor will they ever."

She leaned closer, so her breath fell on his face. "Vanity, vanity, all is vanity," she husked. "You are wound about with the ropes of Ego."

Now he did fall back, cheeks burning. "It is my will which runs this City!" he almost stammered. "Mine! My will alone that keeps it from anarchy!"

She advanced on him, backing him up like a pigeon on a sidewalk. "For how long, little man? The Plains are awash in anarchy. Disorder is a sea which breaks in waves upon your doorstep. How long before the tide advances to swamp you, to bring all your bright fine towers of Order crashing down in ruin?"

His butt collided with the table. He gasped. Then he slammed his fist on the polished wood surface.

"No! It shall not! The rule of One must prevail. Dallas . . ."

A word too late he bit down on the flow of speech. She laughed again, and laid a finger on his lips.

"Do not fear, Little Brother. You have let nothing slip I didn't know. I too observed your so-secret conference—and your ice princess spying as well. Such a fine and frosty figure, that one. She will never give you what you want, Little Brother. She will never give any man what he wants. That is her nature."

"How *dare* you . . ." Posen raised a hand as if to strike her. Quick as a diamondback, her hand was at his throat. He felt the bones of his neck creak as she raised him from the floor.

"You speak of the Rule of One," she said in a voice like oiled silk. "How little you know of Oneness, you who know nothing but division and conflict within. Were it the will of the True One, I would let you strike me—or burn me at the stake, for that matter.

"Were it the will of Oneness, I could also snap your neck as easily as I snap your fingers. You are in the presence of a vessel of great Power, Little Brother. Learn that fact well, and your City shall know the greatness you desire."

She let him down. He fell back against the table, rubbing his throat. "I could call my guards," he croaked.

She laughed.

His face twisted. He sidled away, sought the open floor. "If you were spying," he said in a clearer voice, "you know of our secret treaty with Dallas."

"I know many things. It is my gift as a servitor of True Oneness. Likewise my burden."

"Big talk, as you say. Try running a City sometime."

"That is not my karma."

"Anarchy cannot stand against order, if order be backed by strong will. My will is harnessed with the will of Duke-President Austin now. The nomads will be crushed as by the jaws of a vise."

She came toward him. He tried to keep mind and eye from the way her hips swayed.

"That long-haired colonel, Selfridge, is a Hero," she said. "Also a fool. He will find death upon the Plains. Arms alone will not defeat disorder, Little Brother."

He fetched up against the wall. He hadn't known he was backing away again. She stopped inches from him. It was as if they both gave off similarly charged magnetic fields, as if the mutual repulsion was trying to squirt him away to the left or right. But yet another force pinned him to the wall.

"This very night we strike a blow against the Plains scum," he croaked.

"Arms alone will not bring you the death of Tristan Burningskull," she said.

"He's just a barbarian," he said, in something between a hiss and a squeak. "An—an outlaw. He can't stand against us."

Her laugh was as full-throated as a man's this time. "He is touched by Power," she said. "It is you who cannot stand against him. Not without the Power of the One. Not without yielding to Fusion."

"What—what do you want?"

Her face was close to his. "It is the ice-bitch's nature to deny men what they want," she murmured. "It is mine to give men everything they desire."

She stepped back. Seemingly of its own accord her saffron robe slithered down her long body and legs to the floor.

She stood before him nude in the doomed moonlight. Her body was perfection. Not the ice-sculpture perfection of Elinor Masefield, but warm perfection, vibrant with life, with an energy Dirk Posen could not comprehend. She was tautly muscular, with only the slightest hint of padding to soften the outline. Her breasts were full, the nipples dark wide circles. She was shaven below as above.

She reached to him. A small sound escaped his throat. She seized the stuff of his jumpsuit with her hands and pulled. It tore.

Dropping to her knees, she peeled the garment down his body, his trembling thighs. With a wrench of her wrists she tore open his underwear, let it fall.

His cock was rigid. It seemed to vibrate in the chill air of the room. He moaned as her hand closed hot about it. She steered it into her mouth. Her slanted blue eyes traveled up his body as she did so, caught his, held them, challenged them, as her lips enfolded him.

In the City sex was for procreation, and that of course was closely regulated, to keep the population in line. Sex as recreation was strictly frowned upon. Pleasure distracted the masses from their duty.

Pleasure distracted the Chairman of the PDU. Pleasure broke down all his barriers and walls. The woman slid her warm clinging mouth up and down his cock, and her tongue swirled round and round. Urgently she sucked, insistently, until he grasped her smooth head in his hands and his own head banged back against the wall in uncontrolled rhythm, an he spent himself in surges in her mouth.

His knees sagged. He moaned again, and drool trailed from his lips. Her eyes burned his face like torches.

The pressure of her mouth was painful on his suddenly sensitive prick. She did not relent. He tried to force her away. She smiled around him and continued to suck.

Impossibly, he grew rigid again in seconds. Pain turned once more to pleasure. He began to tremble with building need.

She released him. He gasped. He had the urge to seize her gleaming head, impale it again on his rigid dick, force her to free him from the torment she had laid upon him. He knew that it was not within him to compel her. She would break him like a stick.

She smiled, licked her lips. Then she turned from him.

Quivering, he watched her. Her waist was narrow, swelling to buttocks like compressed spheres, round and perfect. He watched them. His throat was as dry as the heart of the Jornada del Hell through FlameLand.

She crossed her forearms on the table, and bent forward to lay her cheek upon them. Her buttocks went round and taut. It felt as if his cock would explode.

She smiled back at him. "The Way to Power lies open to you," she said from the depths of her throat. "Walk it. *Take it*."

He kicked free of his ruined clothes and shuffled forward like a man in a dream.

7

With a flick of the wrist Tristan had his Bolo out. Something whirred, and the slim-barreled pistol was struck from his hand. He danced frantically back.

The figure sprang into the aisle between darkened tents. An object flashed in a blurred circle between them, then came abruptly to rest at an angle. It was a foot-long staff, separated from an identical staff by a brief length of chain. Nunchakus, then, held in a guard position.

The man behind them was short, dressed all in black, with a black headband tied around a shock of pale hair. His feet were bare, toes splayed to grip the tamped-down earth.

"Who the fuck are you?" Tristan asked. He was standing erect, with his hands down at his sides. It looked as if he was just standing there, unready to defend himself. It was in fact a fighting stance, and a potent one, taught him by Jeremy. The weapons-master based it on a stance used by the sword-saint Musashi, a time-dimmed legend even when the Star fell, which was known as *Open in All Eight Directions*.

Tristan gathered there was some convoluted and mystical explanation behind the name. What he liked was that it made your opponent think you were just standing there with your teeth in your mouth. Tristan was a practical kind of guy.

"My name is unimportant to you, though it shall be sung across the Plains as long as the stars shine down upon them," the man said. "You may think of me as Death."

"Very poetic," Tristan said, "but why don't I just think of you as Bullshit?"

The man bared his teeth. The two-part weapon he held whistled as the intruder released the left-hand rod, whipped it around and over his back, caught it again with his left hand behind him, held it there a beat, whipped it around his body—

Tristan relaxed ever so slightly. This wasn't an attack, yet. The man was showing off.

"You're one of those pencil-dick Apostles, aren't you?" he asked. He shook his head. "I've whacked five of you already. When are you clowns going to get the idea—"

The samurai shrieked *"Death!"* and launched a horizontal attack at Tristan's left temple.

It had not failed to occur to the Lord of the Plains that the bravura display would make a fine, distracting setup for an opening move. Tristan dropped. At the same instant he scythed out with his long legs, sweeping the nunchaku artist's legs from beneath him. The man fell on his ass with a grunted "Woof!"

The Burningskull weapons-master had taught his second-time-around pupil—for it was Jeremy, as the dorm rat named Ferret, who had taught the adolescent Tristan a knife art levels beyond anything known on the Plains—that the best way to overcome the advantage of a long-ranged hand-to-hand combat weapon was to cancel its range. In knife or sword range, the most common engagement distances for face-up fights, the nunchakus were a deadly and subtle weapon, difficult to counter.

At belly-to-belly range, they were damned near useless. A true master—and Tristan had no doubt that was what he faced—would know tricks for jabbing with the ends of the metal rods, or getting them around a joint or his neck for a nutcracker crunch. But master or no, that was damned hard to accomplish against a foe doing everything possible to disturb your concentration.

Tristan was not an expert wrestler—he had always preferred the striking arts, and the one conspicuous weakness in Jeremy's art was ground-fighting as well. But the two had picked up a few useful tricks between them. And Tristan had a knife—a weapon far easier to use when rolling in the dirt than the nunchakus . . .

The samurai understood the limitations of his weapon of choice. He simply threw himself away from Tristan's attempted scissors lock, rolling along the ground until he was well away from his opponent, and springing to his feet as if little wires hanging down from Mother Sky to his shoulders had snapped him erect.

As Tristan got up, not quite so spryly, he heard Jovanne moan. He advanced, to put himself between the assassin and her. He didn't want any hostage situations developing here.

With his eyes alone—keeping his face squared toward his foe—he cast about for his Bolo. No joy. It was lost in the shadows somewhere, worse luck. It would of course be the worst possible sportsmanship to end a match with a samurai and Apostle with a gun.

Too bad Tristan never thought Death was a game.

As he advanced slowly he drew his knife, a Bowie whose foot-long blade made it as much a shortsword as a knife. Tristan had actually toyed with the notion of continuing the fight barehanded, on the grounds that the samurai unquestionably devoted more of his practice to fighting a knife-man than any other kind of encounter. He abandoned the notion quickly enough. Even for an expert bare-hand hassler, and Tristan was, the difference between *unarmed* and *disarmed* could be pretty damned subtle. Man was a tool-using animal; any kind of weapon jumped your fighting abilities if you had the least idea how to use it.

The samurai was doing his thing again, whipping his weapon in a blur from one station to the next, pausing to let Tristan admire his pretty pose and then lashing to a new one. *Trying to lull me, distract me,* Tristan thought.

He walked forward, holding the knife reversed, its broad blade cool along the inside of his right forearm. Parrying a stroke that way ran less risk of getting the weapon knocked out of his hand—those 'chakus developed a hideous amount of torque.

"All right," Tristan said, "I'm impressed. But someone's bound to notice the commotion here and come running. You don't win much glory if my Dog Soldiers shoot you into little pieces. Any dog can die in a ditch."

The samurai showed teeth again. "The partying covers any noise we've made so far," he said, continuing to flash his metal 'chakus around. "And you haven't hollered for your guards yet, Burningskull."

Well, no, he hadn't. The truth was he didn't want to get the rep as a warrior who hid behind his bodyguards when the hammer came down. And he didn't want to think of himself that way.

He kept walking forward. He wanted to force the samurai to

act so he could launch a counter—even a forearm splintered in
a block was a good trade if he could plant a foot of Blood steel
in his enemy's guts. Naturally, the samurai wished for him to
make the first move. If he could get close enough he'd force the
assassin's hand.

The samurai kept backing. They were almost out in the Plains
now. That suited Tristan to the eyeballs. No matter how practiced
you were, no matter how finely honed your warrior senses or
how developed your ki, if you kept walking backwards blind
across broken terrain, sooner or later you were going to trip or
back off the wall of an arroyo or something. And Tristan was
ready to back his foe clear to the Black Hills.

The samurai sensed it. He caught one rod of his weapon in his
left armpit, and instead of continuing his backward posturing
march he slashed it forward in an underhand blow towards Tristan's long chin.

Tristan almost walked into it. He stumbled slightly, trying to
stop and leaning hurriedly back to avoid the blow. The samurai
transferred the weapon's upward momentum to a flat spin once
above his head and brought it down again toward the still-off-
balance Tristan.

Tristan's only defense was to throw himself backwards. The
steel nunchaku slammed the great muscle in his thigh. It was like
setting a bomb off in there.

Tristan staggered backward, went to one knee. *Jeremy would
sure kick my ass if he could see me now,* he thought, *getting my
mind locked in to advancing. Of course, this guy seems to be
doing a pretty good job of kicking my butt right now ...*

The samurai charged. Tristan whipped the Bowie around in his
hand, a flying grip change—a move, generally, that was more
juggling than you'd care to do in a fight, since the slightest mistake and there you were waving your bare fist in the breeze like
your cock, with your blade point-down in the dirt.

Tristan caught the weapon perfectly, though, and suddenly
there was a foot of sharp steel for the samurai to impale himself
upon. The Bowie's star-glinting menace drew a reflex strike from
the 'chakus.

As soon as he sensed—*guessed*, more like it—that the blow
was started, Tristan reversed the knife-flip. The rod cut air an
inch beyond the knuckles of Tristan's thumb and forefinger,
where the blade had been half an eye blink before. Tristan

launched himself off the ground in a lunge and drove the hilt of his knife into the pit of his assailant's stomach.

The samurai doubled as all the air was blasted out of him. With no options Tristan had made himself a projectile; he had no control over where he went. The two went down in a flailing heap. The nunchakus cracked down across Tristan's back, hard enough that he'd be cussing it when the sun came up if he chanced to live that long, not hard enough to make any difference in a fight. He got a couple of good body blows in with his left hand, then brought his right hand up, drove it down.

With a squealing grunt of rage and effort the samurai wrenched himself free and rolled away. Tristan's blade sank halfway to the hilt in grass-bound earth.

Still short on air, the samurai took his time getting up. That gave Tristan the time to yank his blade free and find his feet as well.

The samurai advanced, his weapon hissing figure eights before him. *Uh-oh,* Tristan thought. In the tent city, there had been enough stray light that he could keep reasonable track of the nunchakus. Out here dark ruled like an absolute monarch, and the 'chucks were a blur of black in blackness.

Sensing his advantage, the samurai laughed. He began switching the weapon from hand to hand, to add to Tristan's confusion. It was time for desperate measures; a turn of those strong supple wrists and the steel rod would lick out to crack Tristan's elbow, or his knee, or simply stave in the side of his head for him.

He did another juggling trick then, one that Jeremy would pound his nuts for if he ever found out. It was what you called a *border switch* if you did it with a handgun, tossing the Bowie from his right hand to his left. Then he launched a right front snap-kick to the samurai's nuts.

Like everyone else human, the samurai was wired to respond rapidly to attacks on eyes, throat, and testicles. Even a fighter with no training has a good chance of blocking a shot to those so-vital parts of him. The samurai held one rod out toward Tristan with his right hand, and pivoted the other over and down to crack Tristan's shin for him.

But Tristan's left forearm was in the way. Steel rang on steel as the nunchaku struck the Bowie. Even as he blocked Tristan was whipping his feint-kick down to plant on the ground, launching an overhand right into the middle of the assassin's face.

It wasn't a takeout blow—Tristan had no intention of shattering his hand. It had the desired effect of mashing the samurai's nose in a squash of cartilage and blood and distracting him for a fraction of a second.

Tristan turned his knife, threw his hand up, letting the blade wing out. The samurai screamed as the Bowie severed the tendons inside his forearm. The nunchakus cartwheeled into the night.

The samurai staggered back, clutching his spurting, ruined arm. Tristan flipped his knife blade forward. The samurai dropped into a fighting stance, letting his arm bleed—

Lightning and thunder. The samurai's body jerked. Again the flash and deafening crack, and again the assassin flinched in response.

Tristan's reflexes overruled conscious thought. He dropped flat. Those were *gunshots*, his subconscious realized, and until it knew who they were coming from it was by-God going to put Tristan out of the way of any stray lead.

The shots kept coming. From the warm earth, moist and fragrant from a sunset shower, Tristan saw a tall figure stalking deliberately forward from the tent city, arm extended, flashing fire at intervals. At each flash the samurai jumped, as if those wires from Heaven were jerking on him.

The final flash illuminated Jovanne's lovely face, set in a look of grim concentration. She lowered the elegant .40-caliber Dance Brothers & Park Vindicator handgun that had once belonged to Black Jack Masefield to her hip.

The samurai had fallen to his knees. He stared at her. The whites of his eyes gleamed all round his pupils as Sister Moon momentarily escaped her pursuing clouds.

"That's not," he began, and blood slopped over his lower lip, "not *fair!*"

"Who told you life was fair, sag-nuts?" Tristan asked. The assassin toppled.

Jovanne walked up to the prone body and kicked it vindictively. Despite the fact that the man was beyond feeling it, Tristan winced.

"Adding insult to injury, isn't it?" he asked, massaging his thigh. He had a bad bone bruise, no question. The muscle was knotting up on him big time, now that the adrenaline flow was beginning to cycle back.

"Teach the son of a bitch to crack *me* in the back of the neck," she snarled, rubbing the injured part. She spat on the corpse.

That was one thing about the warrior babes of the Plains. They were even less chivalrous than Tristan. It may have been one reason he favored them so.

She turned a glare on Tristan. "What are you bitching for anyway? I saved your ass, you might notice. Not for the first time."

"Not this time, hon," he said, gimping around in a circle to stave off cramps in his injured leg. "I'd just disarmed him. Thanks for the thought, though."

"Well, fuck you anyway," she growled. "In fact . . ."

She dropped the mostly spent magazine into her left fist, replaced it with a fresh one from the beaded Absaroka medicine bag at her hip. Then she marched up to Tristan, who was circling like a bird with a broken wing, and seized him firmly by the ear.

"Ouch!" he moaned. "What the hell do you think you're doing?"

"I'm going to take you back to the tent," she said, "and I'm going to fuck your eyeballs out. And you don't have any choice in the matter. Okay?"

"I never argue with a lady who just saved my life."

Looking like a cross between a colander and a watermelon dropped from a height, the nunchaku artist advanced, grinning, his steel rods whispering a song of death. Tristan's busted arms dangled at his sides like a rag doll's.

"Can't we talk about this?" he asked the apparition. In response the samurai whapped him in the left side of his rib cage. And again, and again—

"Wake up, O Mighty Lord of the Sound Sleepers," the revenant said in a horribly familiar voice, "and thank your lucky stars I'm not another sag-nuts Apostle."

"But you are," Tristan heard himself protest as his eyes came open.

"Not a chance," said Jeremy, who stood over him, grinning like a skull. "Why would I hang out with a bunch of crummy amateurs like that?"

"But . . ." He shook his head, shedding the remnants of the dream like droplets of water.

The sunlight filtering through the walls of the tent was considerably weakened. It made his brain hurt anyway. He took stock of his hurts. His thigh ached as if one of the kobolds was standing beside the bed pounding it with a hammer in time to his heart. And the fuckard had done a job on his ribs too.

Wait a minute. The Apostle had never connected with his ribs, had gotten in no body shots at all except for a lick across his back—and he felt that too, come to think of it. . . .

"You were kicking me!" he said accusingly.

"You're a smart boy," Jeremy said. "I can see right off why they made you Lord of the Plains."

Beside Tristan Jovanne sat up. She was naked. Instead of using the bearskin robe they had for a blanket to cover herself, she rubbed her eyes.

"Good morning, Jeremy," she said in a sleepy, surly voice. "You'll do anything to get a look at my tits, won't you?"

"Don't flatter yourself," the weapons-master growled. Though as a matter of fact, the Joker Prez had very nice tits indeed, large and pink-nippled, but round rather than protruding. . . .

Tristan realized his mind was wandering. He was mildly surprised he hadn't got all that kind of thing worked out of his system last night. It wasn't for lack of trying, on his part or Jovanne's. Escaping death always made him randy as a blackfoot ferret. Maybe it was a life-affirming thing, or some other such wifty-drifty StarLodge concept. . . .

"Whoa," he said, sitting abruptly upright. "I had a hard night, Jeremy. It usually doesn't take this long for my brain to turn over."

There were two people in camp who had the privilege of entering the Maximum Lord's quarters unannounced, and one of them had been there all along. And no matter how familiarly they treated Lord Burningskull, neither one would ever dream of abusing that privilege.

"What is it, Jeremy?" Tristan said blearily.

"I thought you'd never ask," Jeremy said, and the smile slipped from his pointed near-handsome face. "It's Homeland. Mobile Forces advanced fifty miles last night. Caught the Desperadoes and a few Wild Things camped near where the Big Sandy flows parallel to the big Hard Road. Lost twenty riders killed, ten missing. Survivors got through to us by radio a few minutes ago. Say the MoFos are already stretching fence."

He hunkered down next to the pallet. "Fuckards are moving on us, Tristan. Big time. It's war."

8

The earth was burning. Black smoked poured out of a hole in the ground, defying a heavy rain. It was almost as if the rolling Plains were about to give birth to yet another volcano.

Out of the smoke climbed a woman, her clothes and long black hair smoking. She stumbled, got to her feet, and began to flee east.

From behind her came a snarl of full-automatic gunfire. The woman pitched forward into the lush prairie grass to lie unmoving.

Belly-down on a ridge a quarter-mile away, Tristan Burningskull lowered the binoculars from his eyes. His eyes were bleak.

"Bastards," he spat.

Lying beside him, Jeremy showed no response. His eyes were fixed on the distant scene, lips peeling slowly, subconsciously back from his teeth. To the left and right of them, a dozen of Tristan's handpicked Burningskull riders lay behind their weapons, concealed by the crest line.

They were lying up five miles south of the place where the prairie had absorbed all but a few crumbled walls and cracked plates of ancient pavement of the pre-StarFall town of Limon, to either side of Hard Road 70, itself scrupulously maintained through religious observance and necessity alike. A couple of miles further south the tree-lined course of the Big Sandy was visible, diving away into the southeast after running with 70 for a few miles. With the exception of the long-disbanded Strikers, who had been known to range clear to the Missus Hip when ne-

cessity or even fancy called them, Homeland forces had not pen-
etrated this far into the Plains since the disastrous campaign of
the spring of '23, during Tristan's senior year in high school.

It was a bad omen for the brothers and sisters of the High Free
Life.

A platoon of Mobile Forces troopers had dismounted from
their canvasback trucks and begun to advance in a slow line,
M52 storm carbines held in the patrol position, faces depersonalized behind black shades. Their battle dress consisted of streaky
green cammies and baseball caps. The look was a Purity innova-
tion; the shakeup in the HDF had gone far deeper than the name
change. The rest of the company was deployed along a line of
hill four hundred meters behind them to the west, supported by
four Marauder armored cars armed with automatic 20-mm cannon.

A man on fire burst out of the blazing underground dwelling.
He dropped to the wet ground, rolled the flames out, and lay
moaning. The advancing line began to curve around the burning
house, the men on direct approach crouching cautiously, their
comrades right and left continuing forward.

One of the semi-faceless troopers briefly straightened to fire a
single shot into the back of the moaning man's neck. The flanking soldiers went to ground behind their weapons. Another soldier rolled a couple of frag grenades into the house, which a
mortar barrage had set on fire. A double crack, a fresh gout of
smoke.

No one else came out.

With a muted rumble of its alcohol-fueled engine a Marauder
armored car prowled forward. Its long slim gun like an insect's
antenna aimed straight ahead instead of tracking side to side; the
Mobile Forces were confident, unafraid of the worst these pathetic squatters could do to them. They held Diggers in the same
contempt the High Free Folk did. They wiped them out as casu-
ally as they would pesky colonies of prairie dogs.

The Marauder came to a halt beside the smoking hole. Almost
immediately there was a high-pitched crack.

The armored car blew up. The turret popped into the air atop
a gusher of yellow flame, tipped to the side, and fell onto the unseen roof of the buried house, which promptly caved in in an upward shower of sparks.

From a hilltop off to Tristan's right a puff of white smoke left
by the rocket that had shattered the Marauder was blowing away

in wisps. The MoFos opened frantic fire on it. The engines of the
surviving three cars whined as they hustled to put hills between
them and the hidden rocket launchers. One of them rolled forward to a hill-down position behind the crest. Its long gun
snarled. Small geysers of earth stitched the hilltop.

The shrilling of whistles breasted the wind's flow as unit leaders rousted their men off the ground and sent them forward in
squad rushes. The company line pivoted left as it advanced, to
face the hill from which the rocket had come and protect the precious armored cars.

Armor was a paradox. Against light-armed nomads it could be
lethal—as long as speed or covering infantry kept enemies from
getting to daggers-drawn range with the fighting vehicles, at
which point they turned highly vulnerable. Antitank rockets blew
the equation to hell; suddenly the armored boys puckered their
assholes and hunkered down and prayed the grunts with their
asses in the grass could save them. There was something about
the prospect of burning to death in a big iron can that took the
starch right out of a man's spine.

Old City soldier Tristan watched the MoFos maneuver with a
critical eye. Highly critical. The Mobile Forces had looked pretty
enough putting the moves on a shattered sodbusters' den, with
odds of two hundred to maybe four or five surprised farmers
armed with break-open shotguns. But when it came to a tricky
redeployment under fire, the MoFos were starting to get ragged,
to get in each other's way, cohesion coming apart in the slacken-
ing rain.

"Cargo soldiers," Jeremy said contemptuously. He'd done his
time in the old HDF himself, losing a foot to a comrade's bullet
when he deserted, escaping with his life only because an outlaw
attack fortuitously coincided with his break. "They're fine as
long as they're stacked in the back like so many boxes."

Tristan heard another sharp crack, the characteristic sound of
a shaped-charge armor-busting warhead going off. He frowned,
hunting back and forth with his glasses, unsure what the hell was
coming down.

He heard another as Jeremy grabbed his arm. He lifted his
eyes from the binoculars in time to see one of the distant Marauders explode. A third was already blazing cheerfully.

"What the fuck, over?" Tristan murmured in disbelief. The
sole surviving armored car turned tail and promptly vanished
over the hills.

"Somebody's caught the MoFos' nuts in the wringer," Jeremy said.

"Yeah," said Tristan. "And it's *pretty*."

The MoFos in the grass were beginning to look around in surprise and fear. Nobody likes getting hit in the rear, and no one feels more naked than a leg soldier who's just lost his armor support.

At the south side of what was rapidly becoming an armed mob a commotion broke out. Tristan turned his glasses that way in time to see men leap to their feet and then fall again, thrashing and clutching at themselves.

"Now what?" Tristan asked. He felt Jeremy's shrug.

"Look—there, to the south!" a Burningskull shouted. The wet Plains slid across Tristan's field of vision in a dizzying blur. Movement—he tracked back. Horses with riders, a score or so, vanishing down a draw with tails high. The riders carried recurved bows in their hands.

"I'll be dipped," Jeremy breathed. "The Merry Pranksters."

"Fucking *Beasties*?" a Burningskull asked in disbelief. Not all the High Free Folk were Pure Engine People, but to ride an animal into *battle* put you at about the same point on the nomad evolutionary scale as your mount.

Tristan lowered his glasses. A figure appeared on a ridge to the southwest, a solitary rider, small and slim on a dark horse. The animal reared, stroked the air with its forelegs as its rider brandished a bow above its head. Then the beast wheeled and vanished.

Tristan snapped his glasses back up, but the apparition was gone. He blew a breath out under his mustache. He had come for a look at the revamped Mobile Forces in action. He'd gotten an eyeful . . . more than anticipated, in fact.

He turned his attention back to the MoFos. Some of them were milling around, and it looked as if a couple of squads had flat-out broken and were beating cheeks off over the hills in the Marauder's tracks. The City's noncoms were a solid bunch, though, and squad and platoon leaders were getting their boys dug into a defensive circle off-centered on the burning underground house.

"MoFos are prettier than good," he said, sliding back down from the crest line and rolling over to sit up. "But they won't break easily. All right, everybody, let's putt!"

"Somebody missed a big chance down there," Jeremy said,

standing up out of the City soldiers' range of vision and straightening his arms out behind his back in a stretch.

Tristan hiked up an eyebrow at him. "What do you mean?"

Jeremy laughed. "Horse barbs had the truck troopies running around like decapitated chickens. If they'd just hit 'em hard when they had the chance they could have pulled a Hardriders' Last Stand in reverse. Uh—sorry."

Tristan grinned. Jeremy didn't apologize too often, but he realized he'd just stepped on his prick in a major way.

"No worries," Tristan said, but a shadow passed behind his eyes. The Hardriders' Last Stand was the standard by which nomad military disasters were measured—and Tristan had been one of two survivors on the Stormrider side.

Jeremy went gimping off down the slope to where the bikes were parked. A frown notched Tristan's brow as he watched his old friend go. Jeremy was an unparalleled fighter, and not without tactical sense. But he lacked a master's eye at any scale beyond man-to-man, and he'd just displayed the fact.

As far as Tristan was concerned, they had just witnessed a minor masterpiece. A handful of horsemen, armed with a few modern missiles and *bows*, for Mother Sky's sweet sake, had dropped a few troopies—symbolic casualties, really, except of course to the poor bastards who got punctured—and three expensive armored cars. They had done so at no visible cost to themselves.

Had they tried to press the attack, the MoFos still had their automatic weapons, their storm carbines and machine guns, not to mention mortars. The horse barbarians would have been ground to dog food in seconds.

Somebody had just inflicted absolutely the worst defeat possible on the arrogant MoFos, given the resources they'd sent against them. That was *art*. Tristan knew he could have done no better himself. He honestly wondered whether he could have accomplished as much.

If I could use the High Free Folk that well, he thought, pulling at his chin, which most people would have said was already plenty long, *we could tell Homeland and Dallas both to just go whistle.*

Thoughtful, he started walking down the hill. His little party had already mounted up, awaiting only his lead to kick their bikes to life.

All clans were his clans; he was Maximum Lord of the Plains, in theory anyway, though none understood the practical limits of his power better than he. But the Burningskulls were *his* clan. Successors to the lost Hardriders. He had assembled them from the finest of the volunteers who'd flocked to his flaming-steer-skull standard. Most of the most noted or notorious clans of the Plains were represented: the Freebirds, the Caballeros, the Seventh Sons, the Seekers. He even had a former member of the Smoking Mirrors, a truly outlaw clan of cannibals and DemonCallers—his mother Jen Morningstar's clan, in fact, from which his father Wyatt had stolen her, not without her help.

A pallidly pretty white-blond woman caught his eye and nodded. She was Pony, formerly of Jovanne's Jokers. By preference Tristan would have taken Sly or the sharpshooter Little Teal. But he didn't want to cut the guts out of his lover's club.

Jovanne, of course, had thrown a major tantrum over the fact that he hadn't selected *her*. He had carefully explained to her that she was too valuable to him as a clan leader to scale back her responsibility to the level of just another fanny in a saddle. He thought she'd come to accept his reasoning. He *hoped*.

He swung a boot over WildFyre, kicked her starter. Her engine turned over at once, of course.

The run thunder rose in his ears, the unmistakable full-throat boogie of outlaw bikes. The MoFos would hear the noise, no question. The Burningskulls didn't care. The Marauders were thoroughly out of the picture, and by the time the truck soldiers clambered back into their cages the nomads would be gone with the wind. If the horse barbarians didn't have them too frightened to move.

Tristan put his ride in gear, and started to roll. Jeremy rode at his right, of course. The Burningskulls started to eddy around him, to take their places behind him in some order of precedence they had worked out among themselves.

From over his left shoulder he heard a cry. He put a boot down and pivoted around in time to see one of his riders topple with an arrow sunk to its black feathers in his chest.

9

"*There's the fuckard!*" screamed Alien, pointing to a ridge a good two hundred meters away. Tristan saw a figure duck away behind it.

"They got Wire," Hawkman snarled. He jacked the slide of his twelve-gauge Cherokee pump. "Son of a bitch must pay!"

Engines revved with a roar. "Wait!" Tristan screamed. "Gods damn it, *nobody move!*"

The engine howl died away down the scale. Heads turned toward him, jaws slack with disbelief.

"Why not?" asked Enforcer. He was as rangy and dark as Tristan himself, with a Mephistopheles beard and mustache. "We can run him down easy. We run on internal by-God combustion, and his ride's powered by grass. And all he's got's a bow."

"We're riding sleds, not scramblers," Tristan reminded him. He signed for the Bone Dancer to see to the injured man. "Besides, it could be a trap. We don't want to ride full-on into the killzone if it is."

Peaches pushed his grimy goggles up on top of his head and scratched his taffy-colored beard. "But Boss," he said, showing the gap where he'd had a front tooth busted out in a dustup with the Misery City heat. "They're *Beasties*."

"You saw what they did to the MoFos. Now, off the irons and into the grass. Set up a defensive circle to cover the Dancer."

The Burningskulls looked at one another. They didn't dare shrug, quite. Tristan was their Main Man. They would not publicly question his judgment. They would most especially never suspect him of cowardice. But they wondered, deep down inside them, just the same.

They dropped kickstands and dismounted, taking up positions around the injured man with weapons ready. They moved kind of slow for picked troops. Tristan had not assembled them for any slavish qualities; he wanted initiative as well as loyalty. But he wasn't too happy.

Damn, he thought. *I can't afford to start losing this bunch. I can't afford to even come close.*

Vengeance snarled as Jeremy goosed her throttle. "He's right," Jeremy said, in a soft voice that carried despite the wind and the rain and the now-muted thunder of 74-cubic-inch engines. "An arrow'll kill you just as dead as any bullet, you stupid sons of bitches."

Though he never referred to the fact himself, that Jeremy had been the famous masked hero called the Black Avenger had become common knowledge. When he spoke the Burningskulls hung their heads, ashamed to have doubted their leader. Tristan could have kissed him.

"What," the small man added in a voice less edged with razors, "did the Lord Tristan pick you for your good looks instead of your brains?"

Everybody looked at Peaches, who was famously ugly, and broke out laughing. Tristan gave Jeremy half a smile, which the smaller man never noticed. For all his lone-wolf proclivities Jeremy was not without leadership skills of his own. But he steadfastly refused anything resembling command.

Wire was still alive and breathing, if bubbling. He was lucky there. If a chest wound doesn't take out the heart and cancel your account right there, it's more survivable than a belly wound by far.

The Bone Dancer, who was sun-browned to the color of an old cypress knee and painfully skinny except for knobbed joints, so that he resembled a collection of beads strung on sticks, ministered to the sucking chest wound as best as possible. Then he assembled a stretcher out of tarps and collapsible aluminum rods which Tristan insisted his men carry for just such occasions, strapped the injured man to it, and slung him between his bike and Pony's. It wasn't easy to ride together hauling a stretcher; the pace would slow way down.

The Mobile Forces might have had a chance to catch them up after all. Fortunately, the MoFos had problems of their own.

● ● ●

"Justice!" raved the bearded man. "That's what I seek, that's what I demand. Some old-fashioned Gods-damned *justice*!" He uttered a piercing scream and began to tear his beard out in handfuls.

Tristan raised his head from the Road Hog rider groveling in the dirt of his tent city to Lonesome Dave, who stood behind him as if playing the sponsor. Though late spring was blending into early summer, the day had grown bitter, and pelted the returning Burningskull reconnaissance party with hail. Always a snappy dresser, the Pistolero Prez sported a gleaming ankle-length black leather greatcoat that he claimed to have gotten off a Dallasite general who'd had no further use for it. Lonesome Dave claimed a great many things. He always had something to back his claims, but it generally fell short of eyewitnesses.

"He came to me with his sad story," said the Pistolero from behind his near-perpetual sardonic grin. "It just tore at my heart, but of course there was nothing I could do without my Lord's approval."

Not for the first time, Tristan swallowed the desire to pound in that too-handsome face. Lonesome Dave had a way of presenting all the tokens of the utmost respect in such a way as to let you know he didn't mean them for a moment.

Tristan looked down at the Hog, who was now wallowing in the mud pounding the ground with big fists. "Come on now," he said, "catch a handhold here. Get up and tell me what's the rattle." The High Free Folk didn't put much premium on keeping the old stone face except when it came to physical pain; expression of Plains emotion could get pretty extreme. But this was a little much.

The Hog got to his knees and shuffled forward, trying to grab Tristan's hand as if to kiss it. Tristan snatched his hand out of harm's way.

"It was those fuckard Beasties," the rider sobbed. "The Merry Pranksters. They 'bushed us big, on the Hard Road to Backroad Bill's. We lost seven fine bros and true in the wink of a eye, all fulla arrows and takin' on most piteous."

Backroad Bill's Roadhouse was a trading post, cantina, and show club on the Hard Road I-70, just outside the demon-haunted and well-picked-over ruins of the Dead City of Denver. Bill himself was a bro, a legendary biker in his day, war chief and Prez of half a dozen clubs before he decided to hang his colors on the wall and settle down. It was fifty miles almost due east of Chaos Central's current site, on the banks of the Beaver.

Tristan scowled and rubbed his chin. Backroad Bill's was like a little bit of Rendezvous year-round, where a brother or sister could kick back, slug down some Taos Lightning, eat a good steak, sluice off the trail dust, stuff some coin into a G-string or two if the mood overtook them—Bill catered to a wide range of tastes in entertainment, none of them unusually refined.

It was in Tristan's mind to wonder what the Road Hogs had in mind in going there exactly. The Hogs were a clan he would have been just as glad to leave out of his Plains federation entirely. They were entirely capable of taking into their small heads the notion of knocking over the Roadhouse.

It would be a conspicuously poor idea. Invitingly wealthy as it was, the Roadhouse was also large, well-fortified, and permanently staffed by a contingent of the Crazy Dogs Wishing to Die MC, a surly and combative Plains Indian club dominated, in its West Plains branches, by former Cheyenne mercenaries pissed off at their two hundred years' subjugation by the rich and powerful Absaroka. They were armed with river guns and kobold light artillery, with copious stocks of fodder for defenders and weapons alike.

Moreover, Bill himself had been a primo razzer in his own day; there were no tricks or ruses that he didn't know and had not his own self run, at one time or another. While all brothers and sisters of goodwill were welcome, as long as they could pay—and he had been known, once or twice, to extend generosity to the well and truly strapped—he had no tolerance for bullshit. The wire perimeter that surrounded the Roadhouse compound was dotted with over a hundred stakes, and on each stake was a skull, placed there by Bill himself. "To encourage the others," as he put it.

"What happened?" Tristan made himself ask.

The Hog sat back on his heels with his big gut spilling over his belt and almost onto Tristan's shins. "Nothin' much to tell, Yore Worship. There he was, ridin' along, enjoyin' being in the wind as is the birthright of every brother born. Suddenly, without warning, the mingy fuckards opened up on us from the side of the road."

He shook his head, saddened by the perfidy of humankind. "Just imagine! Violatin' the sanctity of the Road like that!"

The Road Hogs should have had little trouble accomplishing

that trick, even with their limited imaginations, because they themselves were known for doing just that.

"Our brother here asks for a jihad against the horse barbarians," said Lonesome Dave. "They did desecrate the Holy Road."

"Did they string a wire then?" asked Jeremy, who had come up behind his lord and friend.

The Road Hog's face fisted as his brain tried to assimilate the question. "No," he blurted out, then said immediately, "I mean yes! Course they did, the skunks. Not fit to be left alive, a beast-loving one of 'em."

"They hung you on a wire, did they?" Jeremy asked, not bothering to keep the nasty out of his voice. "The causeway for 70's forty yards wide at that point. That's a hell of a long wire."

The Hog looked back at Lonesome Dave for support. "Our brother here's a bit befuddled," the Pistolero drawled, his face as straight as it ever got. "A reaction to what he went through."

The Hog managed to catch the cue. "That's right," he said, nodding so vigorously Tristan dared to hope he'd dislocate something in what neck he possessed. "We got us the Post-Dramatic Stress Disorder, and it's got our thinking riled up."

Something like a strangled snicker squeezed out of Jeremy's ears. "You mean to tell me you've never bushwhacked anybody on the open Road?" Tristan asked slowly. Barring the unforgivable sin of hanging a wire, the act was considered moderately treacherous. But its practice was too universal for the Folk to get genuinely outraged about it.

The Hog's eyes grew wide in shock and feigned innocence. Given that the area customarily covered by his goggles was the only relatively clean area of his face, if not his entire lumpy body, it gave him the appearance of a photonegative raccoon.

"Why, shorely the Maximum Lord is aware of the Road Hog Clan's undyin' reputation for honor of the most upstanding sort."

"I'm aware of no such thing," Tristan said. "If your clan has an undying reputation, it's as back-shooters and bottom-dealers of the lowest sort."

The Hog picked himself out of the dirt. "If you wasn't the Lord of the Plains hisself, I'd have to call you out," he said, glowering bushily.

"Don't let that stop you doing what your honor demands," Tristan said. "I'm not known for hiding behind my titles."

The man's boar-hog eyes were rolling around in his head so

radically they seemed likely to just **bust loose** and start free-wheeling. Lonesome Dave stepped forward.

"The man is crying for justice, **Lord Tristan**," he said. "Are you going to close your ears?"

It struck Tristan that for the Hogs, pleading for justice was a bad plan, because the just thing to do would certainly be to hang the clan *en masse*. He toyed with the idea. Jovanne and Jeremy were constantly ragging him to act more like, well, a *lord*. That'd show them, plus it would be fun.

"The just course isn't just leaping out at me," Tristan admitted. "What is it you're asking of me?"

"Revenge!" the man howled, spraying him with spittle.

"You're saying the Road Hogs are too helpless to avenge themselves on a pack of horse barbarians?"

The man looked back at his coach. Lonesome Dave shrugged, ever so slightly. The Hog went to his knees again, jarring the ground like a temblor.

"Lord, we're your subjects. Your loyal children. Ain't it up to you to pertect us? If them beastie fuckards can 'bush as they please, where's the point of bein' part o' your Federation?"

Tristan showed his teeth. "Very well," he said. "I will think on this, and give you my decision."

That seemed about the most neutral thing possible to say, but the man started blubbering and grabbing for his hand again. Tristan gave Lonesome Dave one of those looks which, if they could kill, would, turned on his boot heel, and stalked off to his tent.

10

He dropped to a pile of cushions and kicked off his boots with a moan of relief. Jeremy came in after him.

"Mother Sky," Tristan said. "That fat, unwashed bastard had me by the short and curlies there, and he knew it."

Jeremy settled with his back to the wall of the tent. The wind started flinging handfuls of pea-sized hail against its outside with a snare-drum sound.

Tristan had stopped off by the healers' tent to check on Wire. The jaunt cross-country had done him little good. He had not regained consciousness, and looked like death warmed over and allowed to congeal. Nonetheless the Boss Healer, a striking if slightly hefty StarLodger named Andromeda, had assured him the rider's chances were good.

"You picked your Burningskulls tough," she told him. "Now get the hell out of here." He got.

"You could've kissed him off," the small man said, "and nobody'd thought worse of you for it. Everybody knows what kind of low-down scooter trash the Road Hogs are. Plus, he's no doubt lying through those jumbled brown stumps he calls his teeth; Hogs can't tell the truth even when it's not in their interests to lie. It'd make 'em vanish in a flash of blue fire."

"All that's true," Tristan said. "But he raised a damn good question. Better than half the clans of the Plains acknowledge me their overlord. What do they get from the deal?"

Jeremy shrugged. He produced a knife with a slim, tapered, straight-edged blade and began to strop it on a leather band he

70

wore about his wrist. "They get to be part of the biggest, baddest club that ever rode the Plains. The Stormrider Federation, that pinned the Catheads' ears back and told the high and mighty Cities where to get off."

"Yeah, and got the high and mighty Cities to send whole armies into the field to kick our butts too."

Jeremy laughed, and shaved a patch of hair from his forearm to test his edge. The blade shaved him like a razor, but apparently that failed to satisfy him, for he set to work again.

"That shows how powerful you've become. Homeland and Dallas are shit-scared of us now. It's forcing their hand, forcing them to act before we become unbeatable."

"That's the problem. Maybe they're right."

Jeremy shrugged. "I give you rations of shit," he said, "more than you should probably put up with. But I have faith in you, boy. You're pretty sly for a mangy scooter tramp."

"Thanks. But you're not telling me what I'm offering the brothers and sisters aside from a chance of getting washed away by giant Citizen armies."

Jeremy held his blade up, squinted at it in the afternoon gloom, nodded, and made it vanish up his sleeve.

"Everybody loves a winner," he said. "We're front-runners, all of us. You beat the Cats big, after the disaster at Rock Creek, put steel back in the spines of the kindred. They feel *good* riding beneath the Sign of the Burning Skull. They feel part of something big, bigger than themselves—the stuff of epic, of legend."

"You're starting to sound like Jammer."

"Hey. We're all adolescents out here on the Plains, is what it comes down to. Acting out our fantasies is what we're all about, with our big gleaming bikes and our outlandish clothes and hair and our wild-ass nicknames and get-down-till-you-fall-in-the-fire shivarees. Shit, I spent five years dressed in black riding all over the place wearing a black steel hockey mask, for Christ's sake. I'm as bad as any of you bike-trash born."

He shook his head. "Shit, Tristan. You're good theater. You're *entertaining*. That's what you offer the bros and sisses, once the bullshit's boiled off."

Tristan glared hard at him for almost a minute. Jeremy laced his fingers behind the back of his head, gave him a Cheshire Cat grin, and leaned back to let the hard hail fingers massage his back.

Tristan put his head back and shattered the tension with a

laugh. It rumbled up from the middle of him, like a quake from Mother Earth's fault-lined belly.

"You have the annoying habit of being right," he said, when the laughter died away in aftershocks. "Here I thought I offered them law, order, and glory."

"The Stormriders can get their bellies full of glory any time they're seriously minded to," Jeremy said. "Ask your pal Jammer. As for order, I think the brothers are more interested in escaping it than getting a good dose of it. And laws . . ."

He chuckled. "The Plains have their own laws. Always have. Lot of 'em more complicated than anything the Cities throw up, except maybe Dallas. You should know that—you were born out here."

"It's true. But I offer . . ." After the afternoon's events the word practically stuck in his throat. "Justice."

"I think that'd scare the ass off a lot of these bike scum. Take the Road Hog out there."

"You take him—please."

"Old joke. He and his bros were heading off to do a little unsanctioned razzing, something you'd have had to squash them for if you found out about it. I know it, you know it. They wound up catching a good dose of their own salts. If that's not just, I don't know what is."

Tristan nodded, but his eyes had gone storm-gray, a sure sign he was troubled. "But the other bros saw him beg me for justice—Lonesome Dave made sure of that."

Jeremy sneered at mention of the name but said nothing.

"The clans heard that one of their own was victim to an unprovoked attack. What will they think if the Maximum Lord lets that slide?"

"Fuck what they think."

"I can't. Jeremy, don't you see—what happens if they quit thinking I'm Maximum Lord? I'm not exactly an elected official."

Jeremy shrugged. "So politics isn't my strong suit. I could offer to kick their asses for you, one at a time."

It was Tristan's turn to laugh. On the other hand, he wasn't sure Jeremy wouldn't do just that, should he request it.

"So what are you suggesting here? That I not try to lay any payback on the horse barbarians?"

"You don't have enough problems with Dallas and Homeland? I mean, shit, while you're at it, why not declare war on the

Kaybeckers too, for speaking French? That offends the ass off *me*." He shook his head. "Shit happens. Casualties happen. The Pranksters are not a priority right now. If some of the bros can't see that, let 'em grumble."

"I have another problem," Tristan said. "What about Wire? My Burningskulls are pretty hot over watching him taken down and not being able to do jack about it."

"He'll live, won't he?" Tristan nodded. "There you go. He's a big boy. The 'Skulls are all big boys and girls. If you say suck it up, they'll suck it up."

Tristan frowned.

"Listen, Tristan," the smaller man said, leaning forward over crossed legs. "Not a man or woman in the whole damn Federation doubts you're the toughest hombre on the Plains. You wouldn't have come near this far if they did.

"And besides—what's so damned rewarding about being Maximum Lord anyway? What's it ever won you besides major pains in the head, gut, and butt? Why not just shuck it and ride off into the sunset?"

Tristan blinked and rocked back. The idea hit him like a blow. He had been so single-minded in his purpose since—since escaping Homeland, really, in a hail of Purity gunfire—that the thought of turning aside, of abdicating as Maximum Lord, had never occurred to him.

"I—can't," he said at last.

"Yeah, you can." Jeremy grinned at him. "You just never thought of it."

Sometimes having people know you to the bone was a positive detriment, Tristan reflected. He touched himself on the breastbone.

"There's something won't let me do that," he said. "Something—*here*. I have plans. I can't—won't—let 'em go."

Jeremy shrugged, spread hands in a *well, I tried* gesture.

"I don't understand you, Jeremy. One breath you're ragging my ass for not being dictatorial enough. The next you're telling me to pitch it all over and go for a putt on WildFyre."

"Just want you to keep your mind clear. If you're going to do it, do it right. But I thought you might want to ask yourself if it's worth the damned hassle."

Tristan sighed, then laughed at himself: the mighty Tristan Burningskull, Maximum Lord of the Plains, sighing in self-pity like a love-struck adolescent.

"I still say don't sweat this Road Hog crap," Jeremy said. "Sure some people'll bitch if you kiss 'em off, but you have to know you'll never please everybody. Bottom line is, the bros will follow you as long as you show class."

Slowly Tristan nodded. "You're right again, Jeremy. Damn your eyes."

He stood up, stretched. "And you've shown me the Road I'm going to take."

Jeremy looked up at him, surprised. "You mean you're going to toss your hand in?"

"Hell, no. I mean, if the Road Hogs want justice, I'll give it to them—good and hard."

"You're gonna hang 'em?"

"I mean, if I'm going to be just, I have to listen to both sides. So what I'm going to do is go find the Merry Pranksters and ask them *their* side."

11

"Tristan Burningskull, you are stone-cold out-of-your-skull crazy!"

Jeremy's parting words rang in Tristan's mind like a bell as he rolled his scrambler forward into the cluster of Plains Indian-style tipis. Gritty ash from a mountain-busting volcanic explosion many miles northwest in the FlameLands crunched under his cleated tires. No people were in sight.

His best friend was undoubtedly right again.

It had taken two days of good old-fashioned Striker-style snooping and pooping to catch up to the party of twenty or so riders—twenty!—who had laid such hurt on the MoFo company. Tristan was a skilled tracker. He couldn't come close to a Cree, say, but the truth was the horse barbarians, contemptuous of their truck-bound Citizen foes, had not bothered to hide their tracks.

That signified to Tristan that, while they were cunning and bold, and directed by a keen tactical intelligence, they had a tendency toward overconfidence. Useful to know, possibly.

The band seemed to be headed northwest. He guessed that they were near rejoining a larger party of their comrades. Little factual was known about the horse barbarians, no more by the Folk than by City intelligence. He had no way of judging whether the raiding party would hook up to the main Prankster body or merely a part.

He thought of trailing them to their rendezvous, and rejected the notion on several counts. First, he could afford to take only a limited amount of time away from Chaos Central. The Plains were vast, and no matter what Homeland and Dallas intended, or how hard their field commanders pushed, it would take many days before they could truly compel the Stormriders to react to them. Still, he had no desire to surrender the initiative completely to his foes.

Second, the great advantage the Beasties had over Pure Engine types was that their chosen mode of transport was *quiet*. Tristan would have to shadow the horsefolk at a considerable distance to avoid alerting them. It would be impossible to keep them always in sight. That meant it would take not just skill but plenty of luck to keep from overrunning them if they happened to stop for a piss break or a mount gone lame.

Finally, if things went sour—and obviously the Pranksters harbored no great love for the High Free Folk—he'd rather be stuck facing twenty of them than *all* of them.

The disadvantage of horses, of course, was that they were slow. They could traverse terrain even a scrambler couldn't handle, but this wasn't such country. The roll of the Plains was beginning to turn into chop, preparatory to becoming the wooded Rocky Mountain foothills. Assuming the horse barbarians tended to the path of least resistance—as their tracks said they did— Tristan could guess the path they would take. It was a simple matter to swing far enough wide of them that they would not hear his engine, then position himself in their path and wait.

Toward midday he saw the riders approaching in a line. The sky was clotted and gray and sporadically leaking; the animals' hooves raised no dust. Hidden behind a ridge line Tristan waited until they were within fifty yards, then mounted his scrambler and rolled up to silhouette himself against the clouds.

The brief snarl of his engine and his sudden appearance threw the column into a flurry. Animals reared; hands fumbled bows from shoulders or skin cases, grabbed at black-fletched arrows in quivers. He held up both hands.

"I'm unarmed," he called out. "If I wanted trouble I could have picked off half a dozen of you from up here."

During the handful of heartbeats that took to sink in, he took stock of the first Pranksters he had ever seen up close and personal. They were a wild-looking crew, even to the Lord of the outlandish High Free Folk. Some sported bright-dyed mohawks, some feathers, some dreads, and one tall dark-skinned woman bravely attempted all three. Some of them painted their faces like

Tommy Hawk. They looked like nothing so much as a bunch of Lakota far gone on a heavy Trad trip, but of all colors.

Tristan was making no attempt to conceal the butt of his Saskatoon Mk. V Scout carbine. The Pranksters were smart enough to grasp the sense of what he said to them. Nonetheless, he noticed that several hands were slow to drop away from weapons.

"Can we talk?" he said.

They could. He waited the rest of the day. He spent the first part of the wait fretting, but then he made himself lie on his back with his head resting on his hands. A hawk drifted into his field of vision, a big bird, with a pale-and-orange underside: a red-tail.

The red-tailed hawk had always had special significance for Tristan, since the vision of one had sustained him through the claustrophobic nightmare of his first imprisonment in the Hole at McGrory. Later, after he escaped from Homeland, he'd found himself in the very setting he had dreamed of back in solitary in the Diagnostic & Developmental Institute, watching such a hawk. As he gazed at the bird kiting above him now, he felt himself let go of his anxieties and fears. He had made his decision; he had done what he thought best. What would come, would come.

The bird folded its wings and dropped suddenly, to rise up in moments with a mouse hanging limp from its talons. Tristan smiled farewell to the hawk. He enjoyed the rest of his sojourn alone.

The next morning, a party of six riders met him, at a place agreed upon.

A Star fell from heaven. It had destroyed the old order of Earth, reasserted the might of Nature over Man and righted the balance of things. The High Free Folk were born of the star-stuff brought down from the sky, so that for each of them, man and woman alike, a star shone in the sky. Stars were their souls.

So Tristan had been taught as a boy.

He had learned more, in later years, as a captive of the City— which was not to say he had learned *otherwise*. As a high school student he had found such freedom as he had known in the long-neglected stacks of Homeland's Library, under the blind eye of old Bayliss, the Librarian. He had supplemented legend with first-hand accounts of the falling of the Star.

The Star had been a comet, in fact. When it struck the atmosphere it broke into pieces, striking hammer blows all across the

Northern Hemisphere. By the time of its arrival it was already becoming apparent that the long climatological and geological peace—so rare in the planet's turbulent history—which had permitted human civilization to rise and flourish, was coming to an end. The truce was off—and the comet strike set off a virtual war.

The world Tristan had grown up in—the only world anyone had known for over two hundred years—was savaged by an endless succession of storms and earthquakes and volcanic eruptions. Such humans as survived the shocks of StarFall itself, and the plagues and famines and disorders which ensued, had been driven within the squat reinforced-concrete walls of a handful of Cities—or turned out into the wilderness to live as nomads and squatters. Humankind, once so proud and unassailably powerful, was brought low.

But the natural world thrived. Herds of bison blackened the Plains, pronghorn jumped and jostled like living yellow seas. Flocks of big, aggressive wolves stalked them, culling the herds of the weak and slow. Hawks like the red-tail Tristan had watched dotted the sky on a spring or summer day, as much resting before once more stooping on one of the tiny animals that swarmed in the grass or brush, or slashing through a cloud of songbirds, as hunting.

The world was cooler than it had been before StarFall, Tristan knew, and the ice was advancing from the north. Though the practice of science had largely been abandoned, as possibly suspect and in any event too much work, observation and measurement of the surrounding world still continued in many places. Sometimes the results found their way to the Library, through commerce or personal travel or the transmissions which lapses in the pervasive atmospheric interference permitted to get through.

To countervail the cooling, though, the heavy rains lavishly irrigated the whole of North America, including many areas that had once been desert. The volcanoes cast up great clouds of ash which, while they could smother all life from an area on which they settled too densely, also provided excellent fertilizer.

The result was an explosion of vegetation even greater than that of animal life. The Plains were furred with thick green grass, high in some places, short in others, depending on which species predominated. The former deserts of the Southwest had been overtaken by thick brushy chaparral of piñon and juniper, where they weren't overrun with the lava-blasted desolation of the BlackLands and the Jornada del Hell.

And the forests were advancing. The unknown demon-haunted land east of the Mississippi—unknown to the High Free Folk, at least—hid behind a virtually unbroken wall of jungle for most of the length of the Great River. In the West, the foothills of the Rockies had in many areas been overrun by hardwoods once largely confined to the East, which liked the wet cool weather better than did the conifers of the heights. From his reading Tristan knew these were what a botanist might term "escaped" populations, composed of trees grown for shade and ornament in the stricken pre-StarFall Cities.

The camp of the Merry Pranksters was located in a stand of young oak engaged in life-and-death struggle with elms. The trees gave good cover from casual observation. When Tristan's escort first stopped and motioned him to proceed alone, he thought he was riding into uninhabited woods.

The hide tipis—his nose noted gratefully that they were well cured—resembled natural growths of the forest. They were far less gaudy than the brightly colored synthetic tents favored by the Folk. Still, there was a stagy, contrived quality to them Tristan could not quite define. After all, they *weren't* naturally occurring, and their occupants weren't Plains Indians—who except for the odd obsessed Traditionalist wouldn't be caught dead in one of the things.

Rolling in low gear between the apparently deserted hide tents Tristan noted handprints and symbols scrawled on them. Some of the symbols he was familiar with, like the A in the circle, the eye of Horus, the yin-yang, and the pentagram, all of which were common among the Folk. But there were others he had not seen, notably yellow apples and designs incorporating them with yin-yangs and pentagons.

He noticed that the place was well kept and neat, and that the apparently random placement of the tipis would prevent intruders on bikes from rolling from one end of the encampment to another, firing as they went. They would have to dodge around the tents, putting themselves at the mercy of inhabitants lurking behind them with bows or, for that matter, baseball bats.

The camp was arranged in the shape of a donut, centered on a natural clearing. In this clear space in the temporary village's midst waited a hundred Merry Pranksters, as wild and various in their appearance as the party Tristan had tracked. All were armed, with bows, knives, spears, even the occasional crossbow. No firearms were in evidence. No arrows were nocked, and no weapons leveled at Tristan.

That could change in a hell of a hurry, he didn't have to be told.

He rolled right up to the front of the crowd, slewed his bike sideways, and dropped his boots to the leaf-mulched earth. "I'm here to talk, not to fight or make demands," he said, raising his hands. "Take me to your leader."

That goosed out a bubble of laughter, not altogether friendly. A big black-haired man with sideburns extended along the line of his jowls and up to meet beneath his broad nose, from which hung a huge gold ring, spoke up.

"We have no leaders," he said. For his part Tristan wondered just exactly how he ate with that thing stuck in his face. "We are the Merry Pranksters, all equal in the sight of the Goddess."

"Hail, Eris," the crowd muttered. "All hail, Discordia."

"Hail, yes," Tristan said. "So who do I talk to? All of you at once?"

"There is one who speaks for all of us," Ring-Nose said.

"And that one is me," said a crisp, high female voice from behind Tristan. He turned.

A woman stood there, young, slim, and slight, brown hair cut around the face of a tough pixie in a boyish bob. The eyes were huge and hazel. She wore a buckskin jerkin with a thong laced up the front and tight tan leggings.

But that wasn't what Tristan saw. He saw a girl, gawky and coltish in early adolescence, skinny and all leg, with a snub nose and a shock of unruly hair. She wore grubby torn jeans and a grease-stained T-shirt, and she could ride a scrambler as well as any man among the Hardriders save Quicksilver Messenger— and considerably better than eleven-year-old Tristan, a year or two her junior.

The speaker for the Merry Pranksters went pale behind her woods-runner's tan. She sagged slightly at the knees, but caught herself quickly enough and stood sapling-upright once again.

"Tristan Hardrider," she breathed. "So it's true. It is you. And all these years I thought you were dead! Oh, *damn.*"

12

"Is that any way to great an old bro, Jamie?" Tristan said. It was hard to get the words out, what with the knotting in his throat and all.

"Are you okay, Eris?" Ring-Nose asked. Tristan glanced over his shoulder. The crowd was giving him a notable hard eye.

He looked back in time to see Jamie—Eris?—flip her hand in a calming gesture.

"I'm fine," she said. "I just saw a ghost."

Her eyes narrowed on Tristan's face. "I thought I saw a boy I once knew. But I realize he really is long dead."

The words rocked Tristan back on his heels. "Come on," the woman said to him. She slipped past him, almost touching but not quite, and walked into the crowd. It parted politely for her. Tristan followed, conscious of the hostile looks pressing on him from both sides.

He noticed that her hair was not bobbed all the way around. She wore it in a long, thick braid in back.

She led him to a large tipi painted with a huge yellow apple with a bow above it. She gestured him in, then followed, letting the flap fall to behind her.

"Sit," she said, so he did, dropping his butt to the ground and crossing his long legs. She sat across the ashes of a cold fire from him. Though light flowed in the smoke hole at the top of the tent he could barely see her; his eyes were slow adjusting from the cloudy daylight without to the gloom within. It was warm and a little close. The day was chilly, up here in the foothills, so the warmth was not unwelcome. Still, he'd be just as glad not to get stuck in here with a dozen disputatious Stormriders on a muggy summer night.

Without necessarily realizing it, he had over the years rehearsed again and again what he might say to his oldest friend, should chance ever cause his Road to cross hers. He never once anticipated what he actually found himself saying.

"Why did you say I was dead, Jamie?" he asked in a gentle voice.

She sat with her slim legs drawn up and her arms wrapped around them. A smile flitted across her face like a humming-bird's ghost.

"They call me Eris here," she said in a faraway voice. "Jamie . . . I haven't heard that name in years. It brings back painful memories."

"I apologize," Tristan said deliberately. "I did not know."

"Will you take water? Cider, hard or soft? Since you come before me as a lone traveler, I won't deny you basic hospitality."

"Hard cider's fine." Jamie—what did they call her? Eris?—poured a handleless earthenware cup full from a stone jug and passed it to him. She poured her own cup full of water.

He drained the cup at a toss; he hadn't realized how thirsty he was. The cider was good—Española Valley in the heart of the BlackLands, if he was any judge, where the Mexican farmers divided their energies between fighting crows, Smoking Mirrors, and the lava and glowing clouds from the River of Fire, and growing the finest apples known on the Plains.

"Now," he said, wiping his mustache with the back of a hand, "what's all this about me being dead, and denying me hospitality? And what the hell am I supposed to call you?"

"The Pranksters call me Eris."

"Yeah. I heard 'em out there going 'Hail, Eris' a lot. You the boss?"

She shook her head. "The Merry Pranksters acknowledge no 'bosses,' as you call them. I am . . . an influential person. My people have agreed to allow me to speak for them in this case."

"This 'hail' stuff sounds mighty bossy to me."

"No. Eris is their Goddess, the Goddess of Discord. It's Her they hail, not me."

"They must think plenty highly of you."

Another thin smile came and went. "Perhaps." She held up the jug. "Will you take more?"

"Water would be nice."

She refilled his cup from another jug and returned it. "Now you—am I wrong, or are you truly the Tristan they call Tristan Burningskull, Maximum Lord of the Plains?"

His teeth shone white in the dimness. "That's me, all right."

"So I feared, when I first began to hear of your exploits." She sighed, closed her eyes, lowered her head. "The boy I knew—loved—was a true child of the High Free Folk. Wild, brave, and free."

She lifted her head. Her hazel eyes fixed his. Even in the poor light he saw that now they were green, with amber rings around the iris.

"Now you come before me as a tyrant."

"Say *what*?" He sprayed water down the front of his unbleached linen shirt and into the ashes.

"The self-proclaimed ruler of the Plains. Despoiler of the squatters—Diggers, you call them, I believe? A man who would grind even the proud Cities beneath his boot heel."

"Well, you got the last part right, I gotta admit. First one too. But what's this about despoiling the Diggers?"

"Do you deny that you send your men to kill them and pillage their farmsteads?"

"Damn straight I deny it! I let the bros razz the Cities all they want, at least Homeland and Dallas, and Misery City, which has been acting surly toward us. But I sure as hell don't let 'em prey on the Diggers." He shook his head. "It's not exactly a move that wins me any popularity contests either."

"Ten days ago," Jamie/Eris said, watching him the way a hawk watches a field mouse, "your men wiped out a family of what you call Diggers near Bijou Creek. Ten people were killed. The youngest was a two-month-old infant, who was thrown alive into the flames of the burning farmhouse.

"Her mother was an eighteen-year-old girl. She was gang-raped, stabbed, and left to die. And she did die, but not before we found her. She gasped the story to us with her final breaths.

"We lay in wait for the marauders, who were bound for Backroad Bill's Roadhouse to sell the paltry loot they'd gotten from their victims. We killed seven. The rest fled. We will hunt them down in time. And we will kill them all."

She paused. "Your men. Do you deny you sent them?"

"Yes. Gods damn it, *yes*!" He slapped his thigh with stinging force. "I swear by any Gods you like—Jesus, Brother Wind,

Mother Earth, Mother Sky, Buddha, this Eris of yours, anybody—I swear I had no knowledge of this. Nothing to do with it. It is a violation of my laws, and a bad one. I'll see the guilty are punished for it."

"There you go," she said, "speaking of *your* laws and *your* punishments and what *you* permit. Can you still deny that you're a tyrant?"

"Hey, my people are free. The High Free Folk are still that way."

"They are ruled. That is not free."

"I didn't exactly force anybody to join!"

"The fact that your people—that *your* again—chose their status doesn't make them free. It wouldn't be the first time in history people chose freely to become unfree, far from it. Does the word *democracy* mean anything to you?"

"Yeah, as a matter of fact." He felt momentary triumph: *See, I'm not just an illiterate saddle tramp. So there.* "I've read history. I know that democracy was all about free people governing themselves."

"Is your Stormrider Federation a democracy?"

"Well, no . . ."

"And did democratic societies never vote freedom away?"

"Well . . ."

"What about the country that once existed where we now sit? The United States of America. Was it free when the Star fell? Or was it a place a lot like Homeland, where the government prescribed its citizens every act, where everything not compulsory was strictly forbidden? *Where even motorcycles were outlawed?*"

"Uh . . ." He realized he was not being any more articulate than your average member of the Road Hog MC here. He rubbed his jaw and tried to force his brain to work halfway right.

"Okay. I've seen newspaper stories from the time, books, articles, all like that. Folk back then thought they were free—too free, according to some. Mighty like those Purity pukes back in Homeland. And no, they weren't free. And yes, they put themselves there!"

"Very good." She smiled. "You do know your history. You've impressed me at last, Tristan."

The smile slipped away. "Knowing what you do, how can you set yourself up to follow in the hoofprints of Genghis Khan."

"Ouch," he said. "That isn't what I want."

"You're a nomad chieftain, and a conqueror. How would you describe it?"

"Well, yeah. I am and I am. But I'm not into the pyramid of skulls thing."

"That was Tamerlane. Genghis Khan believed in mass murder without too much embellishment."

"Whatever. I mean to harm those who take up arms against me, make no mistake about that. But I don't make war on non-combatants, don't war against women and children."

. "In war, how can you make such distinctions?" she murmured.

"When you 'bushed the Road Hogs—and they *are* under my protection, as I guess those Diggers were under yours, though something tells me the Hogs have forfeited their claims on me— when you took them down, were you sure every man you got an arrow into was actually a gang-banger or baby-burner? Maybe some of 'em stood there watching their buddies and wishing they had the power to make them stop!"

"Everybody was guilty. They chose to be there, and they chose not to interfere."

"It seems you make some awful convenient distinctions." He sipped water, watching her over the cup rim. "What happened to you?" he asked in a gentler voice.

"I grew up," she said. "What happened to you?"

He shrugged. "The same, more or less."

He laid the cup carefully down on the packed ground before him. "There's also the matter of the rider in my party you feathered—Wire, his name is. He hasn't been involved in any unauthorized razzing; he never did anything to you at all. Why did you shoot him?"

"*I* wasn't the one who did it," she said tartly.

"The group you speak for did. Don't dodge the question. Why?"

She stared down at the ground. "As a warning. The Merry Pranksters were still angry at the farmhouse raid. Then you came riding in, more of the men who did it, all arrogant and proud."

"I'll cop to the 'arrogant and proud' stuff. But beyond that somebody was pretty badly confused, if he or she took my Burningskulls for Road Hogs."

"You are all one nation. Isn't that what you're all about?"

He groped through memory for a phrase from the Library, long ago. "So you buy the concept of collective responsibility then? If one of us does something, everybody did it?"

Her eyes went wide, and the color dropped from her cheeks. "Never! We are individuals, dedicated to preserving the sanctity of the individual, against you and the Cities and the Fusion alike!"

"Jamie—Eris," he said, looking at her hard, "have you forgotten what it was like to grow up among the Folk? Pretty hard-core bunch of individualists, weren't they?"

She opened her mouth as if to argue, then shut it and nodded.

"Do you really think any of the Stormriders would put up with me one second if I messed with their individuality? It's difficult trying to get any given group of them to ride in the same direction. How the hell far do you think I'd get if I tried to lockstep them into some kind of City order-trip?" He shook his head. "If I didn't get back-shot or my throat cut while I slept, I'd be gray in two weeks and dead of old age inside of half a year."

"Still," she said, picking her way carefully across the field of words, "you have begun the process of amalgamation. Of centralization. The very fact that the High Free Folk permit it is a sign they may be turning their backs on their old individualistic ways."

He shook his head. "It's been a while since you rode among us, hasn't it? We're still as rasty-assed, crazy, and mean as ever."

He stood. "Well, you speak for your folk, so I guess you recognize my right to speak for mine. The Road Hogs I'll deal with my own way. But Wire—I'll have blood-price for his pain, or I'll fight you."

She got up slowly. "You say something like that, in the middle of a hostile camp?"

"If your Pranksters want to try me on for size, let 'em come. Might be I could lay hand to an influential hostage somewhere round here."

He realized she was grinning at him, and she broke into his half-veiled threat with outright laughter.

"Tristan, Tristan, you are still as full of shit as any person I've ever met in my life. It's good to see you haven't totally changed."

She came to him and hugged him. He hugged her back, and felt strange feelings, and didn't know what he was thinking at all. It was an uncomfortable feeling; he was used to knowing his own mind, even when he was otherwise clueless.

She stepped back. "Your man Wire deserves compensation. We made a mistake there. And it is true, with Homeland and

Dallas on the roll, this is no time for us to be fighting one another."

"Glad for the acknowledgment I'm not an enemy as terrible as a pair of City armies."

"As you say, the High Free Folk stand for vestiges of freedom, at least. Homeland and Dallas stand for none, in spades."

"That's for damned sure."

"I will take counsel among the Pranksters. We will send a messenger to discuss the blood-price for your man."

"Fair enough." He stood a moment, feeling heavy and strange. "It was real good to see you again, uh, Eris. I never thought I'd see you again."

She regarded him a moment in the dimness, a small, scrappy figure, at once formidable and cute as hell.

"I'm glad you didn't die, Tristan," she said softly. "I . . . missed you."

"Me too. I mean, I missed you."

"Wait—before you go. Why did you come? I mean, why you in person? Why did you take the bother—or the risk? You could have sent emissaries to talk about the Road Hogs, and even about Wire."

He cocked his head to one side. "I'll answer a question with a question, 'cause you know I've always been a ring-tailed pisser: Who cooked up the plan for that hit on the MoFos?"

"I did."

He nodded. "Thought so. I saw some pretty sharp tactics there. It came to me I could use the mind that thought 'em up on my staff. I'm going to need every bit of help I can get to handle both Dallas and Homeland at once."

She shook her head. "It can never be, Tristan. I . . . I'm sorry."

He hunched a one-shoulder shrug. "Hey, when the MoFos and the Rangers shake hands out in the middle of the Plains, and start planning where they're going to put the concentration camps, you can let me know what it feels like to be *real* sorry."

She glared at him.

"Now you tell me something," he said. "You were the best rider in the band, save for the Messenger himself, and he was only about the best as ever lived. What in the name of Mother Earth's green backside made you give up your scrambler for a . . . *horse*?"

She laughed. "I told you. I grew up. I found a better way. Really, you should try riding a horse sometime. It's exhilarating."

"Not me, babe. I feel funny about sitting on anybody who has a mother, unless of course it's someone who gave me real cause to shove their face in the dirt. Course, I reckon there're some horses would be happy to oblige me there."

"You're right about that. They do have minds of their own."

"Sleds don't, thank the Gods. Though sometimes it seems that way. Jamie, Jamie, what *happened* to you?"

The glow of old-friends joy snapped from her face. Instead, her eyes flamed with an anger so terrible it rocked him back on his heels.

"Don't ever ask me that!" she cried. "Never!"

She drew three deep breaths through flared nostrils. "Now, get out of here."

"I'm gone."

But I'll be back, he thought.

13

"Just what in the name of Hell is going on here?" Tristan demanded, twisting his scrambler to a stop in the well-churned mud of Chaos Central's main plaza.

It was getting crowded there. At least a hundred riders on their big cruiser bikes were packed into the plaza in the chill afternoon drizzle, bristling with guns. They raised a ragged cheer above the growl of engines when they saw Tristan.

"It's Lord Burningskull! He's back!"

The armed riders parted to let their overlord roll through their midst. The nearer ones moved right briskly when they caught a glimpse of his expression.

At the core of the mob, to Tristan's utter lack of surprise, were twenty Road Hogs and Lonesome Dave. The Hogs had clearly been fortifying themselves liberally with bottled courage; they were weaving in their saddles already.

Lonesome Dave's expression flickered when the crowd gave way and Tristan appeared. He recovered almost instantaneously.

"Welcome back, Lord Tristan," he said out the side of his usual crooked grin.

"Hey!" bellowed Sweat, the Road Hog boss who'd put on the original song-and-dance for Tristan's benefit. "Looky there! It's Burningskull his own damn' self. Shoot. And we was just fixin' to come rescue you, Your Lordship."

"No shit." Tristan dropped his kickstand twenty feet from Lonesome Dave and started to walk toward him. Apparently feeling that some kind of masculine ritual was going on, Sweat dismounted and came hustling up at the waddle, belly slogging greasily above his belt.

"You got back jest in time, Lord," he puffed. "We was all ready to go pay back them Beastie bastards, and spring your lordly butt did it happen you required—"

Tristan lashed out and nailed him across his hairy chops with a cracking backhand. Sweat staggered back three steps, blood streaming into his beard, and then sat down on his wide ass, more from shock than the force of the blow. He held up a grubby paw to his mouth, staring goggle-eyed at the blood on his finger-tips.

"Hey," he said, "you hit me!"

"Get up," Tristan hissed.

Grunting, Sweat climbed to his feet. Tristan waited until he stood as close to upright as he generally got and kicked him in the balls.

"Thought you'd make a fool of me, did you?" Tristan asked.

Sweat doubled. Tristan straightened him with a knee to the face, then rocked the Road Hog's head around on its virtually nonexistent neck with a roundhouse kick.

"Thought you'd do a little razzing on the sly, didn't you? Only you dumb fucks ran your fat asses into some payback. *Didn't* you?"

He spun a back-kick into Sweat's midsection and sent him flying back to knock over half a dozen Road Hogs bikes and riders like big chrome and leather dominoes.

"You thought you could trick your bros into taking out the witnesses, didn't you? Guess what? You lose."

News of current events was finally beginning to penetrate the alcoholic fog inside the Road Hogs' skulls. Their Prez was getting his butt roundly kicked here. The ancient Plains law of *one for all and all on one* kicked in. They started to go for their weaponry, the identity of the ass-kicker notwithstanding.

Because part of the pretext for this happy hunting party was a possible rescue of Tristan, the Burningskulls were out in force. When their Main Man arrived they reflexively fell in behind him. They had *not* been drinking on the job—Tristan had picked them better than that. With a cricket clicking of safeties they held down on the slow-handed Hogs.

Seeing that even on one of his better days—which this was not shaping up to be—Sweat would take a while to get himself sorted out of the heap of bros and bikes, Tristan wheeled and began to advance on Lonesome Dave. His blue eyes blazed like vents to the heart of a gas-fired boiler.

"You put these dim fuckards up to this, didn't you, Dave?" Tristan demanded. His voice was low and dangerous. "They pooled all their brains together in one big pot, it'd take 'em all year to get one solitary idea to bubble to the surface."

Lonesome Dave fell back a step. His right hand slid inside the open front of his rain-shiny black Dallasite greatcoat.

He froze. His blue eyes swiveled right. They could not traverse quite far enough to come to bear on Jovanne, who stood behind his shoulder with Black Jack Masefield's .40-caliber Vindicator held at the full extent of her arms, hammer back and muzzle socketed into the little notch right behind Dave's ear.

"Don't let me interfere with your plans, Davey," she said in a poisonously sweet voice. "Go ahead and draw on the Maximum Lord. I want to see if it's really true what they say, that your head's inflated to eighty p.s.i."

Dave smiled—a brave effort, but a tad on the sickly side. He let his hand slide *slowly* out of his coat. He dangled a white handkerchief between his well-manicured fingertips.

"I was just going to offer this to the Lord," he said, "in case he wanted to wipe his brow."

"I think he more has in mind wiping his ass with that pretty yellow hair of yours." She let him feel the cool hardness of the Vindicator's barrel for another two heartbeats, just to let him know she wasn't buying his line, then stepped back and slowly lowered the piece.

Lonesome Dave looked around to see Tristan planted squarely in front of him. "Talk," the Lord of the Plains said.

Lonesome Dave laughed. Tristan had to give him credit for balls. The strength—and sass—was coming back into his voice already.

"I'm hurt, Lord Tristan," he said.

"Not yet, you're not."

"You're in a hurry to suspect me," Lonesome Dave went on with barely a hesitation, "when all that I have in mind is your continued well-being."

Yeah, Tristan thought, *interrupting it.*

"Lord Tristan," a voice called from behind him.

He glared at Dave a moment longer and turned. A couple of his Burningskulls had taken Sweat by the arms and hauled him out of the tangle. They were keeping a grip on the dazed and bleeding Road Hog. Their comrades were efficiently disarming the rest of the clan.

"Good boys and girls," Tristan said. "That's using your initiative."

The Burningskulls glowed. "What shall we do with this?" said one of the men holding Sweat.

"Throw him at my feet."

To hear was to obey. Sweat plowed a furrow in the mud with his potato nose, almost to the tips of Tristan's boots.

Tristan glowered down at him while he struggled to his knees. "You know the penalty for unauthorized razzing," he said when the operation was done.

Sweat clasped fat hands before him. "B-but Lord," he sobbed, "they was only *Diggers*."

A hush landed on the crowd like a sheet of lead. "Yes," Tristan said, underscoring the obvious, "and it's only my law."

Sweat rolled his eyes upward. A moment too late it was dawning on him that he had just unzipped his fly, flopped his pecker in the mud, and commenced to perform the Mexican Hat Dance on it. Few if any of the bros loved the Diggers any better than he did. But one and all they had agreed to abide by Tristan's laws. Sweat had just blurted out what amounted to a confession of having broken one of the sternest.

Tristan smiled. He bent forward and hooked his fingers into the filthy denim vest of Sweat's colors.

"Nooo!" Sweat squealed in the voice of a frightened child. Tristan straightened, set his jaw, grunted with effort. The vest tore free of Sweat's bulk with a ripping sound that seemed loud as a gunshot in all this silence.

Tristan held the torn colors above his head. "Let everybody see the penalty for breaking the Law of the Plains!" he announced in a ringing voice.

He cast the colors down beside the blubbering Sweat and ground them into the mud with his heel. A gasp rose from the crowd like a startled flock of gulls.

"Strip the rest of these low-down mangy curs of their colors," he directed his Burningskulls, "and burn them." It occurred to him that the more zealous of his riders might gleefully misinterpret that order, so he quickly added, "The colors."

Wailing, the Road Hogs were stripped of their colors. The ragged, grimy vests were tossed into a heap in the center of the plaza, doused with gasoline, and set alight.

From the way the Road Hogs took on, it might as well have been them burning out there.

Tristan stood watching until the colors were well and truly alight. Then he turned to address the mob.

"I have damned few laws," he announced in a voice pitched to carry over the grumble of many engines just turning over, "but those I have are not made to be broken. The cost of free-lance razzing is known: the death penalty."

A collective gasp rose from the crowd. The death penalty did not mean death for an individual, but for a club.

"I might have chosen to be merciful," Tristan declared. "But the Road Hogs compounded their crime by lying to me, and trying to make you—all of us—accomplices to their deeds. They turned on their bros, and no worse crime is known between Mother Earth and Mother Sky.

"So Stormriders, hear my judgment: The Roads Hogs are no more. Let them ride forth from our midst and not return. And let it be known that any found bearing the colors of the former clan shall be fair game for any who would take his life!"

The ex-Hogs mounted their sleds and rolled away through the crowd, which fell back away from them as if they were contaminated. The gesture of fine outlaw defiance would have been to crank the throttles and roar away on a wave of noise. But the Road Hogs were nut-cut. They had no defiance left in them. They eased onto the gas and sort of faded off into the broken land until a drifting curtain of rain hid them from view.

Tristan stood watching them go. When they vanished he realized his lips had peeled back from his teeth.

He turned slowly. Lonesome Dave stood watching him with his hands in his pockets. The usual sardonic grin was missing from his face. His eyes held no more expression than a doll's.

"Your Lord is back," Tristan announced. He spoke to the riders crowded into the midst of Chaos Central, but his eyes held the Pistolero President like claws.

He started to walk away. As the crowd began to break up, intent on driving their rides back to their own encampments and getting them out of the rain, the whine of a solitary scrambler soared above the general motor murmuring. Tristan turned back.

What rolled into the cleared space looked as if someone had tried to mold a sculpture of a motorcycle and rider out of mud. It stopped, and reached a mud gauntlet up to skin goggles up over mud-caked hair. Blue eyes stared forth from a shocking mask of pale skin.

"Lord Tristan," the courier said, "the Dallasites've busted out past Fort Hammond. They'll camp tonight on the Great Bend of the Arkansas!"

14

"What do we do now?" Tramp, the Sand Kings' President, said through the fingers that covered his face. He looked up at the others grouped around the Council Table. "Dallas and Homeland're fixin' to squash us like a juicy old bug. What're we gonna *do*?"

"Well, we could fold our hands and start studying to live like good little Citizens," Jovanne said. "Or we could figure out a way to fight."

"Like what?" demanded Buzzard, the Bandido Prez. He had long greasy strands of graying black hair hanging to the shoulders of his age-darkened colors, and the strange and terrible staring eyes of his namesake. "We got the fuckards closing in both sides of us."

"What does a woman know of ways to fight anyway?" asked Rico of *Los Tremendos Gavilanes*. He was a steady man and keen, but he had an old-fashioned outlook on women.

"Got that right," growled Buzzard.

Color was slowly draining from Jovanne's face. Tristan realized it was getting time to intervene. She would take his head off for presuming to help her—as if she couldn't handle a couple of blowhards like Buzzard and Rico. But what he would *not* do was leave one of his main lieutenants twisting in the breeze. He had to show confidence in Jovanne in no uncertain terms . . .

"She knows quite a bit about fighting," drawled the Pistolero Prez, who sat at the far end of the table, legs crossed and languid in his chair, drumming long ring-studded fingers on the tabletop.

"Our Jovanne's a proven hassler—as you two would know if you ever bothered to look past your bellies."

That was calculated to piss off both Rico, who was whip-lean, and Buzzard, who had a truly impressive biker gut. Both glared toward that end of the table, but said nothing. The blond man smiled blandly at them.

Lonesome Dave looked like a totally useless pretty-boy. It was a mistake to take him at face value. Gonzo, former warlord of the Spawn, had made the error the year before. Lonesome Dave had called him out bare-handed. He'd popped both Gonzo's eyes from their sockets and force-fed them to him before breaking his bull neck.

Dave laced his fingers together and placed his hands on the table. "I'm interested in hearing what you have to say, Jovanne."

The Joker Prez eyed him warily. She had told Tristan face-up that she thought Dave was powerfully cute—it may have been a try at making her lover jealous, which was a waste, since he felt no possessiveness toward her at all. In any event she also made no secret of the fact that she thought Lonesome Dave was an irredeemable sleaze.

"I trust your judgment, Jovanne," Tristan said, feeling as if he were taking sloppy seconds to the Pistolero boss.

"Well," she said, "it's pretty damn clear we can't fight both Homeland and Dallas—"

Tramp slammed his hand down on the table. "Well, shit, the bitch shoots off her mouth to contradict me, and when she gets the floor she says the same thing I was!"

"You want to go one on one, Tramp?" Jovanne asked.

"Chill," Tristan told the room at large. "Finish saying your piece, Jovanne. Tramp, save the comments till she's done, or go outside and let the big boys and girls talk."

Jovanne nodded, forcing her temper down with a visible effort. "As I was saying, we can't fight both *at once*. Whether we can whip either of them alone, face-up, is a question."

"We can't," Tristan said quietly, "face-up."

Heads turned toward him. "Go ahead, Jovanne," he said.

"Whatever. The point is, we take both of them on at the same time, they'll mop us up twice as quick."

"What are you suggesting then?" Tristan asked. It was what you called your leading question. He'd already gotten the point; he wanted to be sure some of the less-swift chieftains did too—and got it from Jovanne.

"Our best chance is to drop a token force on one, to keep them busy and to keep them from getting too cocky. Then we concentrate on hitting the other one with everything we got. If, uh . . ."

Her eyes flicked to Tristan, and for the first time her tough and lovely face showed doubt. "—If we got enough to do any good, that is."

Tristan nodded. "We do."

The tent erupted in confusion. Everyone tried to talk at once, objecting, approving, or just pushing air. Tommy Hawk stood listening, his arms crossed over his bare bulging pecs, his painted handsome face settling deeper and deeper into a frown. Finally he raised his right hand and brought it down on the table hard.

The inch-and-a-half-thick wood cracked. The table collapsed. Silence fell along with it.

"I don't know about anybody else," the Freebird war chief said deliberately, "but I know *I* want to hear what our Lord has to say."

"Uh, sure, Tommy," Tramp said nervously. "Anything you say. Why, shit, all of us're eager to hear."

Unmollified, Tommy Hawk glared at him. "Then shut your mouth and open your ears."

Trying not to grin, Tristan said, "We don't have the hair to do either Dallas or Homeland face-up. No, don't get started . . ." He held up his hand to keep the peace. "There is also nothing that says we have to go face-up with the fuckards."

"What's your saying, then?" asked Hercules.

Now Tristan smiled. "We cheat."

"How do you mean?" the black giant warlord of the Dragons asked.

"We're not sluggers. We're razzers. Float like a butterfly, sting like a bee, that's our style. Get 'em looking one way, hit 'em somewhere else. Never let 'em rest. Run off their cattle and piss in their wells."

"Guerrilla war," Hercules said.

"You got it," said Liquid Louie of the Marauders.

"Is it an honorable way to fight?" asked Blue Murder warlord Moonhawk.

"Screw honor," growled Wolfman the Enforcer. "We're low-down scooter trash. I *like* this plan."

"Who do we hit, and who do we let alone, Jovanne?" asked Jesse. Every President of the Outlaws MC was named Jesse by time-honored tradition; this one was skinny, beardless, brown-haired, and not as young as he looked. The Outlaws had been blood brothers to the Jokers since before John Hammerhand's disastrous Rock Creek fight against the Cathead Nation. Jesse could be relied upon to back the Joker Prez.

Jovanne looked to Tristan. "I say we hit Dallas," she said, picking her words with unaccustomed care, "and leave Homeland alone."

Expectant silence filled the tent till the walls seemed to bulge like venison sausage skins. Everybody knew the Maximum Lord's consuming obsession was to invade the City that had enslaved and then betrayed him, and drive Dirk Posen and his white-jumpsuited Purity dogs into the wastelands.

Tristan let his long chin drop to the little tuft of black hair peeking out of his shirt at his clavicle. "How do you see that?" he asked.

Jovanne made a face. "My gut tells me."

Buzzard started to make noise. "Quit bitching," Lonesome Dave said quickly, "and let the lady talk."

Jovanne sighed. She gave the Pistolero a funny look.

"Okay," she said. "I can give you one good reason: Dallas has five times the population of Homeland. They have a bigger army. If we can handle them at all, it'll take all we've got. We can't wear ourselves down punching it out with Homeland and hope to deal with the Rangers."

Still frowning, Tommy Hawk nodded slowly. "It's a good saying." He touched his breastbone with his fingertips. "My heart is good for what she says."

"Anything you say, Tommy," Hercules said dubiously. "Whatever he said, I'm with him. Girl makes sense to me."

"Me too," Tristan said. He leaned forward, a scroll of map around perpendicular to the table's long axis, unrolled it with a flick of his fingertips.

"So let's cut some details."

"Your gut told you?" Tristan asked quietly.

Walking back to their tent in the midnight dark, arms hugging her chest to augment the warmth of her wolfskin-lined jacket, Jovanne nodded. Tristan patted her flat belly.

"Usually your gut keeps its damn peace," he said, "or I sure as hell wouldn't let you into my bed."

"It'd be your loss," she said. She laughed, then shrugged. "I still don't know what it is, but there's something else there—in here." She prodded her own stomach with her fingertips, a gesture reminiscent of Tommy Hawk's.

"I respect your hunches, wherever they hang out," Tristan said. "Even without whatever's riling up your innards, you came up with a pretty good reason for dealing with Dallas first."

She shrugged. "It's the right thing to do. I *know* that. I just wish I could see the whole picture."

He reached out, put his arm around her, hugged her close as they walked. She looked at him. Her breath came in a white puff.

"Tristan?"

"Yes."

"Do we have a chance?"

For a moment his face—his whole body—went taut. Then, "Yes. Hell, yes."

Maybe not a good one. But some chance anyway.

Between slim and none.

15

"Tristan?"

A voice from the shadows. Jovanne jumped. Her hand went instantly to the butt of the Vindicator.

A figure limped into lantern glow showing dimly through the walls of a geodesic tent. "Speak with you a minute?" asked Jeremy.

Tristan looked at Jovanne. She disentangled herself easily. "You boys go ahead and bond," she said. "I'm going to hit the sack."

He patted her on the butt. She slapped his hand affectionately away and sashayed off into the darkness.

Tristan turned to his old friend. "You were quiet during the meeting."

Jeremy shrugged. "Figured the boys were making my share of noise. Also eighty or ninety other people's shares. Why do you put up with those wind machines anyway?"

"They're important chieftains. I can't talk to the clans directly about every little thing. I have to go through the wheels."

"Thank God I don't have to handle the politics."

"You didn't have much to say about the strategy either."

"I'm a one-on-one hassler. You know that, I know that. What I know about strategy is that if you gave Jovanne an army, and me the same size army, she'd have my dick in the dirt inside a week." The smaller man shrugged again. "She's better. I don't have any problem with that. I also know not to open my mush when I don't really have anything to say."

"You've always known that," Tristan agreed. Even back in the Dorms, Jeremy had been ready enough to offer an opinion when he had one—but he had never been one of those people who feel obliged to have an opinion on everything.

"You sure handled those bozos briskly."

"Bozos?" For a moment Tristan thought his old friend meant the Council. Then comprehension dawned. "Oh, you mean the Road Hogs."

Jeremy nodded. Tristan scrunched his mouth up.

"I suppose you're gonna tell me I was too quick on the draw, to trash their colors and exile them on the basis of what a stranger told me. I've been waiting for somebody to jump my shit for it."

"I don't think it's too likely. The Road Hogs were not what you'd call a popular club. They did it, everybody knows it, and even those who, shall we say, might not care that much for your laws still reckon the Hogs had it coming. They were stupid enough to get caught. There is one thing I've been meaning to ask you, though."

"Ask."

"I've been out on the Plains longer than you have as an adult. But you were born out here, and you know the Folk better. What the hell's to keep the Road Hogs from re-forming under another name?"

"Nothing at all," Tristan admitted. "In fact, that's likely what they'll do. The bros need a clan to belong to; the life of a non-affiliated is too much for most of them to handle. They'll feel lost on their own. And there's not many clubs that would accept a member who had his colors burned before his eyes. So they'll probably come up with a new name and new colors and turn outlaw for all fact."

He rubbed his jaw. "Then we'll probably have to hunt 'em down and wash 'em away."

Jeremy laughed, a sharp, quiet sound, like a muffled coyote yip. "See? You were too lenient again. You need to learn to be a righteous hardass, and you'll have fewer problems."

Tristan grunted.

"But there's something else I wanted to ask you. A favor."

"It's yours," Tristan said without hesitation. "Shoot."

"The Silk Stocking Strangler," Jeremy said. "I want the case."

Tristan looked at him a moment. "You *what*?"

"You got a killer on the loose here, Tristan. I want the case."

"What's all this 'case' crap? You been watching old *Dragnet* episodes on satellite out of Eddie City?"

"Somebody's got to do something. The fuckard needs to die. You sure don't have a clue what to do about him."

" 'Clue.' There you go again with the cop talk. Face it, Jeremy: We're motorcycle outlaws. What the hell do we know about investigation and police techniques?"

"Ever hear the old expression 'Set a thief to catch a thief'?"

"Yeah. What, you're telling me you're a secret serial killer? I know you've dropped the hammer on Brother Wind's own plenty of times, but you never struck me as a lady-killer. At least, not that kind."

"I have a fair amount of experience with police techniques, as it happens."

"What the hell are you talking about?"

Jeremy showed teeth in a coyote grin. "Why do you think I was in McGrory? I sure wasn't orphaned bike trash like somebody I can name."

"So you were a juvenile offender. What does that teach you about cops? Hell, they *caught* you."

"After a while. I was an adolescent. Adolescents are by definition stupid. It was only a matter of time before I managed to get more stupid than the cops."

"What are you telling me here exactly?"

"Tristan, I do know something about how cops work, something about investigation. I grew up having scrapes with cops; hell, I got pretty friendly with some of them before the Therapeutic types made 'em run me in. I got street smarts—which is more than you or any of the brothers can claim."

"Plenty of bros know what it's like to be downed by the Man's law."

Jeremy grimaced. "They know what it's like in the Man's slam. Prison survival is a useful skill, no question—if you're sag-nuts enough to get caught. But it won't help you catch your killer."

Tristan sighed, looked around. Snatches of *mariachi* music, tinny and off-key, floated his way on a wind that had begun to swirl up out of the hills. The *Gavilanes* must be camped nearby.

"Tristan, have you ever known me to bite off more than I could chew?"

Tristan looked down at his friend. There was an unfamiliar

note in the smaller man's voice. A note of pleading—desperation almost.

"Jeremy, what is it about this dude?"

"Don't you want him, Tristan?"

"I want him bad."

Jeremy's lips compressed. He nodded. "Yeah. You want him. But the need to catch this fuckard—catch him and kill him—it doesn't burn in your guts. Does it."

Tristan gazed off across the broken land. Somewhere a coyote chorus tuned up.

"No," he said at last. "I want the bastard downed. But I have other priorities."

"Okay." Jeremy nodded almost eagerly. "When you need a blade at your back, or a nasty bastard to take on razz against the Rangers, you know where to find me. But I'm no good at this strategy and tactics stuff, and I'm useless at planning. Let me hunt this fuck."

"What is it about this guy?" Tristan asked again.

Jeremy gave his head a taut little shake. "Don't ask, Tristan. Does it really matter?"

Tristan rubbed his chin. "Nooo," he said, "no, I reckon it doesn't."

"I don't ask often, and I don't ask much. You know this. Let me have him, Lord."

"What the fuck, over? I sure as hell wouldn't want you on my trail."

Tristan clapped his friend on the shoulder. "Go for it, Jeremy. Find the fuckard. Bring me his head."

"Do I have to leave a piece that big intact?"

Tristan guffawed. "No. Bring me anything. A hunk of his hair. Or nothing at all; I'll take your word for it."

"Thanks, Tristan."

"A word with you, gentlemen?"

Tramp, Buzzard, and Rico looked up from the barrel where they sat playing cards between the tents by the light of a lantern. A few piles of gold coins glinted dully on the table.

"Want us to deal you in, man?" Rico asked, showing a flash of gold tooth in his lean dark predator's face.

Lonesome Dave smiled. "No, thanks. I've got conversation on my mind, not cards."

Tramp gusted laughter. "Thank Bro Wind for that! I ain't eager to play with you, bro. You're too sharp for me."

"I'll take that for a compliment, brother," Dave said, pulling up an empty crate for a chair. For just a flicker his mask of easy affability slipped. Tramp recoiled from what he saw.

"Thank Brother Wind for that too," Lonesome Dave said, so quiet it was hard to pick his words out from the breeze whistling between the darkened tents. Every man heard him loud and clear just the same.

"What's on your mind, bro?" asked Buzzard, tossing his hand in with a last look of disgust.

"Tonight's Council meeting," the Pistolero said. "Doesn't it strike you gentlemen that our Lord is a little . . . distracted?"

The three passed looks around like a goatskin full of wine. Each reacted to the taste in a different way. Rico frowned. Buzzard sat back and dropped his blunt fingertips on the barrel head with a thump. Tramp stared at his cards.

"How do you mean?" Tramp asked. A glint came into his eye.

Lonesome Dave made an easy gesture with his right hand. "I mean the responsibilities of his position are great. Who'd want to be Lord of the Plains really?"

Rico lightened up enough to laugh. "Not me, man. He's welcome to it." But Buzzard leaned in a little closer. It did not escape Dave.

"Not me either," Lonesome Dave said. He reached inside one of the voluminous pockets of his greatcoat, and brought out a bottle of fine Eddie City whiskey. He twisted off the top, and passed the bottle to Buzzard. "The High Free Life for me. That's for sure."

"Damn straight," said Rico, as Buzzard took a hit and passed the bottle to him.

"What's his problem?" Tramp asked, staring morosely at the barrel head. Then he answered his own question. "That slash has got him wrapped around her little finger. Check it out: listenin' to a mouse instead of us proven bros."

"Lady Jovanne can be mighty persuasive," Lonesome Dave said.

"You were ready enough to take the bitch's side," Buzzard said, wiping his beard with the back of his hand.

Dave grinned. "Just trying to keep the peace. It doesn't do us any good to be fighting against each other."

"Doesn't do us any good to be fightin' two fuckin' Cities at once neither," Tramp said, and took a hearty swallow.

Dave accepted the bottle from him and handed it immediately off to Buzzard, who was ready enough to take another hit.

"Maybe not," Dave said. "As I said, the Lord Tristan's toting a heavy burden. Can't be easy on his mind. Maybe it seems clear to you and to me we should just blow away from Dallas and Homeland on the breeze. The Plains are wide."

"Yeah. Why don't we do that?" Tramp asked.

"Fuckin' Tristan's got a bee in his bonnet about Homeland, that's why," growled Buzzard. "He's goin' down hard because of it, and he's gonna take the rest of us down with him."

Rico frowned with the bottle almost to his lips. "Hey, now. Is that any way to talk, man? He's our Lord."

"Fuck," Tramp said. "What do we need a Lord for anyway? Wasn't we doin' fine just like we was?"

"You joined him of your own free will, man," Rico said reproachfully. "Nobody forced you."

"If we got to have a Lord," Buzzard said thoughtfully, "and mind, I ain't sayin' we do, and ain't sayin' we don't. But where is it writ it's gotta be Burningskull?"

"In the stars, man," Rico said. "In the fuckin' *stars*. Don't you remember the Sign of the Burning Skull? The Guest Star in Taurus? Shinin' bright as a new silver ounce when Tristan whipped the Catheads."

"I saw the Guest Star," Buzzard said. "I didn't see nobody's name writ on it."

Rico frowned. "Hey, now. Hey. What are you guys talkin' about?"

"Wind blows," Buzzard said, and took a mighty swig. "You live in the wind, you live with change."

He set the bottle down on the barrel with a thump. "Bro Wind might be due to blow some changes our way."

Rico snapped to his feet, swaying slightly. Lonesome Dave's was not the first bottle to be passed around this night. "I can't believe what I'm hearing, man. I just can't believe it. Tristan's our *Lord*. We promised to follow him. If there's anybody gonna steer us through this shit to the open Road again, it's him. I ain't gonna listen to anybody say nothin' against him!"

He stormed off into the darkness. The three men sat staring after him. Buzzard cracked his scarred knuckles, slowly, one after the other.

"I hope he don't go runnin' his head," Tramp said worriedly.

"Aw, don't shit your britches," Buzzard said, and belched. "He's an okay dude, for a Mex. He won't snitch us off."

"How can you be so goddamn sure?" Tramp demanded. "Everything's gone all upside down the last two years. We used to be high and free. Now we're just lapdogs for this Burningskull bastard. He says jump, we ask how high. He says shit, we drop trou and squat. Nothin's like it used to be. I mean, shit, we used to be big buddies with the Hardriders, rode together to the razz all the time. Does that count for anything now? No, sir, it does not!"

He spun on the Bandido leader and pointed an accusing finger. "How the fuck do you know what that greaseball'll do?"

Buzzard frowned and rubbed a grimy cheek with his fingertips. "You know, brother, there's something in what you say, now I think on it."

"Damn straight! You can't trust nobody no more. And if that pumped-up dickwad Burningskull hears what we've been saying—"

Tramp jumped to his feet, upsetting the barrel and the cards, and began to pace frantically back and forth. He clenched and unclenched big hairy hands in the air before him. "Why, I oughta . . ."

Lonesome Dave rose smoothly to his feet. He laid a hand on Tramp's shoulder.

"What you ought to do," the blond clean-shaven man said, "is go back to your tent and get some sleep. It's been a long day for everybody."

Tramp tried to shake him off. "Easy for you to talk. Shit, you saw what Burningskull did to those fuckin' Hogs, just for burnin' out some suck-ass Diggers! He thinks we're talkin' him down . . ."

Lonesome Dave clamped down with his fingers, holding Tramp in place. The Sand King Prez was an inch taller and outweighed him by twenty pounds. But he could not escape the Pistolero's smooth-fingered grip.

"We have nothing to fear," Dave said, looking into the larger man's eyes. "This is me telling you this."

Without apparent effort Lonesome Dave forced Tramp down to sit on a crate. Then he smiled at both men, turned, and vanished into the dark.

16

Run thunder rose like the rumble of an earthquake. Tristan Burningskull sat WildFyre atop a ridge and watched his motorized nomad Nation of the Plains stream east below his feet.

"Gets in the blood, doesn't it?" asked Jovanne, leaning forward over the bars of Black Death, the big Black Mountain sled that once belonged to the Cathead war-band chief Drago, killed by her Jokers at the Burningskull fight two years ago. She glanced back at Tristan, and her eyes were aglow. "Almost makes you feel like we'll pull it off somehow."

"We will," Tristan said seriously.

Jovanne was not usually given to sloppy in-the-wind sentimentality. But there was something about the roar of hundreds of big outlaw irons all lining out in the same direction, something that resonated deep in the nomad soul. Jovanne was a child of the Plains, as Tristan was, and had grown up knowing when she heard that sound that big things were coming.

An engine muttered from behind. Jeremy came rolling up astride Vengeance. "Impressive," he said.

"Yeah," Tristan said. "It should get even more so as the other clans join up." He grimaced. "That's if they do, and don't decide life'll be a whole lot simpler, not to mention safer, just out blowin' in the wind."

Jeremy laughed. "Live for the moment every once in a while," he said. "It's good for you."

Tristan produced a sour chuckle. "Strange days, when a City boy has to tell a Stormrider to live in the present."

"Life's never dull around you, Tristan," Jeremy agreed.

"Speaking of blowing in the wind," Jovanne said, straightening in the saddle and smoothing her short hair back from her face, "we should be doing that about now, unless we want everybody else getting there ahead of us."

"So, where is the crazy son of a bitch anyway?" Rico asked himself in Spanish. "Wants me to meet him, he says. Got something important to tell me, he says. And so where the hell is he?"

He pinched out the ember of his cigarette between callused fingertips, and tossed it to the shelf of basalt rock beneath the cleated front tire of his scrambler. The last hit of smoke trailed out his nostrils and whipped away on the wind blowing up out of the valley and making the gnarled limbs of the scrub cedar on the ridge top rattle.

He had been flattered when the rider came to tell him that something had come up, that the Lord of the Plains needed to meet with him at a private, lonely place right away. He admired the Maximum Lord greatly; he had been glad to lead *Los Tremendos Gavilanes* to join the great Nation of the Plains after Tristan's stunning victory over the Catheads. He had been honored when he and his clan were chosen to stay behind to harass the MoFos, even though the Lord had chosen to leave overall command to one of his own Burningskulls.

Rico was also nervous. Had Tristan somehow learned about the conversation the other night, about him and Tramp and Buzzard and that yellow-haired devil Lonesome Dave? Tristan was a cunning man, a hard man to fool. He would have his ways of finding out secrets.

"Fuck Lonesome Dave anyway," Rico said aloud in English. He had put the Council discussion out of his mind already, and Buzzard and Tramp had quit grousing about it. He thought Tristan listened too intently to that uppity long-legged squeeze of his, but that was Tristan's lookout. Rico had said his piece at the Council, and that was it.

But Lonesome Dave had come around, with his golden hair and his silver tongue, stirring up trouble.

Rico's fingers fumbled as he was shaking tobacco from his doeskin bag into a paper. The shreds of tobacco blew away on the wind. He cursed and threw down the paper.

If Tristan had found out about the loose talk, Rico would tell him it had only been that: talk. Nothing to worry about. Tristan was a wise man, a man of honor; he would surely understand . . .

Besides, all the worry might be for nothing. Tristan had probably thought of some new plan to bedevil Homeland; he was always full of plans, that one. But where was he?

Rico waited another half hour in growing impatience. Was the Lord playing games with him?

More likely someone was playing tricks on him. A lot of bros thought that kind of thing was real damn funny. He would find out who was behind it and teach them otherwise. You didn't fuck around with Rico or the *Gavilanes*.

He kicked his scrambler alive, turned it around, roared back down the ridge to the dirt road that ran down to the Plains. Once on the road he wound it out to an insistent snarling whine and fairly flew down the mountain.

He had gone barely a hundred yards when a length of wire, stretched taut and invisible between two pine trees, hit him just under the chin. It took his head off cleanly as a blade. His corpse rode on another fifty feet, blood fountaining from the neck, before it went over.

Without his hand on the throttle the engine died. An interval of silence, and then a Steller's jay began to fuss. The standard forest sounds came back.

With a purring of a well-tuned motor Lonesome Dave emerged from the woods, mounted on *Caballo Diablo*, his low-slung Iron Horse sled. He gazed at the head nestled among fallen needles against the base of a tree. Its expression was businesslike but unafraid. Rico had died without time for fear.

Lonesome Dave smiled. "You were easy," he said. "You were too easy. You should have made it harder."

He laughed, and put the bike in gear and left.

At any given time only a fraction of the Plains Nation's total numbers were on hand at Chaos Central. Tristan took most of them east with him, leaving behind a couple of clans. He put Ace, a ranking member of his Burningskull club, in charge. Ace had been a member of John Hammerhand's bodyguard, the self-proclaimed Death Commandos. He had impressed Tristan as a brave man with a brain, which made him all but unique among Hammerhand's ManLodge buddies.

When the discredited Hammerhand had abdicated his post as commander of the armies of the High Free Folk and ridden off

into the wasteland, Ace had remained behind. On learning that
Tristan was putting together his own elite band he had asked to
be allowed to join. Tristan had accepted gladly. He had not re-
gretted the choice.

This journey was a far cry from Hammerhand's sweep east
two years before. The force moved at speed, but cautiously, with
reconnaissance patrols ranging far ahead—something Hammerhand disdained. Tristan did not want to run into any unpleasant
surprises.

The Road to war with the Catheads had been assailed by
spasms of natural violence savage even by the standards of the
post-StarFall world. The disasters—and ill omens—had begun
when a fall of ash from a volcanic explosion had suffocated the
Gipsy Kings MC in their entirety. Floods, stampedes, and Stalking Winds had attacked the nomads like enemy armies.

The weather was not good for Tristan's drive to meet the
Dallasites—it never stayed good long, out on the Plains. Nature
took her toll: scouts caught in flash floods and whirled away to
their deaths, riders struck by lightning. But nothing beyond the
grim routine of life on the Plains.

But the trip was not entirely routine. Mother Earth liked her
surprises.

"Will you look at that?" Tristan parked WildFyre on the hilltop,
took a few steps forward with his fingers hitched into the back
of his belt, and stared out at the plain.

Out in the middle of the flat grassland a black cone poked
thirty feet in the air. It was perfectly symmetrical, like a toy, like
a prop for a hobbyist's model railroad. Thick black smoke
drooled from the tip. Sparks shot upward in a fiery cascade; several seconds later the crack of an explosion sounded.

"A brand-new volcano," Jovanne said, and shook her head.
Her wonder was genuine, almost childlike; one thing all
Stormriders learned was to appreciate the terrible beauties of
their world. Around them riders were pulling their irons up for a
reverent look at the newcomer.

"How long's it been there?" Tristan asked.

A group of Diamondbacks clustered around Tristan and his
companions. They had discovered the caner on a reconnaissance
sweep ahead of the army. The spokesman, a bandy-legged rider
with a gold incisor, shrugged.

"We was this way a moon back," he said, "on our way back to Chaos Central. No sign of the puppy then."

"Shit," Jeremy said. He looked nervous—a genuinely rare sight. He feared no man, as Tristan could testify. But for all his years among the bros he had never entirely shaken the City boy's intestinal dread of the more gaudily awe-inspiring processes of Nature. "How *big* will that thing get?"

Tristan shrugged. "Who knows? It might stop while we're standing here watching. It might just keep growing and growing—who knows?"

Volcanoes springing up in the midst of the sea of grass that was the Plains was not a commonplace occurrence, but neither was it shocking. At one time it would have been. But that was before the falling segments of the Star cracked the Earth's crust, allowing the magma to seep to the surface in dozens of locations that had never before shown sign of volcanic activity. At least, the post-StarFall scientists whose speculations Tristan read in the Library had blamed the comet strike. Interest in science had dwindled almost to nothing within a century of the catastrophe, so in the end not a lot was done to prove or disprove the theory.

"Is it an omen?" Jovanne asked half-seriously.

"Hey," Tristan said, "it beats the ass off me."

Jeremy looked askance at them. "You cycle savages are supposed to be up on all this mystic crap. Don't you even know an omen when you see one?"

Jovanne frowned. Jeremy liked to push the limits of the status he had gained among the High Free Folk, during his days as the Black Avenger and beyond. Tristan laughed.

"All right," Tristan said. "I'll play the expert here; I've had a run-in or two with omens. I officially declare this to be one."

Jovanne turned, crossed her arms beneath her breasts, sat back with her rump against the saddle of her Black Mountain, and gave him a twisted smile.

"All right, O wise one," she said. "what *kind* of omen is it?"

"Uh—a good one. Yeah, that's it."

"Now, if I only believed in omens," Jeremy said.

17

"Are you certain, gentlemen," the man in the tall hat intoned, "that you cannot reconcile your differences in a peaceable manner?"

The handsome young face of Captain Andrew, Baron Taliaferro, was pale, and his eyes indicated he had not slept well during the night just ending. But his expression was resolute. He jutted his jaw, nodded, and spoke firmly.

"The colonel by negligence and willfulness caused my men to be massacred," the captain said. "Since he denies me the opportunity to clear my name at a court-martial, I have no choice but to demand satisfaction on the field of honor."

The dueling party stood on a swell in the ocean of rank grass that undulated away in all directions: toward day, toward night, to north and south. Here an island of short eastern grasses held out amid the tall grass of the Western Plains. A thick white mist swirled about the lonely figures, and pooled in the low places, turning them to bowls of cloud.

"Might I point out that your opponent at present enjoys the rank of brevet brigadier general?" the referee said in tones of gentle reproof. Taliaferro shrugged, and made a negligent gesture with the naked saber in his hand.

The referee swiveled his head to Colonel Selfridge, standing slim and confident in the milky dawn light. The referee was a tall man with a long, lined undertaker's face. He wore a striped tailcoat along with his top hat. The rising sun turned his spectacles to disks of yellow fire.

"Sir Lane?"

Selfridge flipped the basket hilt of his own saber up in front of his striking yellow-mustachioed face. "I never yet ran from a fight, sir," he said in his soft rich drawl.

"Very well," the referee said with ponderous regret. It was fake; he was as eager to see blood spilled scarlet on the green dew-wet grass as anyone. "If you are resolved upon this means of settling your differences, so be it."

He turned and blinked owlishly at the seconds. Baron Taliaferro was seconded by a trio of aristocratic junior officers, each as painfully handsome, earnest, and youthful as he was himself: Captains Bryan and Ellis, both in line for baronies themselves, and a pale lieutenant with slightly bulging blue eyes who had recently succeeded to the title of Count Van Zandt, which despite being a county was the least of the holdings represented. Selfridge's second was his Sergeant Major Dobbs, a huge, dark, beetle-browed man with hanging apelike arms.

"Assume the guard position, gentlemen," the referee said. The two combatants obeyed. "Wait for my signal, and then lay on with a will. Should either of you disregard my order to stop he shall at once be declared the loser, and his name shall be broadcast as that of a coward devoid of honor. Am I understood?"

The combatants nodded. They stood facing one another across their upraised blades. Each was dressed identically, in loose white shirt, white cavalry breeches, and knee-high black boots polished to an obsidian finish. The only color was the red sash wound about each man's narrow waist. White for honor; red for blood.

They were a disparate pair, Selfridge young-seeming, Taliaferro authentically young. Both were slender, athletic men, broad in the shoulders and flat in the belly. Selfridge had his yellow hair drawn back in a ponytail. The clean-shaven Taliaferro wore his brown hair short, as was currently fashionable among the fine young bucks of the officer corps. He was a good three inches taller than Selfridge, with the longer reach, and he was thicker through the chest. Nevertheless it was *his* hairline that showed a fine chain of sweat strung along it.

The sun broke free of the hills to the east. "Gentlemen, commence!" the referee cried.

For a handful of heartbeats the two stood studying each other as the ochre morning sunlight, already hot, began to sting their faces and burn off the mist. Taliaferro braced himself, evidently expecting immediate attack. Selfridge just stood there, a slight smile on his lips, as if to say, *Make your choice, boy, I can wait here all day.*

Cautiously Taliaferro advanced. Like his opponent he kept his left hand tucked into his sash at the small of his back. Selfridge slowly raised his saber until it was held edge up, parallel to the earth and just above the level of his eyes. An unorthodox *en garde* position, but then the colonel was an unorthodox man.

Taliaferro tried a tentative thrust for the face. Selfridge parried it effortlessly by rotating his hand downward and in. The young captain's seconds cried out in excitement at the clang of blades.

Selfridge's unusual stance invited attack on the low line. Taliaferro was not ingenuous enough to accept the invitation un-critically. He traded a few cuts from the wrist with the colonel, who met each precisely, as anticipated. When he felt he had es-tablished a rhythm—and felt that he had a small edge in wrist strength as well as reach—Captain Taliaferro launched a whis-tling overhead cut aimed to split Selfridge's handsome face down the middle. Selfridge whipped his saber up in a block that was no more than an exaggerated form of his guard position.

Steel kissed. Taliaferro disengaged his blade with a quick slide, whipped it down and around, and thrust, point upward, for the middle of his opponent's belly.

Selfridge slid his leading foot back, went up on tiptoe. At the same time he cut downward with blinding speed. There was the impact of blade on bone, a gasp, and he danced back.

His opponent's saber fell to the grass. Captain Count Taliaferro's face was strained and paper-white as he reached up to clutch his right forearm, where blood welled up from a deep slash, shockingly red against the white sleeve.

"Hold!" the referee cried, with only a tinge of disappointment in his voice. "First blood has been drawn! Colonel Selfridge, do you consider yourself satisfied?"

The colonel gazed at his opponent a moment with heavy-lidded blue eyes, then nodded. "I do, sir."

The referee looked to the young captain. The boy shrugged off his seconds, who had clustered around murmuring concern and trying to bandage his wound.

"No!" he cried. He snatched the saber up from the grass with his left hand, leaving the arm to bleed. "No! It isn't done!"

Like a judge at a tennis match the referee turned his head back to Selfridge, who shrugged. "If you insist," Selfridge said sardonically, and transferred the weapon to his left hand with a casual toss.

"A chivalrous gesture by Brigadier Selfridge!" the referee declared in ringing tones. It would have made more impact had the fact that Selfridge was ambidextrous not been such common knowledge in his army.

Taliaferro attacked, with more desperate energy than skill. He was not ambidextrous, and he knew his only hope was to use his superior size to overpower his foe.

Selfridge met his flailing attack and headlong lunges with cool efficiency. He retreated step by step, keeping his blade between them now, so that the tip constantly endangered his opponent's face and restrained the ferocity of his charges. Through it all he wore the same maddening half-smile beneath his mustache.

When Taliaferro's face was flushed and wet and his breath came in heaves, Selfridge went to the offensive. His cuts and thrusts were conservative and quick, the opposite of his opponent's all-out attacks. Taliaferro was reduced to falling back, hacking at Selfridge's blade two-handed in a desperate attempt to drive it far enough off-line for a last-ditch lunge to spit the slim, haughty white-clad figure. But Selfridge refused to match his strength to the younger man's; his blade was like the Plains wind, always moving, constantly changing direction, elusive. When steel did ring on steel the colonel merely used the momentum imparted by his opponent's saber to snap his own around in a circle, so that he was never uncovered.

Taliaferro's seconds stood still and ashen, encouragements clogged in their throats. Dobbs watched impassively, his gorilla arms folded across his chest. The referee's face shone with damp excitement.

With a wordless cry Taliaferro hurled himself forward. Two overhand cuts—still two-handed, ignoring the agony in his wounded arm—were met with straight parries that rang like bells. The third wild swipe Selfridge evaded by stepping lithely back. Before the overextended youth could recover, the colonel flowed forward and ran him through the left shoulder with a sound like a pitchfork stabbing a potato.

Dropping his saber, Taliaferro fell to his knees, face twisted like a rag in agony. "Hold!" the referee cried, stepping forward importantly and waving a white handkerchief in the air between them.

The colonel stuck the bloodied tip of his blade in the moist black earth. "I declare myself satisfied," he said. He looked down at his opponent. "Do you profess yourself a beaten man?"

Tears of pain and rage flowed down Taliaferro's cheeks. "No!" he screamed. He tried to raise his hands, could not, dropped them to his sides.

"Still," the colonel said, "I shall be generous, and leave you with your life." He unearthed his saber, saluted, and spun on his heel to walk away.

"Just wait!" Taliaferro screamed at his back. "You set my men up to die! *You won't get away with this, you coward!*"

Colonel Selfridge pivoted right, sweeping his saber outward in a looping backhand cut. A sound like a rail-splitter striking a post, and Captain Taliaferro's head sprang from its shoulders and went bouncing away across the grass. Blood blooped from the stump of neck, drenching the white front of his blouse in an instant, and the torso fell.

"Or will, as circumstances dictate," the Colonel murmured. He tossed his saber up in the air with a flip of the wrist. It rotated once, lazily, like a knife in a game of mumblety-peg, and stuck point-first in the earth. The heavy hilt waved back and forth in a pendulum swing.

Selfridge turned and walked away. With a scream of rage the youthful Count Van Zandt launched himself forward. He dashed straight at Selfridge's back, seizing the colonel's saber as he ran.

The colonel pirouetted, smiling. From his left sleeve a derringer, two-barreled, intricately engraved, and chrome-shiny, dropped into his palm. He held it up practically against the charging young man's belly and fired.

The tiny pistol made a sound like a cannon. Blood and fragments of flesh exploded out Count Van Zandt's back. He staggered backwards three steps, clutching at himself, then folded forward to the earth.

In the sudden ringing silence a flight of crows burst upwards from a mist-filled depression, black wings flapping. They cawed in alarmed irritation and flew away toward the rising sun.

".41 Magnum," the colonel said. "Works every time."

He tipped the derringer to the clear morning sky. Though fingers and wrists must have been smarting from the terrible recoil, his face showed no expression other than that languid little smile.

"Anybody else want some?" he asked the surviving pair of

seconds. They shook their heads. They kept staring at the stricken Count Van Zandt as if mesmerized.

"All right then." The derringer went away. "Y'all have duties to attend to, I'm sure. Come along, Sergeant Major. Let's go rustle up some breakfast. I could eat a Tennessee walking horse along about now!"

18

"Tristan! *My man!*"

There was a handful of bikes and bedrolls clustered around the remnants of last night's campfire, nestled out of casual view beside a creek that serpentined between soft low hills. A black man with gray liberally salting the tight wiry black curls of his hair and mirror shades before his eyes was walking to meet the approaching party of bikers.

Tristan leaned WildFyre into her stand and jumped off. He ran to meet the man, and caught him in an embrace that pulled the soles of his knee-high Apache moccasins off the dew-damp grass.

"Jammer!" Tristan shouted. "God *damn*, but it's good to see you again!"

"Whoa!" Jammer said, laughing. "Seeing as you're fixing to bust my back and paralyze me and all, I'm purely glad you aren't *pissed* to see me."

Tristan laughed, and set his old friend down and let him go. "Sorry. It's been too long."

"Amen to that, boy." Big cruisers swirled around the campsite. Jammer walked among the riders, slapping hands and swapping hugs.

The Jokers and Outlaws had accompanied Tristan in advance of his main force, about sixty riders in all—the wars had taken their toll on the two clubs, and both of them had become exclusive, jealous of the privilege of belonging, wearing their decreasing numbers as proudly as they did their colors. By unspoken accord they seemed to have decided that the last of both clans would live and die in the service of Tristan Burningskull, Lord of the Plains. If any clubs chose to bear their names in future, it would be to honor legends.

The Electric Skald's companions were half a dozen Mad Things, four men and two women, rangy, crop-haired, and dangerous-looking in fringed black leather hung with shiny weapons. They had a bad-crazy reputation, and were no formal part of Tristan's Federation. But if they were good enough to ride with Jammer, they were good enough for him.

Jammer introduced him to Angela Death, the war-band leader, a woman of no great height, with lank hair dyed jet-black hanging in her eyes, which were rimmed with thick black makeup to match her black lipstick. She might have been pretty had she not looked like a skull in a wig. Her handshake was wiry-strong.

"We've been helping Jammer here keep an eye on the Rangers," she said in a voice raspy from whiskey and tobacco. "Sons of bitches are getting bold."

"Thanks," Tristan said. "I'm surprised, though; you aren't part of the Federation."

"We're with you on this," the woman said. "Dallas needs to get taken down a peg, or they'll fence in the whole damn prairie, build pleasure resorts for their high-ass nobility all over it."

"We heard tell Homeland's on the move, too," said Lurch, her seven-foot-tall sergeant at arms. He was a horrible-looking party, with stone-shelf brows and lantern jaw and a beak of nose, and heavy brown hair hanging in plaits past gallows shoulders. He looked to have some North Plains in him, Lakota or Blackfoot maybe. His voice, though, was high and mild as an adolescent girl's. "They're fencing the Plains already."

"You heard right."

Lurch frowned. It was an awesome sight. "What d'you intend to do about that?" he asked slowly.

"Nothing till we've dealt with the Rangers," Tristan said.

"Sounds like a plan," Angela Death said. "We can't be racing off in all directions at once."

"I hate to interrupt," Jammer said, "but we'd better either break up this cozy like confab or just plain hit the road."

Jovanne had come up, stretching to work the kinks of the saddle from her limbs and surreptitiously massaging her sore rump. Jeremy wasn't along; he was with the main body, about a day's ride back.

"What's the rattle, Jammer?" Jovanne asked. "We just got here."

"I know. But it isn't safe to concentrate in too-big groups, or hang around any one place too long."

Tristan's eyes narrowed. "Rangers are that good?"

As if in reply an engine whined in the not-so-distant distance. A light combat car burst over a low rise three hundred yards away to the east and began to roll toward them. It was a dune buggy as much as anything else, big tires and openwork frame. A light machine gun was mounted to the roll bar. A gunner stood behind it, and as Tristan and the other new arrivals stared, light began to wink from its muzzle.

"Holy shit!" Tristan exclaimed. "Everybody, down! Take up firing positions."

He was in motion, following his own orders even as he issued them. He raced the few steps back to WildFyre, snagged his Saskatoon Scout carbine from its buckskin sheath, and made love to the earth.

Two more light combat cars had appeared over the hill and were charging with the first in a loose wedge formation, shooting as they came. One of the Mad Things, morning-logy and slow to react, grunted and went down as bullets ripped through the campsite like a rainsquall.

The Jokers and the Outlaws were old hands at this kind of scene. Spending two years in the company of Tristan Burningskull did that to people. They had grabbed up their weapons and gone to ground in a firing line as professionally as any veteran City soldiers, and considerably more so than the green-scared conscripts who made up the bulk of most Citizen armies.

Shots cracked from the outlaw line. The High Free Folk were wild and undisciplined in most things, but the perpetual Plains shortage of ammunition had taught most of them since birth to husband their shots and *aim*. Instead of a quick-firing rattle, or the snarl of City automatic weapons, the shots came slow-paced and careful as the blows of craftsmen's hammers.

Tristan did not bother to flip up the leaf rear sight of his Mk V, graded in hundred-meter increments, trusting instead to the battle sights and Kentucky windage. He had done it often enough before, as a Striker and afterwards.

He drew a bead on the gunner in the lead car. The light combats trusted entirely to speed, agility, and firepower for survival.

They had no armor to speak of. Bouncing breakneck over the prairie toward the outlaw band, they were not ideal targets.

But the nomads were well dispersed and hidden in the long grass. The cars could only beat the general vicinity of their enemies with whips of fire and hope they got lucky. The outlaws, on the other hand, knew exactly where they were.

When a target could be seen, it was only a matter of time before it was hit. Tristan fired once to no effect, jacked the quick-throw bolt action in a hurry, and fired again. The gunner dropped into his seat and sprawled to the side—whether struck by Tristan's bullet or another, he couldn't tell.

A blink later the driver's head exploded. The car went sideways, lost it, and rolled. A rearward extension of the roll bar protected the rear-facing sting gunner from being crushed.

Tristan tracked the rifle right, looking for new targets. He saw the next car turn tail, its own machine gun flopping unoccupied on its mount. Then the two surviving vehicles were fleeing back over the hill, sting gunners keeping up a game fire as they went.

With a wild-animal rustle the nomads started to rise. "Stay down!" Tristan snapped in his hardest-edged command voice. "Stay on-line until I give the word."

Obediently the Jokers and Outlaws dropped back into cover behind their weapons. The handful of Mad Things looked to Angela Death. She frowned momentarily at Tristan, then shrugged, nodded. The Mad Things weren't used to taking orders, much less from outsiders with lofty pretensions. The war-band leader might just have decided to humor this hodad who thought he was the Lord of the Plains.

On the other hand, diplomacy had never been the Mad Things' strong suit, and it wasn't a lack they keenly felt. If Jammer chose to hang with them—and the Skald was out here with a purpose, not just beating the high grass for song-stuff—he had a reason for doing so. Angela might well be shrewd enough to have picked up on Tristan's reasoning: Had he been commanding the combat car patrol, he'd give the bike trash thirty seconds to a minute to decide everything was cool and stand up out of cover to start swapping high fives, then roll the cars back from hull-down positions behind the hilltop and hose them down proper.

So the nomads waited, a minute, two. The Mad Things began to stir and mumble. "Wait for it," Angela growled. "We don't want the fuckards to come back and catch us with our asses in the breeze."

A Mad Thing and a couple of Jokers had been crawling around in the damp grass to check casualties. The Mad Thing who'd been caught slow by the Dallasite burst was history. An Outlaw had taken two rounds through the leg, but had started tourniqueting it himself during the brief firefight. He hadn't lost enough blood to kill him, the bone had miraculously not been broken, and with a packet of precious antibiotics poured into the wound he'd likely make it.

Tristan gave it five minutes, scanning the hill with binoculars He saw no sign of activity, which might be significant and might not. Cautiously he stood up, gesturing for the others to hold position.

No gunfire. "All right," he ordered, "on your feet. But be ready to hug Mother Earth in a hell of a hurry."

Gingerly the Stormriders picked themselves up. Jammer came to Tristan's side. "We should be thinkin' about moving on," he said. "We've already been here too long."

"I hear you," Tristan said. He gestured to Angela. "Any idea what the atmospherics are like?"

"Suck," the Mad Thing boss said. "Those Cowboys aren't gonna find it easy to scream for help."

"We don't know how long it'll take them to get back to their pals," Jovanne pointed out.

The Mad Thing leader subjected the taller woman to narrow scrutiny, and nodded slightly, as if subconsciously. "Yeah. Mad Things, let's putt!"

19

"Camp stoves'll never replace bonfires," Jammer said glumly. He leaned as near as politic to the object in question for warmth. The nighttime rain made a constant seamless sound on the walls of the tent, like the wind or a river. The tent was not large, and it was crowded by four slowly-drying bodies, even though they were all clumped close around the little stove.

"You got that right," Tristan agreed without obvious pleasure. His nod was barely visible by the faint glow.

He took a hit from the wineskin and passed it to Jovanne. She accepted it, drank, and swirled the sweet Fort Hammond Red thoughtfully around in her mouth.

"Are the Cowboys so good," she said, unconsciously echoing Tristan's earlier question, "that we can't even show a lantern in this damned downpour?"

"They sure are," Jammer said. "They're smart, for City soldiers."

"Mobile, agile, and hostile," Angela Death agreed.

Tristan rubbed his cheek. "If the Citizens start getting smart, we could be in trouble."

"I hear you talking, Burningskull," Angela said.

"I can't get over how much ammunition they were willing to burn up," Jovanne said. Seasoned as she was, she didn't have a lot of experience hassling with City forces. Tristan had certainly put a lot of effort and ingenuity into avoiding fights with the Citizens in his two years as Lord of the Plains. He had been trying to gather his strength for the big showdown he knew was coming with Homeland.

Whether he'd mustered enough to take on *both* Homeland and the biggest City of all remained to be seen.

"They could just spray the grass at random and hope to hit us," Jovanne said. "A-fucking-mazing."

"Do they have *any* weaknesses?" Tristan asked, trying to keep desperation out of his voice. He'd had a hard ride across the Plains, and found little comfort at the end of it. After the Ranger patrol had taken a swing at them they had rolled many miles through one of those sudden Plains thunderstorms that boil up from nowhere before Jammer and Angela Death had judged they might be safe from discovery by Dallasite sweeps. And they'd emphasized the *might*.

Angela Death looked at Jammer through the gloom. "They got balls bigger'n their brains," the Mad Thing leader said succinctly.

"They're good, boy," Jammer said, "gotta give 'em that. Send out a lot of patrols, cover a mess of ground. The drill is, they advance in a mass, drop a forward base, and start patrolling out of it, reconnoitering for the next leap. Use a lot of scouts."

"Does that maybe mean we can make them use *up* a lot of scouts?" Tristan asked.

Jammer showed even white teeth. "Glad to see you ain't forgot how to think during my extended absence, boy," he said. "We can at that. Blind 'em up some, lay some stinging on 'em, throw 'em a bit off balance.

"Beyond that, the little lady here hit it right between the eyes."

A little V appeared between Tristan's brows, invisible in the dimness. *Little lady?* Angela Death looked like the kind who'd take a man's nuts off with a rusty old can lid for *thinking* words like that about her. Yet she held her peace, sitting there watching Jammer in a way that suddenly set Tristan to wondering.

Jammer was no spring chicken—he had been well into adulthood when Tristan was a kid, and his father, Twelve-String Jake, had run with Tristan's granddad, Anse the One-Eyed. But Jammer had an ageless quality about him, kept himself in trim except for a little bit of incipient paunch, and had enough charisma for a whole cycle clan—as befitted the Maximum Bard of the High Free Folk. It was not impossible he and the dangerous but foxy-looking Mad Thing babe had themselves a little understanding.

"They're arrogant motherfuckers," the black Bard said. "They think their shit don't stink, think nothing can ever touch 'em. Wouldn't be acting so canary around Osage territory otherwise."

"Too bad the tailheads are such chickenshits," Angela said. "They could put some hurt on the fucking Cowboys if they'd come off their precious little farms and out from behind their wire at Broken Arrow."

"They want to make sure they can defend those farms and their city if Dallas makes a major play for them," Tristan said. Timely Osage assistance had been vital to his victory over the Cathead Nation; he felt bound to speak up on their behalf, even though for a fact he'd be happier if they stirred their stumps and weighed in against the Dallasites. "Dallas hasn't exactly emptied its magazine putting this army into the field. They've got more troops behind their own wire than they got facing us."

"Shit," Angela Death said. "Are you serious?"

"He is that, my child," Jammer said. She flashed him a quick grin. *Now I know you're porking her, you randy old son of a bitch,* Tristan thought.

The Mad Thing leader shook her head. "We're in some trouble, aren't we, Mr. Maximum Lord?"

" 'Fraid so." He looked to Jammer. "What about their CO?"

"Name's Selfridge. He's either a brigadier general or a colonel, dependin' who you talk to."

"Probably breveted to general rank," said Tristan reflexively.

Jammer winced. "I don't know from all this City rank stuff. I wouldn't have much truck with havin' a Lord of the Plains even, if I didn't love you like a son and if it wasn't your clear Destiny besides."

Tristan stifled a grin. "So what's this Selfridge like?"

"Pretty much the same as his men. Looks real good in his fancy command car and his tailored uniform, and he's almost as smart as he thinks he is. The word is he's tough as rawhide too, but I can't speak to that."

Jammer's tone indicated he didn't think much of City standards of *tough*. For all his folksy-jiving speech Jammer was one of the most sophisticated of all the High Free Folk, but he was a dedicated Plains chauvinist.

"He thinks with his dick too," Angela Death said. "He is kind of pretty, though. For a City puke-lapper."

"Don't underestimate him, girl," Jammer said earnestly. "He's been moving smart. If Dallas gave him more men, we'd be in the world of hurt for true."

"Why don't they?" asked Tristan, intrigued. Jammer had an instinctive feel for politics, even the essentially alien politics of a City. His years of travels among the myriad clans of the High Free Folk had given him a bone-deep knowledge of the doings of the cussed creatures called humankind. That was why he served as Tristan's intelligence chief—that and the fact that he could go damned near anywhere he pleased without attracting suspicion.

"He's maybe risen a little far a little too fast for some folks' taste. Maybe stepped on a few faces on the way. There's some rumors goin' round that he's got some peon blood to him, maybe even Mex. Have to be a ways back, though, I reckon, with that blond pelt of his."

Jammer settled back on his haunches, rubbed his hands together briskly, then held the pink palms toward the camp stove. "Official line is, his men are all Rangers, all ee-lite, so they don't need more'n two thou to mop up a passel of raggedy-ass scooter trash like us. Truth is, the jealousy, plus I think maybeso Dallas is as nervous about the Osage as the tailheads are of them."

"They don't want the tailheads grabbing off a chunk of their territory," Jovanne said. "They *really* don't want the Osage driving west to Comanche territory, pinching off their little army in the rear."

Angela Death grinned at her, the first sign of friendliness she'd shown the taller woman. "Wouldn't that be a dream!" she exclaimed. "We'd wash 'em away, no problem. City-ass army stranded out on the Plains without their damned convoys—they'd be fucked big time."

It was true. Getting caught high and dry in the middle of nowhere was a recurrent nightmare for City commanders. The Plains were uncompromisingly hostile to the supply-line-dependent City forces. The very few major victories Stormriders had won over Citizens had come about when City armies had gotten cut off, so that their mobile and persistent adversaries, with the Stalking Wind and the rain and the hail to help, could erode them down to nothing.

Jovanne looked as if she were going to say something more, then slapped herself sharply on the thigh. "I've got it!" she exclaimed.

Jammer jumped. The Joker President had come up to a kneeling position, and was rocking back and forth, unconsciously drumming her fists on the taut fabric covering her thighs. Her eyes were looking somewhere far away.

"What do you got, girl," Jammer asked, "and is it contagious?"

Jovanne gave him the slightest grin—a token of how distracted she was by whatever she'd just got, since she generally got a real kick out of Jammer's bullshit. She'd take a lot more off the Electric Skald than she'd ever dream of doing off anybody else. It was almost enough to make Tristan wonder about the two of *them*, except he honestly didn't give a damn.

"I know how we can hurt the Cowboys bad," she said, "and do ourselves some major good in the process."

"So, are you gonna share it with the rest of us, or make us play twenty questions?" Angela Death asked testily.

"Ammunition," Jovanne said.

"Gesundheit," Angela Death. "What the hell do you mean, ammunition?"

Tristan put his head back and began to laugh.

"Don't you see?" Jovanne asked, and what little light there was was dancing in her amber eyes. "Your talking about their supply trains turned me on to it. We start taking *their* ammunition, and we make it *our* ammunition!"

"Beautiful," Jammer said.

20

May-Elle McCoy's voice was twanging her hit "Love Warmed Over" from the loudspeaker attached to the 20-mm turret of the lead Austin armored car. The sun was shining, the road was good, and all was right with the world.

Bob-Ed Varman dozed at the pintle mount of the big old blunt-nose Omohundro cargo truck, somewhere less than half aware of the music and the sun-heated receiver of the Dallas Arsenal .30 caliber machine gun against his cheek.

"Bob-Ed?" The voice of his old buddy old pal Pooter drifted out from inside the square-top cab. "Bob-Ed, is you asleep again, you broke-dick dog?"

Bob-Ed roused himself with a start. "Shit, no!" he snapped right back, then went and ruined it by yawning a big old yawn.

"Bull-hockey!" Pooter exclaimed right off. "You was too! I heard you chainsawing lumber up there!"

Shitfire. Pooter could be a pure pain in the nut-sac sometimes. "Was not!" Bob-Ed declared. Even he knew it was weak.

Pooter just laughed. He had his corporal's stripe. He could afford to laugh.

"Sumbitch," Bob-Ed muttered beneath his breath. "I'm a Ranger and a white man too! Just 'cause you're a corporal don't give you no call to go treatin' me like I was some peon."

"What say, Bob-Ed? Better speak up there, boy!"

"Nothin'. I didn't say nothin'."

"Now, don't go arguing with yourself," Pooter said sternly.

"You're liable to up and lose." And he laughed so hard he didn't hear his sometime pal cussing him out loud.

Scowling beneath the brim of the cowboy hat it was his privilege as a Dallas Ranger to wear, Bob-Ed grabbed the double spade-grip handles of his .30 and swung it in an arc across the prairie. The grass wasn't real high here, and the land was flat. Not good ambush country, he reckoned. He'd never been in any ambushes himself, mind, or seen any action except to be in on squashing a couple of risings by uppity peons, but he was a Ranger, which meant he knew about that kind of thing as a matter of natural course.

There was no chance of trouble anyway. Yellowhair Selfridge was keeping a close eye on both the Comanch' and the tailheads, and their shit had clearly turned to water; they were showing nary a sign of making any moves against the Ranger salient. And the bike scum had been too cowardly to put in an appearance so far. There was a pool in barracks about when the bikers would show. Bob-Ed's money said *never*. They were just chickenshit. They'd never dare to take on the Dallas Rangers.

If they did, though . . . he grinned. He *wished* they would, God damn him for a nigger if he didn't! They had two Austin armored cars mounting twenty mike-mike quickfirers, one each front and rear, and a canvasback full of a squad of troopies, and a dozen big ammo trucks, six of them mounting machine guns like his.

Let the cycle shitbags come. The Rangers'd show 'em what ass-kicking was *all about*.

Meanwhile, May-Elle was singing a sweet country ballad. The sky was mostly clear, for a wonder, and the sun was hot, and his eyelids were getting heavy . . .

"I tell you, boy." Pooter's voice roused him again. The driver had his window open and his elbow out. He had taken a hankering for some palaver with his good buddy. "I just can't wait to get back to Fort Tom Landry. You wanna know why?"

"No," Bob-Ed said sulkily.

Pooter laughed again. Bob-Ed swore he'd never known such a laughing fool in all his life.

"Sure you do, son, sure you do. And I'm gonna tell you. It's Lucita, that little peon gal out to Old Man Cassidy's place. When we get back from this run I think I'll sneak over the wire, go take her for a little 'round-the-world cruise without ever leaving the *rancho*, if you know what I mean and I think you do."

Bob-Ed scowled. He wanted to believe Pooter was all full of bullshit going on about his peon bitch, with hooters out to here and buns like a couple of Española Valley apples. But he was afraid he wasn't.

Pooter wasn't much to look at, God knows, with stiletto-point sideburns and bandy little bowlegs and a big old gut hanging over his belt. But he had a way with the ladies, there was no denying the fact.

Bob-Ed knew for a stone fact that he was *much* better looking than Pooter. He was a long drink of water with brown hair, and maybe he ran a bit too much to elbows and Adam's apple, but still, when he looked in the mirror, the facts stood out plain as the nose on his face. But that fat fuck Pooter seemed to get all the action. It just wasn't *fair*.

"Old Man Cassidy catches you diddlin' his peons," he said, "he'll nail your nuts to his barn to dry."

"Bull*shit*!" Pooter yelled, voice snapping with genuine rage. "He can't touch me! He don't dare! I'm a Dallas Ranger, ain't I?"

Bob-Ed started to say he didn't think Old Man Cassidy gave a rotten Rocky Mountain oyster who Pooter was. But there was a puff of white smoke from the roadside ditch up ahead, and then from the lead car came a brilliant flash and a crack so horrible loud it felt as if Bob-Ed had been hit in the head with an ax.

The Austin swerved into the ditch. May-Elle's sweet voice turned to that blup-blup-blup of a stuck CD. The hatch in the top of the turret popped open, and a man came flying out with his uniform on fire. He dropped to the grass and rolled, extinguishing the flames.

Belatedly a few synapses clanged shut in Bob-Ed's head. "Holy shit!" he yelled. "We're under attack! The Austin exploded."

The smoke puff was drifting away like a big gauzy balloon. He whipped the .30 around and hosed the ditch below it.

"Omigawd, omigawd, omigawd!" he chanted, as the gun clattered and the handles vibrated against his palms. It was as if he was being hung up in the sky on a couple of long thin needles, the one called fear and the other exhilaration.

"Bob-Ed," he heard Pooter say. He didn't hear what else his friend had to say, because right about then the three tons of ammunition stored in the back of the truck blew up.

• • •

Tristan pressed his face hard into the dirt and prayed that none of the chunks of the ammo truck, blown a hundred yards into the sky by the blast, would land on him. "Son of a bitch, son of a bitch, son of a *bitch*!" he said. He couldn't even hear himself; the awful Doomsday crack of the truck going up had filled his ears to overflowing with a persistent ringing.

The grass was wet from a thundershower an hour before. The sun stung his shoulder blades and the backs of his calves through his clothing. He felt a heavy impact vibrate up through his body and winced.

He looked up. Part of the cab had landed not six feet from his head and was sitting there smoking. "Shit," he said.

He glared around at the Stormriders hidden in the weeds of the ditch. "You shitheads! Don't shoot your rockets at the goddam *ammo trucks*. They're what we're *here* for."

A Marauder showed a nervous bearded grin beneath the raccoon-mask left by his goggles, which were pushed up on top of a bush of ginger hair. "Sorry," he said. Tristan more read his lips than actually heard him.

Tristan turned his attention back to the road. The Dallas Rangers were well trained, well equipped, reasonably well motivated. But the only seasoning most of them had was squatting on wretched peons who rebelled against their overlords—usually without benefit of firearms, unless they managed to seize a few from their masters—and against random bandit gangs, who might or might not be High Free Folk.

They were used to holding the whip hand, in other words; they were *not* used to shrewd, resourceful, well-armed foes. What looked like flat grassland to their inexperienced eyes in fact contained vast amounts of dead ground, places where a bro or sis could lie undetected in a slight dip in the earth, waiting with his piece or antitank rocket.

One group of rocketeers, led by Jeremy, lay five hundred yards up the road from Tristan's ambush party. They had hidden and allowed the convoy to roll past them. When Tristan's group had blasted the lead Austin, they'd whacked the rearguard car from behind. Then snipers hidden along both sides of the road had started raking the canvasback troop-carrier truck and taking down the pintle gunners on the cargo-haulers. Firing at targets higher than they were, they ran little risk of the classic fuckup of cross-firing each other.

As usual the nomad fire was precise and deadly. The troop

truck driver was rapidly killed by Little Teal, and the first troopies to tumble out were picked off as quickly as they emerged. Shots began to punch holes through the truck's canvas covering.

A hand waved a white handkerchief out of the rear of the truck. Jovanne, commanding the snipers in the weeds, bawled out the order to cease fire. The picked band of battle-hardened outlaws knew she meant business, and stopped shooting more or less promptly. The surviving Ranger troopies came staggering out in the sunlight with their hands over their heads, and the fight was done.

Tristan's merry band of rocket rangers had gotten a little exuberant and fired an extra that took out the lead ammo truck. Another rocket had missed the troop carrier. The rockets, manufactured in Iron City on the Great Lake, were extremely expensive. The supply was unsure for the moment too, since Iron City had been overrun by the expansionist Kaybeckers that spring, and its main transshipping port, Big Water on the upper Missus Hip, was reportedly under siege.

Still—four rockets, a few hundred rounds of ammo, and zero casualties for five trucks full of ammunition: not a bad trade.

Tristan signaled. The Stormriders rose up out of the weeds whooping and cheering, and swept forward to the convoy to loot. He stood more slowly, stretched, and grinned.

It was a small start. But it was a damned good one.

21

The three-car patrol was blasting balls-out across the Plains, slip-sliding on grass soaked by a thundershower that raked the land while the sun still shone hot as molten silver. The clouds were already breaking up again overhead, and a man could distinguish between them and the black pall over the western horizon that marked where the newborn cinder-cone was sticking its head up.

The nine Ranger scouts of the patrol had no time for appreciating meteorological or vulcanological phenomena. They had heavy news, and the need to pass it along to their boss, Colonel Vandenberg, Yellowhair's intelligence officer and chief of scouts, filled their veins to bursting like Methedrine.

They had just stumbled upon no-shit Outlaw Central: a nomad camp that blackened the Plains like a buffalo herd, two thousand bikes or more gleaming in the early-morning sun. It was the biker main force and no mistake. The scooter scum had decided to take up Yellowhair's gauntlet after all.

Despite the fact that the cloud cover was fracturing the atmospherics were terrible; the radios crackled and spat like boxed cat demons. No chance of driving a message through that, not with the little pissant generators the Omohundro-built light combat cars carried.

No. It was up to the scout detachment to deliver the mail themselves. And when they did, the DEF would sweep down on the unsuspecting bike trash in pincers flung wide as the horns of a longhorn steer. The outlaws would never stand a chance. They would be exterminated, man, woman, and child.

The Plains would be made safe for civilization, Dallas-style. The very least the members of the patrol could expect would be knighthoods and modest little thousand-acre ranches carved out of the fresh-conquered territories, with plenty of peons to bend their backs for their masters' benefit.

And maybe, just maybe, not *all* the nomads would be slaughtered in the coming battle of destruction. If the noise of their engines and the wind and their rattling, banging cross-country passage didn't drown the possibility of speech, the Ranger detachment would have been chattering with excited anticipation. They'd heard stories of those high-assed biker bitches, fiery and totally amoral. They knew how to do anything a man might ask by the time they first bled. Surely Yellowhair would see fit to gift the heroes who brought the crucial information home with a dozen or so of the choicest outlaw cunts each.

They were so wired by their tidings that they took virtually the same route out as they had on approach. Visions of blood and fire and nomad pussy were dancing in their heads when a command-detonated mine went off right beneath the front suspension of the lead car.

The car took flight with the grace of a sandhill crane lifting off, and soared over the grassland, riding a rolling cloud of soil and torn-up grass. The driver and roll-bar gunner were shredded, killed instantly. Fist-sized chunks of frame were blasted into the back of the sting gunner, who would survive a while yet as he bled out. He was a lucky man; he would never regain consciousness.

The car's glide took it right into the path of the left-wing car. That driver, stunned by the noise of the blast, was unable to react as the stricken car struck nose first, right in front of him. The lead car bounced back into the air upside down.

The left-wing's luck was in; it passed right *below* the airborne vehicle. Roll bars scraped, and then the lead car slid off down the arm-thick rear V extension that protected the sting gunner in a cascade of sparks.

Unfortunately, that was it as far as the left-wing machine's luck ran. The driver was just thanking his lucky stars he'd avoided a fatal crash when a tug of movement at the corner of his peripheral vision brought his goggled head around.

He was looking right down two tunnel-sized holes: the barrels of a side-by-side shotgun being held about eighteen inches from his nose by one of those foxy outlaw sluts in person.

This one was slight and black-clad, with hair a few shades too black to be real and lipstick the same shade around a laughing red mouth. The driver had time to register that fact, and then a brilliant orange flash, and then the equipment he registered sensory danger with was blown all over and into his side gunner by a double blast of double-ought buck.

Bikers on scramblers, lightweight, lithe, and nasty, swarmed around the two cars. Screeching like Comanches—which a couple of them were—the nomads overran the right-wing vehicle, blasting bloody chunks from its crew before they had a chance to swing their weapons into action.

The left-wing car was veering madly across the lumpy grassland. The sting gunner had clawed his way free of his seat belt and was trying to clamber over the driver's seat and headless body to seize the wheel. The roll-bar gunner lolled in a moaning heap, a scarlet and gray and purple mess of the driver's brains and his own gore intermingled.

The sting gunner's mouth filled with sour vomit as he slithered over the blood-slick corpse of his driver. Draped over the seat he grabbed the wheel, and prevented the car from running its right tires up a hummock and going over.

The car rocked on its suspension. The sting gunner looked back over his shoulder. A giant figure stood in the seat he had vacated, black and terrible against the astringent blue of the sky. Raven hair hung in braids over shoulders that seemed as wide as the car itself. Yellow teeth showed in a grin above a jaw like a cinder block.

A huge hard hand grabbed the back of the sting gunner's camouflage blouse and lifted him. The gunner grabbed frantically for the custom Osage orange wood grips of the four-inch Leech & Rigdon .44 Magnum revolver snugged in its holster beneath his left armpit. He tried to twist in the grip and bring the piece to bear.

Laughing, the giant seized his gun hand. He *squeezed*. The gunner screamed as the bones of his hand splintered.

The monster released the mangled hand, and cocked his right fist over his left shoulder. The gunner saw it swinging toward his face like a wrecking ball with knuckles. Then it stove in his temple and torqued his head around, snapping his neck.

Contemptuously Lurch of the Mad Things tossed the body out of the car, which was already slowing; the gunner's contortions had knocked the driver's dead foot clear of the gas. Lurch shov-

eled the oozing mess that had been the driver to the grass and
dropped down behind the wheel himself.

Angela Death cruised by, laughing, pumping a black-
gauntleted fist in hot predator triumph. Her band had already
taken possession of the right-wing car.

A flash lit the western sky. The new volcano was having
growing pains again.

Silence fell across the Plains, to await the thunderclap of the
distant detonation.

Over the rush of the wind of passage the security detachment
emplaced in strongpoints atop the giant gleaming fuel semi heard
a rising rumble, like distant thunder or the sound of the new volcano. It was neither.

The noise was nothing natural, but it did spell disaster.

One moment the semi was rolling majestic down the Hard
Road, protected by a squad of twenty Rangers mounted on big
shiny Omohundro motorcycles. The next it was being overtaken
by a pack of fifty or more outlaw bikes, low-slung and lethal, the
riders howling like the human wolves they were.

The semi sported a sandbag-hardened gun mount at either end
of the fat silver tank, and an open-topped armored turret mounting a pair of heavy-barrel .50-calibers on top of the cab. The rear
gunner woke with a start from his heat-induced doze and began
firing his weapon, a ponderous pounding that shook the whole
huge vehicle.

One of those thumb-sized .50 bullets could damn near turn a
man inside out. Four sleds were knocked spinning into the air or
off the road, one exploding in a great flare of orange flame. The
riders behind rode grimly through the curtain of fire, moving too
fast to be harmed by it.

Then it was too late for the heavy MG to fire, for fear of hitting the tanker's own escorts, deployed in front and behind. The
cycle savages had caught up to the ten riders of the rear guard.

The Rangers fumbled with the slings of their bull-pup Dallas
Arsenal storm carbines as the outlaws swirled among them,
slashing them with sabers, smashing limbs and faces with the
spiked-ball heads of long-handled maces, blasting them point-
blank with sawed-off shotguns and big-bore Comanche pistols.

The Dallas cycle soldiers were skilled riders, but they had not
spent their whole lives in the saddle as the High Free Folk did.
And they were mechanized dragoons; they rode their machines

to action, but they did not train to fight from them. The Stormriders seldom actually fought mounted, but by Bro Wind they surehell *practiced* it, and cherished the chances they got to do it.

The rear guard was simply massacred, strewn bleeding on the sticky-hot blacktop in seconds. Hearing the tanker's heavy MG start to hammer, the ten riders up front did as they were trained: split off the road left and right, laid down their machines, and took up firing positions. Since they were lying prone in the ditch, their full-auto firepower would have sufficed to repel the whole strength of the outlaw band had they chosen to charge.

They didn't. Semi and wolfpack went hurtling past and down the road, leaving the cycle soldiers gaping over their battle sights. A score of outlaws dropped away from the pack, dismounted, and took up *their* own roadside blocking positions in case the Rangers wanted to try and catch up to the running fight.

Black and silver, the cruiser-mounted Stormriders surrounded the great tanker, reminding Tristan of nothing so much as ancient *National Geographic* footage from the Library's data files of killer whales besetting a blue whale. What to do now was a bit problematical.

The simplest thing, of course, would be to stand way the hell off in the weeds somewhere and pop high-explosive grenades from a Kobold-made 40-mm launcher at the swollen silver tank. But the object was to seize the gasoline within intact. Blowing the whole mess to Mother Sky would hardly accomplish that.

Likewise firing directly at the vehicle was out. They could try shooting out the tires, but they were almost certainly flat-proof honeycombs the outlaws' small arms could not damage. Sending the semi out of control would probably not be a good idea anyway, even if it were possible.

Tristan could think of only one thing to do. A premonition had led him to leave WildFyre behind today; he swung the late John Badheart's flame-painted cruiser in close by the rear wheels of the semi. Handholds climbed up the curving sun-dazzling flank of the tank. Tristan reached his right hand up, caught one, swung himself to the semi, and clung like a baby raccoon as the sled fell over on its side in the road.

The riders behind swerved deftly to avoid the fallen machine, then closed up on the semi. In an instant half a dozen riders were leaping for the handholds at the front and rear of the tank. Two missed their grips, and vanished beneath the singing semi tires with brief screams.

Tristan climbed hand-over-hand up the rounded side of the tank. He wore his swept-hilt broadsword over his back and his Bolo broomhandle in its break-open holster under his left arm. A Bowie with a brass knuckle-duster hilt rode at his hip.

The barrel of a storm carbine came poking over the sandbags at him, a rage-contorted face above.

22

Tristan reached up, grabbed the weapon by its flash suppressor, and pulled. The Ranger came flying out of the emplacement with a wail, barely missing Tristan on his short flight to the pavement.

Tristan swarmed up over the sandbag parapet, drawing his sword. Two men in Ranger camouflage remained in the emplacement. One rose from behind the .50-caliber. Tristan hacked at his forehead. The Ranger clutched his face, and with blood spurting over his fingers rolled over the sandbag onto the flat metal walkway that ran the length of the tank.

The other man drew a Shawk & McLanahan auto-pistol. Tristan stepped into him, knocking the handgun aside with the single metal bow swept back over the hilt of his broadsword. He slashed backhand, laying his opponent's throat open. The man toppled off the tank to the road.

Tristan started forward, toward the other tank-top emplacement. One of the gunners remained on his feet. Tristan saw him knock a nomad clean off the semi with a storm carbine butt-stroke to the bearded jaw. Then the Ranger leaned over the side and hosed three more Stormriders off the handholds with a long desperate burst.

He looked back then, and saw Tristan walking gingerly toward him. He swung the storm carbine around. Anticipating the move, Tristan had already tossed his sword to his left hand. He quick-drew the Lakota Bolo and fired twice. The Ranger jerked, dropped his weapon, and fell backward over the forward machine gun.

Alone atop the long tank Tristan advanced, bent low so he was almost moving on the knuckles of his sword hand as well as his feet. He didn't feel all that secure, up here on an open walkway on top of a semi cranking down the road at a good eighty per.

About then the two-man crew of the twin-gun turret noticed that he was up there by himself. They traversed the guns dead aft and opened fire.

Tristan flattened. The noise of the two fifties was almost enough to blow him off the tank by itself. The shooting stopped.

He looked up. It was a true Plains standoff. The gunners could probably depress their weapons far enough to nail him cleanly, but if they did several thousand gallons of gasoline would go up in their faces.

As Tristan watched, the two thick barrels dropped a few fractions of an inch. Flame vomited from them. The shock waves of the bullets' supersonic passing buffeted him like giant open hands.

Maybe the Rangers figured they could panic him into falling off the truck or jumping up into the bullet-stream. Maybe they figured they could skim him off—it wouldn't take much more than one of those huge bullets to nick him to send him spinning into space. Maybe they thought the awesome muzzle blast could actually knock him off.

He began to inch forward, driving himself along by sort of paddling with the toes of his boots. *If they think they're gonna scare the piss out of me this way,* he thought, *they're right.* The hot wind of the bullets tugged at the back of his Burningskull colors vest and the seat of his pants.

He reached the forward sandbag emplacement, slithered into it. He crawled across a gunner with a golden handlebar mustache who stared past a small dark hole in his forehead with eyes the color of the sky, and stuck his head up cautiously next to the body of the man he had shot.

The turret squatted there, low and menacing. The barrels seemed to be pointing right at him, but he knew that was an illusion. The men in the turret had no chance of hitting him now if they didn't want to burn.

Evidently they realized that too. A man stood straight upright, blazing away with a storm carbine at the hip. Bullets chewed the bags and stung Tristan with sand. He poked his Bolo over the top and shot the man.

As the man went down Tristan blurred into motion, flowing

over the sandbags, preparing himself to leap the gap that yawned like a chasm between the stretched cab and the tank trailer.

A storm carbine appeared over the turret's frontal shield. Fire flashed. Tristan threw himself sideways—right off the top of the tanker.

A moment. The semi's big Diesel whined. The wind whistled. The engines of the cycle pack growled to either side.

The top of a head appeared over the turret shield. Eyes scanned the mirror-bright walkway. Nothing. The gunner stood up, his storm carbine held negligently at his side.

Hanging one-handed from the top rung of the handholds, Tristan shot him. Then he was up, gathering his strength and his courage for the leap, flying across to the rear of the cab. He rolled over the turret shield, down inside.

The turret was built-in, not add-on or improvisation like the sandbag gun mounts on the tank. An early Count Omohundro had made great strides on building the family's enormous fortune by pioneering the manufacture of armed semi-tractors for the hazardous Plains trade.

One thing the farsighted Count had *not* foreseen was that an enemy might actually get *into* the turret. There was a hatch in its roof that led into the cramped crew quarters aft of the driver's compartment. It was unlocked. Tristan opened it.

A sticker on the dashboard read ASS, GRASS, OR GAS—NOBODY RIDES FOR FREE. Two startled faces turned back to look at Tristan.

He aimed his Bolo at the startled pair of drivers and smiled. "Gentlemen," he said, "your ass, your grass, and your gas are all of them mine."

The night was black, moon and stars walled off beyond apparently impenetrable clouds. The wind that hunted through the waving grass with hollow-voiced booms and hoots carried a chill that cut like a blade.

Two shivering sentries slowly cruised the wire-tangle perimeter of the Ranger forward base in an open Omohundro utility four-wheeler. One drove, the other swept a huge spot mounted to the windscreen across the open country. Both tried hard not to freeze.

Inside the wire the camp was dark. Off to the far side of the compound the sky flared sporadically with the actinic blue wink of arc welders as armorers worked under canvas. Occasional snatches of country music from the mixed battery of 4.2-inch mortars and 105-mm towed howitzers breasted the wind. Otherwise few signs of life showed.

The four-wheeler paused. Its brilliant beam cut across the landscape like a sword, revealing nothing but the tufted tips of the grass waving in the wind. The car rolled on.

Two dark figures rose from the high grass, hard by where the vehicle had hesitated. They raised strange-looking weapons, with open-frame folding stocks, bulky barrel shrouds, and curved magazines winging out to one side. Hints of flash danced at their muzzles. The only noise the weapons made was the clicking of the bolts as they reciprocated, and that was lost in the sighing wind.

The spotlight shattered. The car veered into the wire and stopped. The two sentries slumped unmoving in the front seats.

The black-clad figures dropped back into grass, covering with their Saskatoon Sterling submachine guns with integral silencers. Others dressed in black ran forward, and began to chew through the knife-wire rolls with bolt cutters. They separated a spiral of razor tape twenty feet long, and pulled it aside.

Their exhausts shrouded with thick mufflers—quite similar in design and function to those on the barrels of the Sterlings—to silence the distinctive outlaw blast of their 74-cubic-inch engines, cruiser bikes began to roll in off the Plains and through the breach.

Brevet Brigadier General Selfridge smiled beneath his splendid mustache, took the jack of diamonds from his hand, and dropped it on the three cards in the middle of the green baize table. "I love it when a finesse works," he murmured, and reached out to troll in the trick.

The full lips of Captain Sir James Sliger, seated at his right, writhed briefly in disgust. *And now I know where the queen is, Jimmy Jeff, thank you very much,* Selfridge thought.

The tent was spacious, graciously if not lavishly appointed, and well lit by kerosene lanterns. Selfridge's partner, the current dummy, Baron Lansford, stood at the sideboard in his shirtsleeves, pouring himself a few fingers of fine sipping whiskey. Sliger and his partner, Sir Ronnie Wilkinson, looked on glumly as Selfridge led trump again.

"Yeeee-*ha!*" Out in the night a rebel yell rang. A spatter of gunfire followed. Wilkinson and Sliger looked around with irritation on their aristocratically handsome young faces.

Selfridge froze in the act of reaching for a card in the dummy's hand. He frowned. "If someone's gotten liquored up and thinks he can hooraw the camp," he said in a voice made the more menacing by the fact that he never raised it, "I'll be pleased to teach him different."

"I'll see what's happening, Lane," Baron Lansford said. He was a tall, athletic young man with long brown sideburns framing his face. He was a lowly lieutenant, but he had the distinction of commanding a troop of the Expeditionary Force's few heavy armored cars. Dallas had some tanks, but they were so expensive and hard to maintain in the field that they seldom saw action.

His social rank alone would justify an invitation to cards in his commanding officer's tent, of course, but Brigadier Selfridge preferred to surround himself with men of actual ability.

Lansford walked to the entrance of the tent, raised the flap, and peered out. "Here, what's this?" the others heard him say.

Gunfire hammered. The back of Lansford's white dress shirt bloomed with splotches of scarlet. The young armored officer fell.

Wilkinson made a choking sound. Yellow vomit slopped over his lower lip. "What the hell?" Sliger demanded.

Selfridge was already up, buckling on his pistol belt. "Clearly, gentlemen," he said in a voice of immaculate calm, "we are under attack."

The mechanics' tent was immense, illuminated to the point of false day by banks of generator-fired lights. It was the kind of commander Selfridge was, and why Yellowhair was so admired by his men, that he would refuse himself the luxury of electric light while providing it to his maintenance crews. Despite the wind the tent walls were rolled up; welding rigs were in operation, and ventilation was more vital than warmth.

Three mechanics getting ready to hoist the engine out of an open-topped armored personnel carrier with a pulley looked up in amazement as Tristan rolled into the glare of the lights on WildFyre. "Evening, everybody," he said. He raised his Bolo and cut them down with two quick squirts of full-automatic fire.

He watched dispassionately as the three men fell. They were unarmed, but he felt no compunction about killing them. They were enemies, and they were probably more crucial to the Dallas

Rangers' highly mobile style of warfare than an equivalent number of line riflemen.

He put the sled in gear and rode into the tent, holding the Bolo, cinched to his right wrist by a lanyard, as well as the bars. He turned WildFyre down an isle between rows of parked armored carriers. Two mechanics stood there. They gaped at him for an eye blink, then dodged to the sides. He didn't bother scattering shots after them.

As he reached the aisle's end, near the open wall of the tent, a man stepped out from the side and swung a long-handled wrench baseball-bat fashion for Tristan's head. Tristan ducked below the blow, hunching over WildFyre's bars. The wrench ruffled his brushcut. He put his right boot down, pivoted the big sled around it, and shot the wrench-man twice through the chest as he wound up for an overhead stroke.

Out into the night again. A squad of soldiers jogged around the corner of a tent, storm carbines at port arms. The lead men almost ran into Tristan. He fired a scything long burst, sending them scattering and tagging at least two, gunned his engine, and charged through the center of them.

He rode the length of the tent, and dropped a leg for a racing turn around the end of it as the squad's survivors opened up on him. Not wanting to get caught with his pecker swinging truly in the breeze, he kept the throttle open, whipping between tents, ripping shots at any faces he saw.

He found himself in an open area with cruisers swirling through it. It was oddly quiet. A slim figure stood before a brightly lit tent. The lantern light turned the shoulder-length hair to gold. As Tristan watched, the yellow-haired man raised a Dance Brothers & Park Vindicator left-handed and fired twice. A nomad threw up his arms and fell from the saddle. Riderless, the bike continued to roll across the open space and crashed through a tent.

Seeing the lone man distracted, a rider in Nightranger colors accelerated toward his blind side, swinging a three-foot length of chain. Without seeming to look at all, the slender man ducked the whistling chain and cut backhanded with the saber in his right hand. The nomad screamed as greasy purple ropes of guts lopped out of his split T-shirt and got tangled in his rear tire.

Halted, Tristan raised his Bolo and sighted carefully at the slender figure. The man noticed the motion, turned to him, stood, and looked unflinching down the slim barrel.

Tristan pulled the trigger. The hammer clicked: empty. It was the loneliest sound in the world.

The long-haired man smiled, raised his Vindicator. The slide was locked back in battery position.

"We seem to be experiencing similar inconveniences," the yellow-haired man said in a cultured Dallas drawl. He saluted with his saber. "You wear a blade, sir, and from the wear on the hilt I'd judge you know how to use it. Would you care to trade a few cuts, Tristan Burningskull?"

Around the corner of the well-lit tent an armored personnel carrier appeared. Its pintle gunner saw Tristan and swung the pierced barrel of his .30-caliber his way.

"Another time, Colonel Selfridge," Tristan said. He turned WildFyre and gave her the gas as the machine gun began to rock and roll.

23

"Mosquito bites."

Gathered around a long table in a lantern-lit tent, the Federation Council turned and looked at Jeremy, who stood behind the seated Tristan with his arms folded.

"I don't know much about warfare," the small weapons-master said, "but I do know this: We aren't doing any real hurt to the Rangers."

"Bull fucking *shit!*" bellowed Buzzard. He jumped to his feet so fast his gut jiggled alarmingly, and slammed his hand down on the knife-scarred tabletop. "We been kicking their ass! Kicking their *ass*, I say!"

"Say anything you want," Jeremy said calmly. "You can't change the facts."

"You sawed-off little piece of shit," the Bandido President snarled in a spray of spit, "what gives you the right to run your head in here? What club you speakin' for?"

"The Burningskulls, Tubby," Jeremy said with a half-smile. "You thinking of trying me on?"

Buzzard glowered and subsided. He must have outweighed Jeremy by almost a hundred pounds, though he only stood a few inches taller, and not all of that was beer weight. But Jeremy, cripple though he was, had taken on Tristan himself in an empty-hand face-up two years ago at Rendezvous and whipped his ass bodaciously. As the Black Avenger, he had never stooped to using firearms in his one-man war with Homeland in which he

146

took the lives of scores of City soldiers. Buzzard was loud and no coward, but he wasn't stupid enough to call Jeremy out.

"He's right," Jovanne said through the silence that had gathered around the brief contest of wills. "We're not taking anything from the Cowboys that they can't afford to lose."

Tristan sat in a folding chair listening to the storm of protest Jovanne's words evoked. His men and women had been riding and fighting hard for two weeks. They were proud of what they'd done, and took what Jeremy and Jovanne said as a personal affront.

But for all the outraged noise the Council was making, Tristan knew his two advisers were absolutely right.

"What are you *sayin'*?" demanded Boomer, the hot-blooded Ghost Rider Prez. "We hit their main base like a blue Norther, blew in and out and put a couple hundred fuckards in the dirt to stay!"

"So what?" asked the ever-practical Enforcer warlord, Wolfman. "We lost twenty-two good bros. Who do you think can replace their losses quicker, them or us? There's upward of fifty thousand Citizens behind the wire in Dallas, all just breedin' away like bunnies."

Time to cut to the chase. Tristan leaned forward, rapped hard with his knuckles on the wooden table: once, twice, three times, sounding like pistol shots.

"I hear your pride talking," he said into the slow grudging silence, "and you've earned the right to let it talk a spell. But let that go by; let your heads talk now, not your hearts."

He looked around the smoky tent with his fierce hawk's eye. "Can any of you tell me we've cut an artery for the Cowboys?"

More silence answered him. "Can any of you say we can go forever before the Rangers tag us hard in return?"

"No way," said Clutch of the Nightrangers grudgingly. "They move around pretty good."

"We're takin' down plenty of their scouts," protested Tramp.

Marauder Prez Liquid Louie snorted through his oft-broken nose. "They got plenty more where they come from."

"We all of us know," Tristan said, "that if we get in a slugging match with City troopers, the Citizens will win. We need to find a way to hurt them—hurt them *bad*—before they get lucky and catch us out somewhere."

That drew no argument. "Anybody got a suggestion?"

A moment as the assembled clan leaders looked at one another. At the far end of the table, Lonesome Dave unfolded one black leather-clad leg from the other.

"I do."

Tristan glanced at Jovanne. Her mouth tightened. Tristan looked back at the lean blond Pistolero. "Say on, Brother Dave."

Dave smiled. "I know a target," he said, "fat and juicy as a pumpkin on a fence post. Just sitting there *begging* for us to blow it away."

"What's that?" Jovanne demanded. "Dallas?"

Lonesome Dave laughed. "You're close," he said. "Try Fort Tom Landry."

If he'd unzipped and flopped his cock on the table, he couldn't have produced a looser-jawed response.

"Fort *Tom*?" Tramp demanded. "Fuck Sister Moon in the fanny, you might as well be talkin' 'bout Dallas! It's south of the Canadian, clear into Dallas Territory. There's yellowleg soldiers swarming all over the place!"

Yellowleg was a standard slang term for Dallas soldiers, as opposed to the Rangers, who were technically a police formation. The Dallasite regulars wore yellow stripes down the trouser legs of their dress uniforms. Rangers wore white stripes.

Lonesome Dave frowned, a rare enough sight that a ripple of muttered comment circled the table. "Easy there, Tramp. I think I have better *information* than you."

The Sand King Prez stiffened, went pale. "Sorry, Dave, I'm sorry, Mother Sky, I didn't mean . . ."

Lonesome Dave held up a hand, cutting off the slobbering flow of apologies. "No hassles, cousin. I just happen to know that most of the Dallas regulars have been pulled south out of Fort Tom, deeper into Dallas territory. The Duke-President doesn't want the tailheads even thinking they have an opening to grab off a piece of Dallas property while the Rangers are north of the Cimarron."

He let his head fall off to the side and smiled his dazzling smile. "And we all know Fort Tom Landry is Dallas's main depot in the north. It was set up to service the Rangers and Yellowlegs keeping border watch on Osagerie and the Kiowa/ Comanch'. Right now they have it pumped even fuller of supplies to feed the Cowboy offensive on the Plains. And they've cut its complement to the bone."

Jovanne drew a long breath, let it out through flared nostrils. "He's right," she said, as if each word had been dipped in shit.

"It's a beautiful target. *Ideal.*" She looked at him with something like respect in her amber eyes.

Tristan frowned. *Is that the twinges of jealousy you're feeling, bro?* an internal voice asked him.

The answer—he thought—was no. It was maybe closer to the truth to say that he'd gotten so used to Jovanne hating Lonesome Dave's guts that a change threw him off balance, the way it would if she dyed her hair jet black and started painting her face like Angela Death.

He was about to speak when the tent flap opened and a pair of Burningskulls came in. "Lord Tristan," one said, "there's somebody here asking for you?"

Jeremy frowned. He readily went to suspicious mode. Of course, that was one reason Tristan kept him around. "In the middle of the night? What, did they just march up to the wire?"

The Burningskulls traded sheepish glances. "Uh, no. She, like—she just appeared in the middle of camp."

"Appeared?" Jeremy asked dangerously. He oversaw camp security.

"She?" Jovanne echoed.

"Bring her in," Tristan said.

Before either Burningskull could respond somebody marched into the big tent between them: a slight, winsome woman with big hazel eyes and bobbed brown hair.

"Jamie!" Tristan exclaimed. "Or should I be calling you Eris?"

"Whatever you choose," she said seriously. Then she broke off a beautiful smile. "Jamie's fine with me."

The Council was beginning to grumble, in confusion, annoyance, or appreciation of the good-looking newcomer. "What are you doing here?" Tristan asked.

"The Pranksters owe you a blood debt for the man of yours we shot," Jamie said. "I've come to pay off."

"With what?" Tristan asked.

"Myself."

A dusty black-green bottle of ancient Kaybeck cognac had fallen into Tristan's possession—as booty or tribute or trade goods, he didn't remember. Jovanne couldn't stand the stuff, and Jeremy refused to drink. It seemed a shame to break the bottle just to drink alone, but Tristan was not about to knock the top off and pass it around a circle of bawdy bros out by the campfire. He had been waiting for a suitable occasion.

Now he held it forth past the low-turned lantern and filled Jamie's earthenware cup.

"I can't tell you how good it is to see you," he said.

She sipped. "Me too."

"What made you change your mind?" He took a taste of the brandy, rolled it over his tongue, feeling its sweet burn.

"I didn't," she said briskly. "I haven't come to swear fealty to you or anything."

He frowned. He was determined not to permit anything to break the mood. He was reunited with his oldest friend in the world. He didn't want anything spoiling that.

"You're here," he said. "You changed your mind to that extent. So I'm asking, why?"

She rocked back among the furs piled on the floor of Tristan's tent. "Dallas and Homeland. They're rapers for true. Real bastards. The Pranksters aren't Stormriders; they're just Beasties, and feel as much contempt for your people as your people feel for them. But they live the same kind of life, need the same kind of freedom. And I . . . I'm still of the Folk, down inside."

"So you've decided I'm not such a tyrant after all?" he asked, with a ghost of a smile.

She shrugged. "I don't know what to think about you. I don't think the Plains need a Lord. But I *know* they don't need Homeland or Dallas fencing them in. I know you're the lesser of two evils—or maybe the least of three."

He frowned and tucked his chin to his chest. Being the least of anything didn't much please him, even if it was of evils. "If I'm evil, I want to be a *great big* evil," he said.

She reached out a bare foot and tweaked his thigh with her toes. She had done the same thing often when they were kids.

"You still get that cute pout, don't you?" She laughed. "You sound like you're ten again."

After a moment he laughed too. "Maybe I do."

"And maybe I missed you," Jamie said over the rim of her cup, "just a little."

He grinned hugely, felt foolish, drank again. "How exactly do you propose to pay the blood debt to Wire? I mean, not to be crass or anything."

"For the injured man himself, I brought gold. How is he?"

Tristan shrugged. "Doing fine. Chest's mostly air. If a wound

there doesn't kill you right off the bat, and you don't get in-
fected, you're likely to pull through okay."

"Good. The attack on your men was . . . over-hasty."

"I'll say." He studied her, rubbing his chin.

She looked damn good. He had never thought of her in terms
of how she looked; she had just been one of his bros, his closest
friend, the one person in the whole wide world of the Plains—or
the small world of the Hardrider campfire circle—he could really
talk to and know he'd be *understood*.

His parents loved him, but they were, well, *parents*. There
were a lot of things you couldn't discuss with them. The other
grown-ups, Golden Marcia and Quicksilver Messenger and Nick
Blackhands the wrench, treated him well and taught him much,
but they all had their own incomprehensible adult agendas, and
his concerns were equally unintelligible to them. The other kids
had just been there: playmates, sometimes pals, sometimes rivals,
but nobody to *talk* to.

Now, though, with the lantern light aglow in her eyes, and her
sharp little elf chin resting on one knee, he realized that somewhere along the line little Jamie had grown up. She had gone
from being one of the bros to being a definite babe. He wasn't
sure just how he reacted to that.

"So what was that about paying the debt with yourself then?"
he asked. "What do you have in mind?"

As soon as the words were out of his mouth he wished he
could catch them and stuff them back in. After the way he'd
been studying her, that man-woman appraisal, they had to sound
wrong, horribly wrong.

Jamie laughed. "Do you have any idea of what a terrible face
you're making?"

She came up on her knees, and caught his face in her small
strong hands. She kissed him lightly, on the forehead, and sat
back down again.

"Don't worry so damn much," she told him. "I can read what
you're thinking. I always could."

"More than I can do most of the time," he said, halfway sulky
again.

"You asked for my help, back there in the woods," she said.
"I'm here to help you any way I can."

"We need it."

She grinned. "I know."

Suddenly they were hugging each other fiercely. "It's good to have you back, Jamie," Tristan said into her shoulder. "I thought—I thought I'd lost you forever."

"Me too," came the muffled reply.

Jovanne stalked through the darkened camp, arms wrapped tight about herself to augment the warmth of her wolfskin-lined jacket, her long legs eating up ground without haste. Was this shaping up to be the coldest damn summer of her memory, or was it just her mood? The ice was coming down through Canada, Tristan said. Damn him anyway.

A pair of Dog Soldiers appeared, recognized her, nodded politely. Then they caught a glimpse of the look on her face by moonlight spilling down through a tear in the clouds, and they passed on, giving her plenty of leeway.

I don't know what I'm eating myself up about, she told herself. *It's not like they chased me off or anything. But I couldn't handle feeling like an outsider.*

She felt that way sometimes when Tristan and Jeremy were together, of course. That was one reason she never entirely got along with the diminutive samurai. But that was different. Jamie was female, and real damn attractive, if you went for that underfed big-eyed waif look.

I don't own him, Jovanne thought. *And Mother Earth knows he makes it clear enough he doesn't own me.*

And yet she wished he did. For all her fierce, proud, independent nature. He told her time and again that it wouldn't work, that she had to be her own woman or be miserable. She knew he was right, even. But she just couldn't accept it, couldn't take it and live with it.

I wonder if he's screwing her. She frowned, mad at herself now for wondering. They'd each had other lovers; they always came back to each other.

But this is different too. He and she go back years and years . . .

Jovanne loved Tristan. She knew he loved her. But she knew what love was about: betrayal. Betrayal and abandonment and giving hurt. He would toss her aside, the way everyone she had ever cared about had—except for one, and she had been taken from her.

So what if he throws me aside for her? she thought savagely. *So what? It don't mean nothin'. We'll either all die fighting the*

Cities, or we'll conquer Homeland and he'll go back to that ice-princess City bitch of his . . .

"Jovanne?"

She didn't break stride—quite—but her right hand slipped inside her jacket to be near the worn grips of the Vindicator that she had taken as booty from the captive Tristan years ago. Then someone had fallen into step beside her, swinging along on legs as long as hers.

"Feeling under the weather, Prez?" Lonesome Dave asked.

She gave him a narrow-eyed stare. There was no mockery on his face. *He really is almost too beautiful for a boy,* she thought.

"Who wouldn't?" she asked. "This weather sucks."

He laughed. "You know what they say. You don't like the weather, wait a few minutes." A beat. "It'll get worse."

Despite herself, she found herself laughing. He showed her his lopsided grin.

"Would you like somebody to walk with for a while?" he asked.

She looked at him. "Yeah," she said slowly. "Yeah, I think I would."

The naked woman straddled him as he bucked like a bronco, full breasts bouncing, head thrown back. The muscles inside her contracted and relaxed, playing him like skilled fingers as he spent himself with gasping near-rhythmic cries. His fingers dug into her smooth-muscled thighs like talons. The light of a fugitive moon seeped in through the weathered fabric of the tent, touching her fine hard body with silver.

With a final shuddering moan he subsided back onto the pallet of blankets on the tent floor. She folded herself gracefully forward, down onto him, and twined her arms about his neck. Despite the chill in the tent their bodies were sheathed in sweat. Her nipples were hard against his bare chest.

He blew out a long breath beneath his mustache. "Well, my dear," he said in a soft drawl, slightly shaky now, "I'm a good Christian man, but you keep this up, you might just make me think some serious thoughts about this Fusion of yours."

She raised her head and smiled into his face. Odd to think how her totally shaven head had repelled him at first. Now he found the thought that the only hair on her body was her narrow arching eyebrows and her naturally long black eyelashes strangely . . . exciting.

"I am the matrix," she murmured. "I am the weave that brings all strands together."

"I don't understand all this metaphysical talk, sweetheart." He chuckled softly, and reached to massage the silken skin of her buttocks. "But there are some things I surely *do* understand."

Her indigo eyes, black and Chinese-slanted in the dark, burned into him. "Do you understand destiny?" she asked, smiling faintly.

"That I do parley-voo."

She sat up. In the fractional light she looked dramatic and perfect as a statue. She raised her hands gracefully to the back of her neck, making her breasts ride up her rib cage most fetchingly. Her muscles gave his softening cock a squeeze.

"Ah!" he exclaimed. "Damn you, woman, a man's got to rest sometime!"

"The limitations of the flesh are illusion," she said. "The flesh itself is illusion."

He raised his hands to massage her breasts. "Damned fine illusion, I'm bound to say."

She reached down and grasped his wrists. She did not pull his hands away.

"The trap is laid and baited," she said. "Our ally has ensured it. You hold the death of the upstart Lord of the Plains . . ."

She plucked his right hand from her breast, raised it to her lips, kissed the palm. Her tongue slid out to lick her own sweat from it.

"Here."

He grinned at her. "You're my luck, darlin', and that's no lie."

She smiled. "There is no luck. There is only One."

"Now you're goin' all mystical on me again. Have pity on a poor country boy."

"Pity is for the weak." She began to rotate her hips, around him and around. He gasped, grabbed her hips, feeling himself begin to stiffen again.

She descended toward him. "Now let me draw you closer to the One," she breathed.

24

Brigadier Selfridge's forward base had been an improvised facility, with a quick razor-tape tangle unrolled to keep the Cowboys from waking up with the nomads in their tents. It had not been a total success.

Fort Tom Landry was a permanent installation in a border zone, prone to raids by hostile Kiowa or Comanche or even razzing parties off the Plains. Its defenses were far more formidable. The multi-hundred acre compound was surrounded by two ten-foot-high chain-link fences, each topped by a tangle of razor wire. Between them ran a thirty-foot-wide cleared space that had been sewn with mines. Large coils of knife wire had been placed in front of the outer fence. Tall concrete watchtowers overlooked the fence line at regular intervals. On the inside the perimeter was dotted with prepared machine-gun pits reinforced with sandbags. A straight-up assault without armor or extensive artillery preparation—neither of which the nomads could come up with—would amount to suicide on a massive scale.

The only way into the base was by a scrupulously maintained Hard Road that ran through the huge main gate. Hundred-yard-square patches of bare earth flanked the gate—more mine fields, as screaming yellow signs with black skull-and-crossbone designs proclaimed. The gate was guarded day and night by a security platoon of Yellowleg riflemen in bunkers to either side. To forestall the simple expedient of trying to crash it with a big truck, a ten-ton cement weight, mounted on an ancient flatbed rail car and faced with sharpened I-beams jutting out, could be

155

rolled out to block the entrance on rails set especially across the blacktop for the purpose.

By night the compound blazed with almost the light of day, courtesy of banks of huge generator-fired lights strung along the perimeter. It seemed to exist in its own dimension, an island of light surrounded by blackness on which it seemed to float. It was a forbidding, unapproachable-looking place.

Sometime well past midnight, the perimeter guards were roused from the torpor that steals over most people at that time of night by the roar of a straining engine and the singing of tires rolling high-speed over pavement. The gate security detail stared in amazement as a giant Omohundro semi came hurtling out of the darkness right toward the gate.

It struck the mobile barrier with a crash like plates of the Earth's crust butting heads along a fault line. The impact was ferocious enough to knock the enormous spike-studded blocking weight off its track. But the security detachment, peering cautiously through their firing slits, saw that the gateway was even better blocked then before, with the tractor trailer, engine impaled by the sharpened steel beams, lying sprawled across the road.

Then the several tons of ammonium-nitrate fertilizer soaked in fuel oil that were packed into the trailer detonated in a gigantic white flash that made the lights of the compound seem dim by comparison. A tremendous roar blew out every window in the compound.

When the mushroom cloud of smoke and dust had lifted, the semi had simply vanished, as had the gate, the bunkers to either side, and the security platoon within. The big cement barrier had been split in two and pushed aside. A giant crater had been gouged in the road.

Around the crater swarmed five hundred screaming nomads on cruiser bikes. Rear-area troopies staggered blinking out of wooden barracks, dazed from being thrown half-deafened from their beds and wondering what the hell was going on. The nomads chopped them down in passing with swords and clubs and close-range gunshots.

Followed by Jeremy and ten of his Burningskulls, Tristan steered WildFyre straight for the post commandant's office. Despite the intimidating fortification of the camp the defenders were pretty slack. Or maybe it was precisely because the physical defenses were so impressive that the troops within had grown overconfident. Whatever the reason, the troopies were always going over the wire for unauthorized leave in the nearby town of Cache Creek. Not literally, of course—the mines in the death strip couldn't discriminate between Yellowlegs and outlaw raiders. The common means of going AWOL was to hitch rides on the constant stream of trucks passing in and out of the complex during daylight hours.

It had been a simple matter for the cunning Wolfman and his Enforcers to troll in a few troopies for a little talk about Fort Tom's defenses and treasures.

Base administration occupied a pitched-roof frame building off the central parade ground. The door was locked. A twelve-pound sledge wielded by burly black Hawkman picked it in a hell of a hurry. Jeremy went in first, twin samurai shortswords in hand, followed by four of the Burningskulls. A moment, and they gave the all-clear for Tristan to enter; the headquarters was deserted.

The CO's office proper was located in a front corner of the admin building, looking out on the parade square, which was hemmed by looming warehouses. While Tiger Barb held a flashlight in her black-gloved hand, Tristan began to shuffle through the papers on the desk.

Even with the encouragement of the Plains outlaws' horrifying reputation for atrocity—aided by the appearance of Wolfman, who looked as if he ate a raw baby for breakfast every morning—the captive depot soldiers had only known so much. Tristan was looking for the location of treasures: medicine, ammunition, explosives, heavy weapons, electronic equipment, items the High Free Folk could not make themselves and found hard or expensive to trade for. The truck parks were full of dark ranks of tractor-trailer rigs and cargo trucks, but with five hundred riders and an unknown but limited amount of time before a Dallas relieving force arrived, he wanted to concentrate on grabbing the most valuable goods first.

A paper with an impressive-looking gold seal on it caught his eye. He picked it up, scanned it quickly by the Barb's torchlight. A phrase leapt out on him: *"—prepare to receive, accommodate, and conceal 1000 men of the 2nd Ranger Mechavalry—"*

"Shit," Tristan breathed. He raised his head to look out the window.

On the left side of the parade ground a dozen Stormriders had dismounted before a warehouse. Two of them strained to open the great sliding doors while the rest waited eagerly. As Tristan watched the doors opened. The bikers started to surge in.

A brilliant flash, a thunderclap of noise. Half the nomads were torn instantly to pieces by the thousand steel marbles of a claymore mine. The others reeled back, blinded by afterimage and bleeding from burst eardrums.

Figures in camouflage appeared in the door. Storm carbines yammered and flared. The nomads fell.

At the crack of the mine Jeremy had materialized between the window and Tristan, desire to protect his Lord overwhelming the instinct for self-preservation which normally would prevent him from silhouetting himself to enemies. He turned back.

"We've walked into a fucking trap." He didn't shout. He spoke calmly, in disgusted tones.

"Fuck," Barb said, snapping off the light. "That Beastie bitch sold us!"

Tristan glared at her. *Jamie wouldn't betray us!* But this was not the time to debate or hold an inquest. It was time to *move*.

Out of the building, back to the bikes. The night was alive with the pop-pop-pop and snarl of firefights all over the compound as the Ranger ambushers emerged from their lie-ups to blast the startled nomads. From the direction of the gate came a storm of firing, punctuated by flashes and the delayed crack of grenades.

Tristan and Jeremy exchanged bleak looks. Thirty riders had been left to hold the shattered gate. Obviously, the Cowboys were throwing an overwhelming force against them.

There would be no escape that way.

Four Rangers emerged from the warehouse, crouched low, paying more attention to avoiding the sloppy-wet tangles of guts and disassociated body parts their claymore had made of the nomads than to their surroundings. Firing from the office windows and ground outside, Tristan's Burningskull escort shot them down. Their comrades began to return fire from the yawning black doorway.

WildFyre came instantly to life at a kick of Tristan's boot. "The others!" Pony yelled from her own sled. "What about them?"

"If they haven't figured out it's time to boogie by now," Jeremy said, "fuck 'em."

A grenade flash between warehouses on the far side of the parade ground punctuated his words. Tristan wheeled WildFyre and gunned her back into the shadows. His Burningskulls followed, snapping a few parting shots at the Rangers in the warehouse.

They hurtled through flame-shot blackness, between the blank cliff-faces of warehouses. Dark figures appeared in doorways and the interstices between buildings. Muzzle flashes licked toward the riders as they passed. The Burningskulls snapped shots in reply.

A squad of Rangers came around a corner at a dogtrot, right in front of Tristan. A Cowboy screamed as WildFyre rode him down. The others dove for cover as the Burningskulls smashed through them.

The Rangers opened fire at the receding nomads. The Bone Dancer grunted, arched backwards, grabbing for his back. His bike zigzagged and went down.

"Dancer!" Tiger Barb screamed. She pivoted her own ride to go back for him.

"Wait!" Tristan yelled. Bullets clawed the tall woman from her saddle.

There was nothing to be done but run. "Let the dead bury the dead," Jeremy said. They ran.

They found themselves in the truck park. Trucks were burning here and there, sending underlit columns of smoke twisting into the clear night sky. Dark figures flitted between the big parked vehicles, some mounted on long dangerous outlaw sleds, others crouching on foot. Some instinct was leading survivors of the ambush to gravitate here.

The party reached the inside of the perimeter wire. A few overturned bikes and a mess of sprawled bodies marked where the machine-gun pits had been taken out. With trapped-rat desperation the nomads had simply charged them in a human wave, taking savage casualties from the river guns before overrunning the emplacements.

The first person Tristan saw clearly was Jovanne, sitting her bike hard by the fence. A wave of relief washed over him, weakening his knees and bringing tears to his eyes. *No time for that.* He rode WildFyre to her side.

She was staring out at the cleared strip between the fence lines. When Tristan stopped beside her she sucked in a ragged breath and nodded. Then her iron self-control reasserted itself.

"The mines," she said. "We're trapped."

Tristan looked back at the parked trucks. "Maybe not," he said, fingering his chin.

Tristan's five-hundred-rider raiding force was picked; every man and woman was battle-seasoned and proven. The Stormriders had reflexively formed a firing perimeter in a semi-circle backed up to the wire. The ambushing Cowboys seemed mostly preoccupied for the moment with mopping up trapped pockets of bikers. Autofire crackles indicated where squad-sized thrusts were poking against the nomad line. The Stormriders seemed to be holding without trouble.

That would change. Tristan could see no more than a hundred riders. Others were streaming in constantly, but the Cowboys had them horribly outnumbered. As soon as the ambushers gathered their wits and their stones, it would be the Hardriders' Last Stand all over again.

"No way," Jovanne said. "They've got anti-vehicle mines out there, not just antipersonnel mines. It's suicide!"

A Diesel rumble. An Austin armored car appeared along the fence line a hundred yards from the tiny outlaw enclave. Its 20-mm flared. Nomads came apart in the spray of high-explosive shells. Bullets glancing harmlessly off its armor made a weird tympanic music.

A rider raced toward the car, hunched low over the drag bars of his bike, a satchel charge dangling from his hand by a strap. The long snout of the quickfirer reached for him. Small geysers of earth chased him, but he was moving too fast for the 20's mount to track him.

As he screamed past the car he flung out his arm. The satchel charge bounced under the Austin. The commander popped out of the turret, fired a burst from the top-mounted machine gun. The rider went down.

The satchel charge went off. The Austin fell over against the fence, collapsing a forty-foot length, and exploded.

Another engine gunned with a hoarse whine. Tristan whipped his head around to see a big six-wheeler truck surge forward. The bulky shape of the Dragons' warlord, Hercules, was visible behind the windscreen, hunched over the wheel.

Tristan waved his arm. "Wait!" he shouted. "Don't try it! The mines—"

Jovanne seized his arm. "Don't you think he knows that?"

The truck hurtled past. It hit the wire. With a scream of bursting metal the fence parted. Raw wire ends raked the steel flanks of the truck with screeching sounds as the vehicle bounced out into the death strip.

A mine exploded with a flash, blasting chunks from the honeycombed front right tire. Hercules fought to keep the heavy machine under control. Another antipersonnel mine went off, and another. The truck veered and lurched and tipped alarmingly, almost going over. Somehow the Dragon leader kept it moving forward on its rims.

A sky-splitting crack: an anti-vehicle mine. Yellow flame enveloped the cab of the truck. The truck struck the outer fence, smashed thorough, went rushing out onto the prairie, blazing like a comet.

A moment of stillness, of inactivity. It seemed as if even the Cowboys hurling themselves against the desperate knot of nomads had paused to watch the spectacle of Hercules' last ride.

The eye of the firestorm passed. The muzzle-flashes of storm carbines surrounded the nomad perimeter like a chorus line of fireflies on speed. The Cowboys were redoubling their assault, determined not to let their prey escape.

"All right!" Tristan shouted, standing up straight out of the saddle. "Everybody, *move*! Follow the path the truck took!"

Cruisers began to stream through the breach, out into the enveloping arms of the night.

Moments later a grand open command car picked its way carefully among the strewn bikes and bodies and rolled to a stop beside the breach in the perimeter. Brigadier Selfridge stepped forth. He was dressed in a resplendent white and gray Ranger dress uniform, with mighty gold epaulettes emphasizing his broad athlete's shoulders and a yellow plume in the band of his wide-brimmed hat. Golden spurs jingle-jangle-jingled at the high heels of his pointy-toed boots, made from the skin of a thirty-foot gator he had personally shot in the eastern bayou country.

He stopped to survey the carnage. The expression illuminated by the skyward-soaring flames of Hercules' funeral pyre was not a pleasant one.

A young officer trotted up to him and jumped to attention. His young face was blackened with paint beneath the floppy brim of the camo boonie hat the Rangers wore into action in place of their dress Stetsons.

"Killed a mess of 'em, sir," he reported cheerfully. "Reckon we taught 'em a lesson they won't soon forget."

"Where are the barbarians?" Selfridge asked in a voice so soft it was scarcely audible above the flame-crackle and the distant

gunfire from within the camp as firefights with a few final pockets of outlaw resistance reached their bloody conclusions.

"They—they're gone, sir."

Selfridge nodded, smiling a strange half-smile beneath his
wondrous mustache. "And the barbarian prince? Tristan? What
of him?"

"Uh, the men say he led the escape, sir. But we got a mess of
'em, no mistake about—"

"He escaped? Burningskull *escaped*?"

The officer bobbed his head. "Yessir."

With a chiming of golden spurs Brevet Brigadier Sir Lane
Selfridge kicked his subordinate in the fanny with the pointed toe
of his boot. It didn't bring back Burningskull, but it made his
loss smart that much less.

25

"Three hundred brothers and sisters killed or captured," Lonesome Dave's lips were white with fury. *"Three hundred."*

He turned with a fine swirl of his greatcoat's black-gleaming tails to face the Council of Chiefs, crammed together in a big tent. "Are we going to let the witch get away with selling us like this? *Are we?*"

Tristan glanced at Jamie. She sat beside him at the head of the table. Her arms were crossed. Her face was expressionless, but her pointed chin was raised defiantly high.

"She's one of us," Tristan said quietly.

Lonesome Dave rounded on him, fine lip wrapped around a sneer. "She rides," he said. "She rides *horses.*"

He glanced around the assembled chieftains. "Does that sound like a sister to you?"

Buzzard thumped his fist on the table. "No fuckin' sister of mine lets no damn animals get between her legs!"

The Council roared laughter and approval. Tristan silenced them with the sheer blue candlepower of his glare.

"Are you saying," he asked the Bandido Prez, "that you're a virgin? Help me get clear on this."

The assembly almost blew out the walls of the tent with laughter. What made it worse was that it actually took Buzzard a few beats longer than everybody else to catch Tristan's drift. When he finally realized what had been said, his face turned purple and he swelled up until Tristan almost dared hope he'd call him out.

Tristan had been prepared for some hard questions, and no

mistake. The Council would have to cover some ground to be rougher on Tristan than he was himself. He had led his riders into stone disaster. In his own mind at least, Fort Tom was a fuckup as grandiose as anything John Hammerhand had marched into with his manly chin stuck out. He felt as if each rider lost had been a piece torn out of his own body.

But he hadn't expected this firestorm of suspicion and fury to descend on Jamie. That took him way off guard. *So what* are *you ready for these days, cousin?* an internal voice kept asking him.

He looked at Jovanne. She sat in her customary place at his right hand. But it seemed she sat farther from him than usual, and wouldn't meet his eye. *Or am I imagining things here, letting myself get paranoid?*

Lonesome Dave, of course, was not about to be steered off course by any amount of byplay. "Bloody treason's been done," he said when the laughter subsided. "Blood cries out for blood."

"That sounds mighty fine," said Jeremy, standing as always at Tristan's shoulder. "What exactly does it *mean*, Davey?"

"Our murdered brothers' and sisters' spirits cannot rest until they are avenged," the Pistolero leader said. "Are we going to let them wander the Plains forever with the cold wind blowing through them, crying out, lost and alone? Or will we free them to find their reward in Heroes' Holm?"

Lonesome Dave was taking a few liberties with the admittedly nebulous Plains cosmology there. There was nothing wrong with his rhetoric, though. The Council started in clamoring again like crows squabbling over somebody's abandoned picnic lunch.

"How could I have betrayed your raid on the Cowboy dump?" Jamie's voice cut across the racket, high and clear and sharp as glass. "I never even knew about it. I never heard of Fort Tom Landry until the razzing party came home, for that matter."

"Why, th' answer's plain as the nose on your purty little face," said Tramp, gazing grandly around to make sure everybody appreciated how clever he was. "You been moonin' around the Lord Tristan all the time since you got here. Clearly you got the answer out of him."

That shut the crowd up. The assembled clan wheels turned big eyes on the Sand King President.

Tommy Hawk frowned. With his war paint on it was a pretty terrifying sight. Tristan had ordered him to stay behind from the Fort Tom raid. He'd reckoned the Freebird war chief, hero that he was, was maybe a little too recklessly heroic for the task at hand. Tommy had not yet gotten over it.

But his loyalty to Tristan was unshaken. "Are you sayin'," he asked in a quietly dangerous voice, "that the Lord Tristan *ran his head*?"

All the color dropped out of the bottom of Tramp's pudgy face, which kind of tended to highlight the grime.

He had stepped right in the middle of it big time, by suggesting that the Maximum Lord had had a part in the betrayal of his own plan. Even if Tristan *had* blabbed, it was not real politic to say so. Maybe especially if he had. Tristan now had the right to drop the hammer on Tramp, as hard as he desired, and not one of the Folk would question it.

Tristan dropped his elbow to the table and leaned across it. "Brother Tramp would never suggest any such thing, I'm sure." His eyes bored into the Sand King like diamond drills. *"Am I right?"*

"N-no," stammered Tramp. "I mean yes! I mean no! I mean—I mean . . ." He covered his bearded face with his hands.

"You mean you'd never say any such thing?" Tristan said.

Miserably, Tramp nodded.

Smiling, Tristan sat back in his chair and crossed his legs. "That's what I thought."

"Who thought of this cockamamie scheme anyway?" Jeremy asked abruptly. Heads turned to Lonesome Dave. "Who brought up the whole idea of Fort Tom as a target in the first place?"

Lonesome Dave had gone a little green about the gills. "Would I be so stupid," he said in a clotted voice, "as to bring up a plan and then betray it myself?"

"I don't know how stupid you are, Dave. It might seem like a great way to get the Maximum Lord out of the way, if a man was ambitious enough."

"Who's standing behind the throne?" Dave asked. "Looks to me like you'd stand a lot more likely to profit from a mishap to our beloved Lord than little old lowly me. You were at the Council meeting too."

"And the woman wasn't, I'd remind you." He folded his arms and grinned. "I tell you what. Anyone who suspects me of selling out the High Free Folk in any way, shape, or form, I'm calling you out here and now. I'll fight every man in here, if you'll all stand to accuse me."

A good deal of silence met his words. No eyes met his.

"Just so there's no misunderstanding," Jeremy said quietly. "From this day forth any man who whispers such an accusation about me is a mingy coward afraid to back his words with steel. Remember that, brothers and sisters."

He looked to Dave. "Any further debate here, Dave?"

The Pistolero had his upper lip skinned back from his teeth. He smoothed the expression away into a placating smile.

"Of course not, Jeremy. Everybody here knows you're a man of the greatest honor. Am I right, brothers?"

The brothers all nodded. None of them was real eager to have the former Black Avenger down on his case.

"Besides," Dave continued smoothly, "I don't know why we're going on among ourselves like this. The guilty party is obvious, and there she sits." He flung out a finger and pointed at Jamie.

She sneered at him. "The Lord is right. I've ridden with the folk you call Beasties, and I'm damned proud of it. But I was born a Stormrider—and I have gone Dancin' with Mr. D., as Tristan himself can testify."

Tristan nodded. That day, only weeks before the death of the Hardriders, when he had ridden pillion on his father's scrambler, clutching Wyatt Hardrider's broad back as he and Quicksilver Messenger challenged the fury and unpredictability of the tornado, was clear in his mind as if it were yesterday. Jamie had followed them, hanging grimly over the bars of her own small bike. Tristan and his father had survived, and the Messenger, and Jamie herself, but the Hardrider named Stony Bill had not.

"I can defend myself like a Stormrider, too," Jamie said. "If you're willing to accuse me, *cousin,* then you should be willing to fight me."

Smiling, Lonesome Dave shook his head. "A brother's birth doesn't signify," he said. "A sister's either, all of us know that. Why, Bro Jeremy here was born a City man, and no one here would challenge his right to sit and speak amongst the councils of the Folk. But you . . ."

He shook his golden head. "Your forsook us. You gave up iron for meat on the hoof. You cannot claim the right of the duel. Besides . . ." He let a corner of his mouth quirk up. "It'd hardly be fair, me against a tiny little thing like you."

She growled and started up. Tristan held up a hand. Jamie glared at him furiously. She didn't want to seem to be obeying his gestures like a slave, but her keen intelligence told her this was no time to make a move. She settled grudgingly back down.

"But we can still handle this according to the Law of the Folk," Dave said. "I suggest trial by combat."

"You're offering to fight to prove her guilt?" Tristan asked.

Lonesome Dave held wide his hands in apparent surprise. "I? The President of such a small and insignificant club as the Pistoleros? My head isn't that swollen. Instead, I nominate a man far more worthy than I to defend the honor of the High Free Folk: Tommy Hawk of the Freebirds."

Everyone turned and looked at the Freebird war chief—except Dave himself, who was staring fixedly at Jeremy. Jeremy's reputation as a face-up fighter was great. Tommy Hawk's was greater. He was widely regarded as the primo hassler of the age by the Folk, who had a fine eye for such things.

Tommy Hawk looked thunderstruck, as far as anyone could tell with broad vermilion stripes painted diagonally beneath his eyes, winging away from a stripe across his nose. His great chest rose and fell.

"I . . ." he said and stopped. He was clearly uncomfortable. But he was no man to resist a challenge. "Sure. I'll do it." He sounded anything but happy.

Lonesome Dave turned back to Tristan. "There you have it, Lord. Let the accused name her champion."

Tristan sighed, rose, unhooked his sword belt from the back of his chair, and strapped it on.

"No need for that," he said. "If she has no standing here, then the choice is mine. And I nominate . . . *me*."

He nodded toward the entrance of the tent. "I wish it were any way but this, Tommy. Shall we step outside and settle this, my friend?"

In the corner of his eye he caught the look on Lonesome Dave's face: a grin of sheer triumph. The Pistolero hated Jeremy—because he feared him, Tristan guessed. Dave thought he had concocted an ideal scheme to neutralize a foe he knew he could never defeat. But here, instead, he had a chance to see the Lord of the Plains taken down by one of the few heroes among the Folk who could likely do the job.

Obviously, Lonesome Dave was altogether broken up at the prospect.

A big fat tear rolled down Tommy Hawk's cheek, drawing a vermilion line down across his jaw. "N-*no*!" he moaned. "I can't! I—I swore on my life and honor to defend the Lord of the Plains. I won't raise my hand against him. If anybody wants to say Tommy Hawk ran from a fight ..."

He couldn't finish. With a choking sob he ran out of the tent.

Tristan stood looking after him, feet planted, hand on the pommel of his sword. Then he turned his gaze to Lonesome Dave. The Pistolero sagged.

"Well, Dave, looks like the combat is decided by forfeit," Tristan said. "Jamie's innocence is established; let's hear no more of this bullshit.

"As for Tommy Hawk—let any who think to say that he ran from a fight know this: I'm calling you out myself in advance. Slander the Hawk ..."

His broadsword sang free of its scabbard. Lantern light shivered along its razor-sharp blade. "And face my steel!"

"Jovanne."

At the sound of Tristan's voice the Joker Prez froze, though his tone had been soft as a rabbit's fur. She was walking between the tents of the nomad encampment again. She had been doing that a lot lately.

He came up to her and stroked her short hair. She stiffened.

"You were quiet in there," he said.

"I didn't have much to say," she said. She gave her head a little flip. "Aren't you glad I managed to keep my mouth shut for once?"

He looked at her strangely. "I don't mind hearing what you have to say, Jovanne. I respect your opinion. It's why I keep you around."

"Well, I'm glad to see there's *some* reason." She walked away and left him standing.

"Tristan?"

Tristan straightened up into the tent and let the flap fall to behind him. "Yeah, Jamie?"

She was sitting on the pile of furs with her back to the wall of the tent and her knees drawn up. She had her arms around her legs and her cheek on her knees. With a pang he realized that he had often seen her that way when they were both young, and again he knew how sorely he had felt her loss over the years.

"Where do you want me to stay? I don't really feel comfortable just wandering around camp, somehow."

He shrugged and sat down across from her. "No reason you can't stay here, kid."

" 'Kid.' " She glared at him in mock anger. "I'm still older than you are, Tristan."

"Yeah." He grinned. "But I'm bigger."

"Won't I be in the way?"

"Not really."

"What about your lady?"

"I don't think she's coming back tonight."

"Is it me?"

Another shrug. "It's happened before."

Jamie shook her head. "I don't want to cause you trouble."

"It's a little late for that. But it sure as hell wasn't your fault what happened in Council."

"That Pistolero, Lonesome Dave—what's his problem?"

"Damned if I know. He's a smart one, a skilled warrior." He rubbed his chin. "He's got something in for me, that much I know."

"No kidding."

"I don't know if he's jealous of me, or what. He manages to just skate past being openly disloyal. He never quite does anything you can pin him for. Who knows? Maybe he wants to be Lord of the Plains. Though I don't really see him as the ambitious type."

"Maybe he thinks it makes him seem higher to see you brought low."

He looked at her, frowning. "I thought you wanted to see me brought low."

"No. I don't care what you call yourself, and if people choose to follow you, that's their lookout."

He sighed. "I sure can't see him as Lord of the Plains. I don't even know why the Pistoleros chose him for their Prez. I wouldn't trust him as far as I can throw him."

"I think you're wise there. So that's what he has against me? He thinks he can get at you through me?"

He sat staring at nothing in particular for a few moments. "That's part of it. I don't think it's the whole, but what the rest is, I couldn't tell you."

They sat for a time in silence, listening to sounds of distant revelry around the fires. The main outlaw camp was big enough that Tristan decided it didn't matter whether they showed fires or not; if Cowboy scouts came near enough, they'd spot the camp anyway. Besides, he had to allow the brothers and sisters of the Stormriders he had lost to give them the traditional outlaw send-off. He owed his people—living and dead—that much.

"Tristan?"

"Yeah?"

"When you came to our camp, what were you looking for?"

He held up an open hand and looked at the palm as if maybe he'd find a few cues written there. "I'm a pretty fair warrior. But I can't take Jeremy hand-to-hand, sawed-off little shit though he is. I have a clue or two about strategy, but Jovanne could fake me out of my socks. I'm a cunning devil as a war leader—I watched that hit on the MoFos, the way your Merry Pranksters whipsawed the fuckards, and I realized I couldn't have done it any better, if I even could have done as well."

He looked at her. "You were there, weren't you?"

"Yes. I rode straight back to camp after the raid. Some of the Pranksters stayed behind to keep an eye on the MoFos and see how they reacted."

He nodded slowly. "See, I'm good at a lot of things. It's why I'm so stuck up and full of myself that I think I can be Lord of the Plains. But I know there are people who are better than I am at any one of those things."

He looked at her. "So I decided to hunt up the people who were better at the things I thought most needed to be done, and see if I could get them on my side. That's why I came alone to the camp of your horse barbarians."

"It didn't have anything to do with your long-lost boyhood chum, huh?"

"Hey, I didn't know you'd turn out to be the straw boss of the Merry Pranksters, remember that. I figured you were dead."

"Not boss," she said firmly. "A speaker, a planner. No more. And, gee, you sure gave me a lot of credit, thinking I was dead."

"You thought I was dead."

"I was almost right, wasn't I?"

"Yeah. Yeah, I guess you were."

"You wanted me to be your tactics master then?"

"Yeah." He looked at her. "I guess it sounds a little funny, huh?"

"Do you still want me to do that? To give you advice, whatever?"

He stared at her. He felt a peculiar tingling sensation, and his heartbeat speeded up.

"Yes." He drew the word out long.

She lowered her legs, tucked them under her. "Then I think I can tell you how you can hurt the Cowboys. *Really* hurt them."

He produced a bitter laugh. "I seem to recall having heard that recently," he said. "You must have heard how that turned out."

"Tristan, do you trust me?"

He looked at her. "Yes, I do." He looked down at the bed. "It's me I don't think I trust."

"Just listen to what I say," Jamie said, "then judge."

He drew in a very long breath, shuddered, let it out.

"We need something," he said. "The Cowboys are going to join up with the MoFos in days—a couple of weeks at most—and cut the Plains in two. Not Jovanne nor I nor anybody have any idea how to stop them. If you have any clue, let's hear it."

26

The nomad army came out of the grasslands beneath a leaden sky and struck the Rangers like the blast wave from a volcanic explosion.

The first to feel the outlaws' fury were the scout camps north of the Arkansas, in the Smoky Hills and along the Saline. While he was careful to throw up a wire perimeter around his main bivouacs, Brigadier Selfridge did not believe in giving in to the fortification mind-set that had plagued commanders through history. Fighting a mobile, agile, well-dispersed foe, he kept his main force together, in order to keep the option of concentrating against the nomads. But he also kept a swarm of scout patrols, in platoon, squad, and three-car half-squad strength, out in the field, to keep an eye on the enemy, and to maintain the element of flexibility.

The idea was to find the outlaws where they hid and destroy them. So far the outlaws had done a somewhat better job of picking off the patrols. But they'd taken their losses too.

Selfridge knew perfectly well who could better afford a strategy of attrition. For all the pious Dallasite propaganda about the outlaws swarming out on the Plains, a-sexin' each other and breedin' like prairie dogs, he knew that the nomads in fact did not reproduce enough to keep up their numbers, and had to rely on misfits and outcasts from the Cities, or refugees from the hellacious lands east of the Mississippi, to keep from dying out. He also knew that their resolve would melt away—and as a consequence, so would their army—long before they took enough actual casualties to threaten their existence as a people.

The scouts' other goal was to seek out the outlaws' main body. If they found it, they were supposed to alert Dallas Expeditionary Force command—by radio if possible, by messenger in the more likely case that it wasn't—while keeping contact. The brigadier prayed daily to his stern Citizen God for a chance to match strengths with the outlaws. He doubted he would be given the chance, and so he placed his faith in his strategy of attrition.

But this morning his prayers were answered.

The patrols had ranged far to the west, the farthest out a hundred miles from the body of the Expeditionary Force, so far that it was expected that they would make contact in a matter of days with the forward elements of the Mobile Forces of Homeland under Brigadier General Webbert, advancing in a bloc at a more stately juggernaut pace. They were also presumed to be far to the rear of the outlaw prince's main force.

The outlaw offensive perhaps resembled an avalanche more than that most feared of volcanic threats, the glowing cloud. It started comparatively small, from around the North Fork of the Solomon. It was more than large enough to roll over the scout camps. Whether they went down at once like scrub oaks or managed to stand momentarily against the flow like lordly firs, they vanished tracelessly, without slowing the onslaught in the least.

Eastward swept the offensive, sweeping up the dispersed outlaw bands and gaining strength from them, swallowing the Cowboy patrols in its path. So rapid was the nomad advance that when the first scout survivors reached the Expeditionary Force's main camp west of Lake Milford around noon, they judged the outlaws to be no more than half an hour behind them.

A more conservative commander would have huddled behind his wire tangles and hastily strewn mine fields and hunkered down to weather the coming storm. That was the classic City strategy. Given the preponderance of firepower the Citizen armies enjoyed, and the outlaws' weakness in heavy weapons and their normal headlong style on the offensive, it had worked well in the past.

But Selfridge gave his enemy more credit. His intelligence officer, Colonel Vandenberg, had provided a dossier on the outlaw prince, Burningskull. It had involved no little espionage against their current—and purely temporary—allies, the Homelanders. The story did them little credit.

Burningskull, then known by the adopted name of Tomlinson, had been trained as a soldier of the Homeland Defense Force. He had distinguished himself both by his skill and courage and by his insubordination. In time he had transferred into the Strikers, the highly mobile scout force created and commanded by the old Plains warrior Black Jack Masefield.

Tristan had been born a barbarian. But he had trained in the ways of City warfare, had obviously acquired a veneer of civilization. Not for him the all-or-nothing warfare of his fathers.

Brigadier Selfridge understood the weakness of his own position. The barbarians could live off the Plains; his logistics-intensive City army could not. If he stayed behind his perimeter he would be virtually safe from direct attack. He would also be doomed to starve, if Tristan were sophisticated enough to besiege him, and Selfridge knew in his bones that he would be.

If the outlaw horde surrounded his camp, he would have the choice of breaking out—which even if successfully would mean a humiliating retreat in the face of the cycle savages—or waiting for relief from Dallas. But the rapid rise of Colonel Sir Lane Selfridge had annoyed many powerful men from old, established families. Important factions would be pleased to see the upstart and his army wither away out on the storm-wracked Plains.

And a relieving force would have to come from the army, not the police-paramilitary Rangers, who had committed the bulk of their combat strength to the DEF already. The Yellowlegs did not love the Rangers. They would not race to the rescue. They would drag their heels until the last possible moment, so that they could rescue the haggard, trapped remnants of a Ranger force about to go under for good. The seemingly safe course, the by-the-book course, was political suicide for Selfridge, and likely literal suicide as well.

Besides, playing it safe was not Selfridge's style.

As soon as the first messengers staggered in on light combat cars or scrambler motorcycles battered to the point of breakdown by a desperate cross-country race over the prairie, the Cowboys rerolled their razor tape; and streamed out through the safety lanes they had left in their mine fields. Selfridge intended to meet his foe head-on.

In the time-honored manner of defeated troops, the scouts exaggerated the speed of the enemy advance—if not by much. Instead of thirty minutes, the Cowboys had just over an hour to break camp and deploy in firing line.

A light rain had begun to fall when a sound like thunder was heard. But it wasn't the thunderheads beginning to pile up to the east, visible through occasional fractures in the cover overhead. It came from the west, and it went on and on.

They appeared as a black line that seemed to stretch from one end of the horizon to the other. A ripple of something like shock ran through the Ranger ranks. They lay in the comparative shelter of the shallow firing pits they had scooped out of the earth, moist from days of rain but still tough from the matted roots of the prairie grass. They were backed by the automatic weapons of their light combat cars, the heavier rapid-firers mounted on the Austin armored cars, and the howitzers and big mortars of the artillery battery. They were tough, trained, and confident.

But there was something elemental and terrifying about the apparition of the outlaw horde, black against the gray of the sky. Something that stirred dark fears within, as they rolled over a swell of earth and disappeared into the high grass, leaving only the thunder of their approach and the certainty that they would soon strike the dug-in riflemen with the fury of a thunderstorm.

In the rear the artillery began to chug. Red-earth fountains sprayed from the midst of the sea of grass. The big tubes were firing without many good targets, hoping to dishearten the outlaws and encourage their own.

Selfridge had deployed his firing line along a couple of low gentle-sided ridges. The high grass still provided a troublesome sight barrier. Selfridge had sent unoccupied Buffalo personnel carriers to run up and down before the line, flattening the grass beneath their fat tires. They had more or less cleared a firebreak of a hundred yards; now they scuttled quickly for the shelter of the rear.

The engine roar mounted like a rising Plains wind, like the howl of an approaching tornado. Tension mounted among the waiting Cowboys. When would the Plains scum appear?

The line of huge bikes broke through the wall of grass, seemingly on top of the Rangers already. The tension held the rifle line a beat. Screaming like mad creatures the outlaws hurtled across the brief cleared interval toward them.

The bubble broke in a crashing outburst of fire as Cowboy fingers clenched around triggers and held them down. The entire front rank of the shrieking horde went down in a welter of blood and spinning wheels and gouts of orange flame.

Their comrades flowed around them, dropping boots to the ground to swerve, firing through their handlebars with their throttles locked wide. Barely slowed, they struck the dug-in line of riflemen.

Here was the horror of an outlaw charge: with their sawed-off shotguns and big-bore Comanche pistols, their primitive edged and smashing weapons, the barbarians were all but unbeatable in close-in combat. It was the turn of the Cowboy front rank to die.

The first ranks of the outlaw army passed through the Cowboy front line without pause. As their comrades behind closed for the kill, the nomad front-runners ran into a fresh firestorm from the secondary line the canny Selfridge had dug in thirty meters down the military crest of the hill. They faltered, broke. The outlaws streamed back in retreat, leaving their brothers and their bikes entangled with the torn bodies of their victims.

A third line of Cowboy riflemen rose from their positions, and trotted through the second rank to reoccupy their former front line. The outlaws had gone to ground in the high grass and begun to dig in for a firefight. Mortars and car-mounted machine guns hammered the front.

As their grass cover was chopped down by bullet and blast the outlaws fell back. But they kept cohesion, kept hurting the City riflemen even as they absorbed hurt. Time and again they launched full-out bike charges. Each charge took terrible losses before it struck, and each left terrible casualties among the Cowboys when it was finally beaten back.

So the long afternoon passed until the day drowned in blood. Around sunset came a break in the fighting and the clouds alike, though shots continued to crack at random from out in the grass, and it was worth any Ranger officer or man's life to show his head; the accuracy of the Stormrider snipers was unerring.

At the start of the battle the barbarians enjoyed a substantial edge in numbers. According to Colonel Vandenberg the Plains army had swollen to a size of three thousand combatants, the largest the nomads had ever scraped together. They faced two thousand Rangers.

Selfridge felt honored rather than concerned. He knew better than to believe his men's mess-hall bragging that one of them was worth ten cycle savages. As a practical matter, he knew his men had the advantage in training, discipline, and the all-important supply.

More than that, they held the defensive. Since high-volume firepower had become a reality of warfare, back during the War Between the now-forgotten States of America—Selfridge knew his history too—the advantage had always rested comfortably with the defense. Only heavy armor and massive bombardment had managed to shift the odds back to the offense, and neither side had either asset now.

Selfridge trusted his men and his deployment. Both served him well.

When full dark settled in the outlaws attacked again, dark roaring shapes and flickering points of flame. The Cowboy front line was overwhelmed almost without loss to the nomads, and many brave and hopeless deeds were performed on both sides before the massed fire of the automatic weapons backing the Dallas line threw the outlaws back over the hill.

Selfridge ordered spotlights rigged along the line, driven by alcohol-fired generators. Back in the tattered grass, Stormrider snipers shot them out. Selfridge rolled his vehicles to the crest of the ridges, to illuminate the night with their headlights. The barbarians shot out some of their headlights too, shattered radiators and engine blocks with carefully placed shots. Ever-resourceful, sensitive to every nuance of the constantly changing situation, Selfridge had the rest pulled back to just below the crest line.

The nomads charged. The concealed vehicles rolled forward, slammed on headlights and spots. Their beams turned the battle zone to a white facsimile of day, dazzling the oncoming riders. Machine-gunners and riflemen shot them down like jacklighted deer.

After that the nomads became more cautious. When their attack was repulsed the cars doused their lights and rolled back to cover. Once the Stormriders' keen feral eyes readjusted to the dark they began to pick off Cowboys again, sometimes sighting in on nothing more than the vagrant gleam of starlight on a shiny-blued storm-carbine receiver.

Along portions of the line platoon leaders ordered their men back behind the military crest, out of sight of the enemy. It did not take the nomads long to discover the fact. Actually moving on foot, leaving their beloved cruisers behind, parties of outlaws infiltrated to the ridge top, fell upon the Cowboy lines with their swords and sawed-offs, and butchered them in their shallow shooting-pits.

As false dawn lightened the horizon behind the Cowboys, a massive charge roared out of the night to exploit the break-through.

Heart pounding so that it seems to drown the deep-throated roar of WildFyre's mighty 84-cubic-inch engine, hunched over the moderately swept golden bars, Tristan rides full-speed up the slope. He reaches the top, roars over, up, an interval of flight, heart-stopping, exposed, and exhilarating. Faces like pale balloons turn to follow him as he flies over them and beyond.

Then down, flexing legs and and superb shocks taking up the shock of reunion with Mother Earth. Tires bite in a squeal and spray of torn grass-knotted dirt. Then speed and power in the seamless union of earth and machine and man. The riders behind him are slaughtering the riflemen along the ridge in their pits. The screams and shots follow him, but he gives them no mind. His eyes and being are focused forward.

A figure, rising up as if from the depths of the earth, cammie-mottled—fleeing, not fighting. Before even Tristan's rattlesnake reflexes can react WildFyre's front tire has spun between the pumping legs. The big quartz headlight strikes the running Cowboy in the buttocks, smashes him down; the tire eats him up, and a strangled scream is squashed from him with most of his stuffing as over nine hundred pounds of bike and rider roll over him.

Flashes in the night as dug-in troopies blast at Tristan, weapons set to full-on rock'n'roll. Darkness and speed are his shields; the bullets miss, though they crack in his ears like constant lightning. He locks the throttle open and sprays back with his Bolo. He doesn't expect to hit anyone, just hopes to throw off aims and keep heads down.

He is among the Cowboys. They roll to their knees and rise from their pits to fire after him from the hip. He lets his Bolo drop to the extent of its lanyard knotted to his wrist, pulls his broadsword over his shoulder from its scabbard.

He backs the throttle down, relocks it one-quarter open. He turns his mighty sled aside to roll along the line of firing pits. Faces rise up before him. He splits them with savage chopping strokes of his sword. Around him ride his Burningskulls, cheering and slaying.

The sun appears above the eastern horizon, a blinding molten-copper arc. The battleground becomes a bowl of amber light, grass, machines, and humanity. WildFyre glows as if she burns.

The High Free Folk have lost the cover of darkness now. The front two Cowboy lines lie choking in their own blood. But the traitor light of Father Sun falls upon the Children of the Fallen Star. The big vehicle-mounted guns of their enemies can see them, and in seeing, slay.

Tristan thrusts toward an open mouth. A crunching impact along his arm, a scream and gush of blood along his blade. Deadweight bears his blade toward the ground.

He halts WildFyre beside the twitching flopping body, plants a boot on the sternum, pulls. With a squelching sound his sword comes free.

A sound rises around him like the noise of mighty tree boles being splintered by a hurtling boulder. Earth-geysers surround him, splashing higher than his head, spraying him with stinging particles of soil. He stares around wildly in a moment of fear and disorientation.

The line of ridges where Selfridge deployed his front line is backed by another undulating series of rises. These are topped with heavy Austin armored cars. Their long-snouted 20-millimeter cannon are ripping at Tristan and his outlaws, regardless of the Cowboy riflemen who might still live in the first and second lines.

For a moment Tristan poises there, sword held high in defiance. More and more auto-cannon reach out for him, until it seems that a hundred new volcanoes are being born about him, to join the cinder-cone that now rises more than a hundred feet above the high grass, miles to the west.

Then the Lord of the Plains turns his legendary ride and flees as fast as her wheels will carry him.

27

"Mark that man! Mark that man down!" Brigadier General Sir Lane Selfridge roars. He stands on the second line of ridges, among the armored cars which are brutally punishing the latest outlaw advance. In his guts he feels it, in his mouth he tastes it: His victory lies within his doeskin-gloved grasp.

The tall black-haired man on the giant golden bike steers between the bursts of 20-mm fire as if he knows they are coming, dodging, juking, hurling the huge machine this way and that as if it were an extension of his own body. It is as brilliant a display of riding as anyone there has ever seen, Cowboy or nomad.

But that doesn't matter. What matters is the *direction* his magnificent ride is taking him: west.

He is running away.

The Lord of the Plains disappears over the ridge on his legendary ride. Brigadier Selfridge pounds a gauntleted hand on the door of his command car.

"Follow! After them!" His words boom out over the loudspeaker fixed to the windscreen frame. *"We got them on the run!"*

The outlaws stream up and over the ridges where the Cowboy front line had fought and died again and again. With a spontaneous rebel yell the Ranger reserve on the secondary ridge system sweeps forward. They crash across the depression between the swells, up the ridges, pulping the bodies of the injured and dead, friendly and enemy, beneath their cleated tires.

When they hit the crest there is no mistaking the fact: The outlaws are in full retreat, swarming westward over the prairie like a swarm of motorized locusts. The prairie is black with fleeing barbarians.

The atmospherics are benevolent today. Selfridge's radio crackles with inquiries: "Orders, sir? What do we do now, sir?"

"What do we *do*?" Selfridge's classically handsome face is thunderstruck. "We attack, of course. We follow, follow, follow! We got 'em whipped, boys. Now we run them down and destroy them all, like the pack of mad dogs they are!"

The crowds herded together in front of Government House were subdued. When Dirk Posen, appearing on the balcony without the figurehead Mayor on hand to distract the masses, told them the news that the nomad menace on the Plains was ended, they raised barely a murmur.

He understood that the Clients might be feeling a certain disorientation. They had all grown up hearing stories of the barbarian hordes outside the wire, how only the benevolent City regime stood between helpless people and unimaginable outlaw excesses. They were having trouble internalizing the news, coping with the magnitude of it. It was like being summoned to your parents' room to learn that the bogeyman was dead.

He was disappointed, though, when he announced the official celebration: a week of expanded Civic Service and political indoctrination meetings. The crowd actually groaned at that.

He stepped back inside shaking his close-cropped head in sadness. "Obviously," he told the person who waited there, "the Citizens have a good deal to learn about the pure joy of Duty."

"Obviously," said Elinor Masefield in a voice that matched the coolness of her eyes.

He glanced at her sharply. Was she being sarcastic? It was so hard to tell with the woman. She wasn't at all like . . . he banished the thought from his mind.

To commemorate the great tidings Elinor wore an all-white Purity jumpsuit. It was a rare sight. She claimed the outfit washed her out, made her look spinsterish, withered, and severe, though it struck even Dirk Posen that she did not help soften its effects by wearing her hair drawn straight back in a ponytail.

If he were a little more attuned to such things he might have suspected that the high spots of color on her cheeks were the result of makeup, a commodity banned to Homeland's Client citizens. On the other hand, while he disapproved of such indulgence, it was also a Purity doctrine that Administration had its privileges.

"Have you heard anything more?" she asked. Word of the colossal Dallasite victory-in-progress had been received by radio at General Webbert's forward base, and transmitted along to Homeland by telephone lines that had been strung to reduce the vulnerability of City communications to the vagaries of the weather.

"Not yet. I gather the atmospheric interference has blocked communications again for the moment." He shrugged. "What more remains to be learned? Brigadier Selfridge will continue to pursue the barbarians, and destroy them whenever they dare to turn and fight. It's all over but the shouting, in effect."

He drove a fist into the palm of his right hand. The vehemence of the gesture wasn't mirrored in the austere features of his face. "It's a great day! A great day for civilization. And for Purity."

"And the Cowboys?"

Posen shrugged. "They've served their purpose. Now they will have to give way to the historical inevitability of the Purity regime."

She leaned back against a desk. "You think they'll simply fold their tents and slip quietly away, now that they've done your dirty work for you?"

He only smiled. The Acolyte had offered him certain visions. Homeland was smaller than Dallas, enormously less populous and wealthy. But the moral vigor of Purity, working in harmony with the mysterious but potent forces at the command of the Fusion, would overcome the imbalance. Posen did not hold much brief with mysticism, as a general thing. But he trusted the evidence of his senses, and inexplicable as the Fusion's powers were, the Acolyte had demonstrated them beyond argument.

At that very moment she was tending to certain modifications in the security arrangements at Purity House. Purity House was his personal residence and headquarters, the heart and soul of Purified Homeland. The former mansion of the man Posen still thought of as the Traitor Masefield. Elinor's father, mentor of that mongrel bastard Tomlinson.

It occurred to him that Elinor had been teetering on the brink of saying something for several moments while he was lost in thoughts he definitely did not care to share. That was unusual. She was not talkative for a female, but if she had something to say she usually wasted no time getting it out. She hated to defer the gratification of watching her barbs hit home.

He arched a brow at her. She cleared her throat.

"Is there any news of Tristan?" she asked.

"The barbarian leader?" He bobbed his head to the side. "Not yet. I'm sure it's only a matter of time until they identify the body. At the moment, our noble allies are a bit preoccupied for graves-registration work."

She turned her face from him. He smiled. It was rare that he managed to create that effect in her.

"Tell your precious jumped-up buddy General Webbert," she said in a low voice, "that he shouldn't drop his guard. If they haven't seen the body, Tristan isn't dead. And if he isn't dead . . ."

She tossed her head as if shaking hair from her eyes, and fixed Posen with a glare that rocked him on his heels.

"Then he's coming after you!"

She strode from the room. He brushed his hairline, receding prematurely under the onslaught of the cares of office, and found it clammy with sweat.

It's nothing, he told himself. *She's just hysterical. Perhaps it's the time of the month.*

Of course Tristan was dead. The outlaws had been stupid enough to match strength with civilized men, and had gotten their just deserts. Why, hadn't Tristan been seen in the thick of battle, at the moment the tide turned? Hadn't he been forced to turn tail and flee in total disgrace?

The Chairman looked at the clock on the wall—he refused to carry a watch himself, since that implied he was bound by the same constraints as those he ruled. To be truly effective, a leader required scope, unlimited freedom of movement. He could not be tied up in rules or schedules.

He decided it was time to call it a day and return to Purity House. He was feeling a certain urge, one that could only be assuaged by seeking the counsel of the mysterious woman who called herself the Acolyte.

Of course Tristan's dead. It's only a matter of time until we get the confirmation.

Only a matter of time.

The pursuit continued throughout the day. Brigadier Selfridge drove his men and machines to the limits of their endurance— and beyond. Broken engines and overheated engines left vehicles strung in a steadily lengthening chain behind the headlong advance.

Selfridge didn't care. The nomads had given him the opportunity he had longed for, prayed for, but never dared believe he would get: to meet them head-on, strength to strength.

Now he had the chance to wipe them out, root and branch. He could smash the presumptuous Plains nations so savagely that they wouldn't dare trouble civilized folk again for a generation, if ever. The biggest real barrier to Dallas's expansion would be gone.

He didn't count the Osage or the Kiowa/Comanche. His Expeditionary Force had already turned their flanks, and they had not dared respond—as he had argued before the Duke-President and his staff that they would not. They had grown decadent. Impotent.

Destiny had unfolded the Plains at the spit-shined toes of Selfridge's boots. He would subjugate the wildlands and claim them for Dallas, that the land might be civilized, contained, broken to harness for the great work of making Dallas the dominant power on the North American continent. And if those white-shirted prudes in Homeland thought to interfere with Dallas's manifest destiny . . . he smiled.

The bald witch, the Acolyte of the Fusion, had filled his head with enchanting dreams. She had power, that one, and no mistake; power he couldn't understand, but power nonetheless. He had no intention of shaving his own flowing flaxen locks and espousing the muddy mysticism she had spouted to him. But he could use her help. He would continue to play her, as subtly and masterfully as he had. He knew she loved it.

Periodically the outlaws would stop and fight back briefly before taking to their wheels once again. Or, overtaken, battle with trapped-rat ferocity before going down in a welter of blood and fire. Refusing to be deflected, Selfridge met each pocket of resistance by peeling off a detachment to deal with it, while the pursuit continued unhindered.

Racing west, the Rangers got strung out to a considerable extent. There was no help for it. Obviously, there was no harm in it either. The outlaws were clearly too disheartened and disorganized to turn and mount an effective resistance.

The sun crossed the zenith, shining hot and brilliant as if clouds had never been invented. Selfridge cruised his command car back along the leading column of his army. He stood erect behind the armored glass windscreen, magnificent hair streaming in the wind, waving his hat with the glorious yellow plume. In their canvasbacks and slab-sided Buffalo armored carriers his men cheered their hearts out.

The Hard Road here was in poor repair, pavement buckled by frost, washed out in places. The grass grew high and close to either side of the road. To the north a giant herd of pronghorn grazed on the lush grass, turning the land to a tawny sea. The antelope looked up at their passing, and fled away from the motor sounds with graceful leaps to what they considered a safe distance. Then they dropped their horned heads to feed again, no longer concerned with Man or his bloody disagreements.

Behind the Ranger columns other creatures of nature were far more interested in the human drama being enacted on the Plains. Vultures wheeled in the sky like black paper crosses caught in a dust devil, then dropped to earth to mob the all-you-can-eat buffet that the humans had so thoughtfully spread for them.

A crack, a column of smoke rushing into the sky like a black elevator. Selfridge frowned, called to his driver to turn about, and sped back to investigate. The troopies, unconcerned, kept hollering and waiving triumphantly.

Another explosion from the head of the column. Selfridge's radio operator was looking stunned, trying to sort out the babble in his headset. Starting slow, singly and then in sporadic spatters, building like a slow-approaching rainsquall, came gunshots.

"What the hell is going on here?" the commander demanded.

The radio operator tore the earphones from his head. "The barbarians are behind us, sir! Our boys are being hit from both sides, they're screaming for help!"

Brigadier Selfridge saw the gunner at the pintle mount of a Buffalo clutch himself and slide down out of view. "I mean *here*, damn you for a peon!"

The radio operator's eyes suddenly bulged halfway out of their sockets at the sudden catastrophic overpressure of a rifle bullet passing through his cranium. His brains blew out all over his radio and the brigadier's spotless uniform.

Jamie's plan was simple: sting the Rangers hard, then let them win.

It worked. Tristan led five hundred riders into the frontal fight with the Cowboys. Their job was to hurt the dug-in Expeditionary Force as badly as possible. Not with any hope of breaking them, which the whole of the Federation army could not have done. But to convince them that the outlaws had taken their best shot, had been broken themselves, and forced into full flight.

The fight had been brutal. Only the personal leadership of Tristan Burningskull himself could have kept his outnumbered and outgunned force returning again and again to attacks they *knew* they couldn't win. Of five hundred riders he had lost another three hundred.

But this time the fallen weren't lost in a debacle, as they had been at Fort Tom. They gave as good as they got, and then some. Deeds worthy of song had been done in that day and night of battle. Few of even the most ferocious Stormriders were anything but pleased and relieved when Tristan finally led the way into headlong retreat.

With the kind of man and commander Selfridge was, Jamie predicted, he could never resist the bait. He did not.

The real advantages the Cowboys had were their cohesion and their firepower. If they lost the first, the second would be greatly diminished. In pursuing their fleeing foes, the Rangers had strung themselves across fifty miles of Plains—just the way they were supposed to.

Meanwhile, the bulk of the outlaw army waited, arrayed in a semicircle that faced the onrushing Dallas Expeditionary Force like open jaws. The DEF charged right in.

When the jaws snapped shut on the spearhead of the Dallas advance, the six or seven hundred men Selfridge still had with him were surrounded by two thousand screaming nomads.

28

On the road the Cowboy vehicles were ablaze from one end of the column to the other. Mines and antitank rockets had taken down the Austin armored cars. The firefight on the road—if it could truthfully be called *fight* instead of *massacre*—had accounted for the rest.

A quarter mile south of the road a little round hill stood above the sea of grass like an island. A handful of vehicles from the doomed column had reached it. They now stood drawn into a defensive circle about the top. Several of them burned, creating clouds of thick stinking smoke that rose to join the clouds that had begun to assemble overhead.

The defenders on the hill traded shots with the horde of nomads who surrounded them. The High Free Folk had drawn back to a range at which their superior marksmanship could take a steady toll, while the Cowboys' storm carbines were largely ineffective. Time was the outlaws' ally now. Though listening conditions had deteriorated all afternoon, the radio reports they had received confirmed that the Dallas Expeditionary Force was finished as a fighting unit.

A spatter of hail fell. The wind began to whistle. A lone figure approached the besieged hill, the afternoon light that slanted beneath heavy slate-colored shelves of cloud turning his ride to a cycle of fire, a white flag fluttering from a metal pole in his hand. The firing slacked.

Fifty yards from the hill Tristan stopped WildFyre. Conscious that if he had misjudged his man, he would soon be dead, he raised a battery-powered megaphone to his lips.

"Is Brigadier Selfridge still alive?" he asked. "I want to talk to him."

A moment, and then the amplified reply came back: "I'm alive. You are Tristan Burningskull, I presume?"

"You presume right. I want to discuss surrender terms."

"If you surrender unconditionally and at once," the Dallasite said, "I offer my word as an officer and a knight that your life will be spared."

Tristan put his head back and had a good laugh while the wind played with the short black hair on top of his head and whipped the longer hair in back around his shoulders. It was a dodge he'd read about before, but he had to give Selfridge his due for trotting it out here and now.

"That's very good, Brigadier. I'm impressed. But you know what I'm talking about: the surrender of you and your men."

"Out of the question. A Selfridge never surrenders."

"Be reasonable, Brigadier. We have you surrounded. If you have a working radio you must know that you're not going to be relieved any time soon. We can lie out here in the weeds, pick you off when you offer us a target, and generally wait for things to get mighty hungry up there."

An interval of nothing except the boom and whisper of the wind and the impact of occasional scatters of raindrops on Tristan's cheek and torn, formerly white shirt. Tristan felt a muscle in his cheek wanting to twitch, told it the hell not to. He could imagine the diehards and glory-hounds up there on the hill, urging Selfridge to let them nail the outlaw chieftain now that he was in range. Of course, that would mean the death of every man on that hill, and the lucky ones would probably be the ones who caught a bullet in the process, for the nomads would be in no happy mood after seeing their Lord fall to Ranger treachery. But the tough boys were arguing that that was worth it; there's a fanatic or two in every crowd.

Tristan was gambling, again. It wasn't that he didn't think Selfridge was as capable of a pretty turn of treachery as the next Dallasite. He just did not believe that, if Selfridge agreed that Tristan needed to get dead, he would not want to see to it himself.

"I have a proposition for you, Lord Tristan," the brigadier's amplified voice came back, "if I may presume to speak to you as gentleman to gentleman."

"It's fine by me," Tristan said. He wanted to pump his fist in the air and shout *yes!*

"Are you brave enough to face me in single combat, face to face? If you win, my men surrender—on your promise of humane treatment, of course. If I prevail, we are to be allowed to leave with our weapons."

"You aren't precisely in a position to dictate terms in the case of my victory," Tristan said, "but I'm willing to guarantee that your men won't be harmed if they surrender. Dallas can have them back, with my compliments."

"You agree to face me then?" The eagerness in the voice was unconcealed.

"I do."

"Give me ten minutes to select my seconds and make my peace with God."

"You've really gone over the top this time," Jeremy said. He had his right arm in a sling. A sliver of shell casing from the Dallas artillery had pierced his biceps during the attack on the Cowboy lines.

"He's right, Tristan," Jovanne said grimly, helping Tristan on with a black leather jacket that made his shoulders seem even broader than they were. "Why don't you just let us wash these fuckards off the hill and have done with it? I hear this guy's some kind of king-hell duelist back in Dallas."

"We won't wash them off the hill without taking casualties. And I for one have seen enough of that. We still have Homeland to contend with, remember?"

Jovanne set her jaw and looked mulish. "We know Homeland can't conquer the Plains all by its lonesome. Why don't we just let that whole thing slide?"

"As far as I'm concerned, it's a little too late to go changing our plans." He zipped the jacket to the throat and glanced at her. "And speaking of lonesome, where's your friend Lonesome Dave? He hasn't been much in evidence these last couple days."

Her eyes bounced away from his as if they'd just been magnetized to the same polarity. "The Pistoleros were supposed to hold back and help mop up stragglers," she said. "You approved that yourself."

"Yeah. I guess I did. How do I look?"

"Fine," Jovanne said, still not looking at him.

"Like an idiot who's going to get his ass killed to no good end," Jeremy said.

"That's what I like best about you, Jeremy. Your total abject deference to me, combined with your vast confidence in my abilities."

"The only way he'll agree to meet you is sword to sword. I know this fuckard's rep, Tristan; he's better at it than you are."

"That's why you're going to insist on the terms I told you about," Tristan said. "Now let's saddle up and go. We wouldn't want to keep a knight waiting."

Their sleds battered and mud-splashed—except for WildFyre, whose finish resisted nicks and scratches and repelled grime as if by magic—Tristan, Jovanne, and Jeremy rode to the foot of the hill. Brigadier Selfridge's command car rolled down to meet them, looking somewhat the worse for wear.

The big vehicle parked thirty feet away. Jovanne and Jeremy gave a final glum look to Tristan, who stood astride his iron with his arms crossed. He showed them a big grin. They trudged off to meet the young officers, one in a plumed hat, one bareheaded, whom Selfridge had chosen to act as his second.

Time passed while the two Stormriders explained Tristan's terms to the seconds, and while they transmitted the terms to Selfridge, who sat in the car looking perfectly at ease. The two sets of seconds conferred again, and then Jeremy and Jovanne came trooping back.

"You're on," said Jeremy, who seemed surprised, though not pleased, by the turn of events. "He agreed to your terms."

"He's such an arrogant prick," Jovanne burst out. "He thinks he can beat you no matter what you do!"

"He may be right," Jeremy said sourly.

"Let's hope not," Tristan said.

They faced each other across a ten-meter circle rolled in the grass at the foot of the hill by outlaw cruisers. Tristan had shed his jacket, Selfridge his tunic, so that each wore a white shirt. Selfridge's was of obviously finer stuff than his foe's, but by this stage of the proceedings no cleaner.

Half the circle was ringed by bikers rowdy in the saddles of their sleds, and half by a subdued collection of Rangers. The hill face was covered with spectators, likewise half nomad, half Cowboy.

Brigadier Sir Lane Selfridge smiled, and swept the hilt of his saber up before his face to salute his opponent. Impassively Tristan returned the gesture with his broadsword.

Lurch of the Mad Things served as fight referee. Though they had fought alongside Tristan's people they were technically not part of his Federation. Smiling, Selfridge had acknowledged the Mad Thing sergeant at arms was as close to a neutral as he was likely to see, under the circumstances. Despite the chill drops of rain that occasionally came slanting down, as if the spirits of the upper air were spitting to show their contempt for surface beings, the giant was naked from the waist up except for a bloodstained bandage wound around his ribs. He had been shot in the chest by a storm carbine during the fight at the Cowboy lines, but apparently it had done him no serious harm.

He held a six-foot aluminum tube meant for use as a tent pole horizontally before him, open ends aimed at the opponents. "Obey my commands," he said in his soft childlike voice. "If you don't I'll pop your head for you, no matter who you are."

Tristan for one believed him. The Mad Thing straightened, turned the pole upright, struck it against the beaten-down grass.

"Begin!"

The two men each walked cautiously forward, keeping their sword arms advanced, until the blades were tip to tip. In his left hand Tristan carried a knife which Hog the famed Head Case bladesmith had created to his specifications. It had a fairly classic Bowie blade, the sort with parallel edges, not the belled cutting surface, twelve inches long. The false edge of the clip on the back of the blade was honed as sharp as the blade itself.

What made it unique was its hilt. A forward-curving guard on top was conventional enough, but the lower guard extended backwards in a stout brass bow that reached clear to the pommel, forming a hand guard studded with sharp milled-steel cones. The knuckle-duster could be a formidable weapon in its own right, but what it mainly did was enable Tristan to parry with the weapon with little fear of exposing his hand to damage. Though he had an excellent broadsword, he was not a terrifically skillful swordsman, and knew it.

For his *main gauche* Selfridge had chosen a classic Bowie similar to Tristan's, but with a normal guard. To be fair Tristan had offered the Dallasite a weapon identical to his own, volunteered by one of his Burningskulls—the pattern had of course become trendy as soon as the Lord of the Plains was observed wearing one. But Selfridge had turned it down with scarcely a glance.

In fact, he seemed to have only agreed to use a parrying blade as a concession to his barbaric opponent. Dallas saber-play was renowned on the Plains, but it was also quite rigid. A real sabermaster wasn't supposed to *need* anything but a length of good steel in his right fist.

Tristan wished he could shake the nagging fear that Selfridge was right. *Why did I agree to this anyway?*

The Stormriders chanting his name from the sidelines reminded him: *because they're my people, and if I can settle this by risking my own ass rather than losing more of theirs, I owe it to them to do it.*

They circled counterclockwise. Selfridge kept his saber extended and his knife tucked back by his left hip. Tristan had adopted something resembling a boxer's stance, right foot and arm advanced, but with his body squared, and his left hand almost as far forward as the right. A contemptuous smile raised one end of Selfridge's mustache when he saw this.

"A highly novel approach, my barbarian friend," Selfridge said. "But I expect to show you that classical ways are best."

He lashed out suddenly, knocking Tristan's sword aside with his own.

29

A slash as Tristan jumped back, and then he was brushing his right cheek with the thumb of his left hand and finding it bloody. The watching Cowboys cheered.

"As I expect to prove that civilization is superior to barbarism," the brigadier finished smugly.

"Really?" Tristan smiled. "I bet you can't do it again."

"You're a brave man, my friend. But, I fear, a trifle naive."

He launched a straight wrist cut at Tristan's forehead. Tristan rotated his wrist inward to parry. Blades kissed; Selfridge's disengaged quick as thought, whipped in a backhand cut for the right temple, again delivered from the wrist alone. Though he had been expecting something of the sort, Tristan had to hack wildly outward to keep the stroke from connecting.

It was a feint, of course. No sooner had he reacted than Selfridge's blade whipped up, allowing Tristan's to pass harmlessly below. Then it flashed around and down, intent on raking a gash in Tristan's left cheek to match the cut on his right.

Instead it clanged against the studded knuckle-bow of Tristan's combat knife. Selfridge's eyes widened in surprise. Tristan lunged.

The smaller man danced back with incredible speed. But not quite fast enough; the very tip of Tristan's broadsword had found a target. A ragged red circle appeared beneath the Dallasite noble's right armpit, and began to expand.

"Pinked me there," Selfridge acknowledged.

"I'm just full of surprises." Tristan grinned back.

They began to fence. Though Tristan was stronger than Selfridge and outreached him by a good margin, he quickly found that the Dallasite was much the more skillful. *Big surprise there.*

As Tristan also anticipated, though, the defense his parrying weapon and well-honed knife-fighter's skills gave him was something new and baffling for the cultured Dallasite. Though he inflicted minor cuts on Tristan, and received small wounds of his own, Selfridge seemed puzzled. He himself had no clue as to the use of a left-hand weapon, and did everything but tuck it into the back of his pants.

But he was learning—as Tristan found when the brigadier suddenly lunged at him while delivering a flailing overhand cut. Tristan parried with his up-flung broadsword, and then Selfridge was against him, grinning up into his face. That genetic wiring whereby males of the species protect their balls caused Tristan to twist his hips counterclockwise at that point—which saved him from a knife-thrust to the groin. As it was, the Dallasite got an inch of his Bowie into Tristan's thigh before he had to jump back to avoid a desperate slashing counterstroke from Tristan's knife.

They backed off and faced each other. Each man was breathing heavily. The events of the last thirty hours or so had been enough to exhaust any ordinary man. That description fit neither combatant, but they still had their limits, and they had just about reached them.

I gotta do *something,* Tristan realized. *He's a damn quick study.* The problem was, the full-length blades were by far the more powerful weapons system, and Selfridge's mastery with the saber stretched back years. As he learned to adjust for the parrying weapons, and factor them into his tactical decisions, Tristan's advantage eroded. It was only a matter of time before the Dallasite picked up enough to let his superior swordsmanship take command.

Realizing that for all their savage reputation their barbarian foes were not going to fall on them and slaughter them out of hand—or if they were, there was sweet fuck-all they could *do* about it—the Cowboys had thrown themselves into the spirit of things, whooping and jumping up and down and throwing their boonie hats in the air. Tristan's initial successes against their boy had quieted them down proper, but they were starting to get rowdy again. Tristan didn't think that was a real good sign in and of itself.

Jovanne and Jeremy naturally led the cheerleading for Tristan. As Tristan's weapons-master, Jeremy was continually shouting advice and instruction to Tristan. Tristan was not usually used to letting others kibitz on his fights, but he reckoned the time had just about arrived.

"Power him down, you big monkey!" the small City-born outlaw was shouting. *Always respectful, that boy.* "You got strength and reach on him. *Use* it. But don't open yourself up."

Trusting momentarily to his peripheral vision, Tristan glanced reproachfully at his friend. *Thanks a whole hell of a lot.* As a multi-sport star in high school, he had pitched for his baseball team, as well as playing center and short. One time when he was getting roughed up on the mound, his coach had come waddling out with this advice: "Don't give him anything to hit. But don't walk him either." Jeremy's advice tasted the same way.

"He's a rule-bound fighter, boy!" Jeremy yelled. "Be flexible!"

Tristan grinned like a wolf seeing a newborn buffalo calf drinking alone at the water's edge. *That* was something he could get his teeth into.

With a scream of fury—only partly feigned—Tristan threw himself forward to the attack. His first mad overhead cut almost beat down Selfridge's block. Then he was hacking at his enemy, madly, wildly, the genuine rage that flooded through his being like lava adding strength to his arm until it seemed he must simply smash his foe to the earth.

But Selfridge was quick and strong and skilled. He gave ground, back and back until the crowd had to break apart to let them pass or be slashed by whining blade. Almost to the foot of the hill Tristan drove him.

Then Selfridge leapt back with the agility of a frightened pronghorn. Tristan's broadsword hacked into the ground. Selfridge lunged forward, his own saber an arc glittering in the rays of the setting sun.

Tristan dropped. His combat knife came up to block the cut on its knuckle-bow. At the same time he thrust out a foot and caught Selfridge in the balls.

Selfridge buckled, reeled back, almost sat down. Tristan leapt up, knocked the Bowie feebly thrust at him spinning away, and raised his broadsword high for the killing stroke.

But Selfridge wasn't out of the fight. As Tristan cocked his sword over his right shoulder the Dallasite staggered forward and thrust. Desperately Tristan tried to pirouette away.

Cold steel entered his chest. He felt the saber grate between ribs just beneath his left nipple. Pain exploded through him.

Selfridge tried to withdraw the saber. It was stuck. It was his turn for desperation to show through the sheen of sweat that masked his face. He tugged frantically.

Screaming, Tristan brought his raised blade down. The broadsword hacked through Selfridge's right arm just below the elbow.

The brigadier sat down, staring at the blood pumping from his stump. Rangers rushed to his side. Tristan staggered back. Still clutching the saber, the severed arm drew the hilt down. The blade slithered free of Tristan's chest. He gasped and went to his own knees.

Instantly Jeremy and Jovanne were at his side. He saw nomads raising weapons. "No!" he shouted. Reluctantly the guns came down.

He batted away his friends' helping hands, fought his way to his feet. He aimed his bloody sword at his still-kneeling opponent.

"Last man standing won the fight," he declared. "You lose." Selfridge stared at him, face pale with shock.

Tristan let his sword arm slump, and turned away. Gently Jeremy pried the basket hilt of his broadsword from his fingers. He turned to face Jovanne.

She had her jacket off. She wore her shoulder rig today, over a holed black T-shirt. Her heavy breasts swayed fascinatingly within as she leaned forward to inspect the stab wound in his chest. He watched them, duly fascinated.

She straightened, frowned into his face. He transferred his attention to hers. He was freewheeling now, not altogether in control of his own actions.

She wiped the corners of his mouth with a scrap of cloth from somewhere, and studied it and him in turn. "No blood, no sucking," she said in grim satisfaction. "Missed the lung, you lucky bastard. Your Sign's still strong."

Then she stared past him and her eyes grew wide.

Tristan's mind was still wandering Happy Valley, but his reflexes took over. His right hand grabbed the butt of Black Jack Masefield's old Vindicator while his left hit her a straight-armed palm blow between her breasts. She went straight down as Tristan spun.

Brigadier General Sir Lane Selfridge was standing up on his knees. From somewhere a shiny, ornately engraved derringer had appeared in his left hand. He was raising it toward Tristan at the full extension of his remaining arm.

"Die, barbarian scum!" he said through features twisted with pain and hate. *"Die!"*

The derringer came on-line. Tristan saw its twin barrels yawn like pits of Hell.

Thunder cracked.

And kept on cracking as Tristan emptied the Vindicator into his foe. As he fell backward the Dallasite loosed both barrels at the unheeding clouds. Then the slide of Tristan's .40 locked back, and all the world was silent. Except of course for the wind.

Major General Brace Webbert—Posen had boosted him a grade after Selfridge's breveting to brigadier general, just to let the Dallasites know what was what—believed the best defense was a good offense. But once he had taken the strategic offensive, he believed the best defense was walls, wire, mine fields, spotlights, towers, and guns.

Now, Brace had to admit that Selfridge was a pretty good old boy, for a stuck-up Dallasite cocksucker. And he had some pretty-sounding theories about why you shouldn't fort yourself in too much when you took the warpath against the motorized savages of the Plains.

And look what had happened. The cycle scum had reached out and touched him, big time.

Homeland's armies, as the HDF and later the Mobile Forces, had much greater experience fighting the scooter trash than the Cowboys did. Brace Webbert was not an imaginative man, and the fact didn't bother him. The old ways were best, as far as he was concerned.

Time-honored Homeland doctrine said if you were going out upon the Plains to stay, you picked a spot to settle and by God you fortified it. Brace believed it. That settled it.

Despite the lights and the watchtowers, someone managed to creep right up to the perimeter wire the morning after word of the decisive trouncing of the barbarians came through. Maybe it had something to do with the victory celebrations of the night before. The troops knew Webbert as an easygoing commander, who found Purity regulations against the consumption of alcohol and other mood-alterants as obnoxious as they did. He was a man who knew how to *party*.

The unknown party got very close indeed. Close enough to heave something small, round, and heavy over the wire and well into the compound.

When a sleepy-eyed sentry came stumbling out of a cement-hardened machine-gun pit to investigate the thump he heard, he found himself staring by the dawn's early light into the features of Brigadier General Sir Lane Selfridge's detached head.

The brigadier looked almost as surprised as he did.

PART THREE

COMIN' HOME

30

When the grisly trophy was brought before Major General Webbert in a soldier's kit bag, the general went pale and spent the next half hour worshiping the porcelain god in his personal portable commode. Then he got busy about the serious business of panicking for real. An outlaw shitstorm was about to strike Fort Purity, and no mistake.

No mistake. The outlaws came in waves, starting at noon. The waves broke harmlessly against the wire and sandbag and cement perimeter and were thrown back, leaving the Plains black with bodies and red with blood.

By this time atmospheric interference had let up enough to allow a few fragments of traffic from the widely scattered survivors of the Dallas debacle to get through to the powerful and sensitive receivers in the fort. Enough to permit Webbert's intelligence staff to make a few shrewd guesses as to just what had overtaken the Cowboys and why.

To Chairman Posen's screamed demands for action at day's end, General Webbert returned demands for immediate reinforcement. The barbarians had just no-shit massacred an elite army out of *Dallas*, for Christ's sake, the most militant of Cities. It would be suicidal to face the triumphant savages with anything less than every swinging dick Homeland could scrape together.

It was a good argument. It quieted the Chairman down considerably, and he agreed before he rang off to send what reinforcements he could.

Brace Webbert hung up the phone with a sigh of relief and

sweat beading the line of his fine blond hair, clipped as always to a silvery plush. The conversation had actually calmed him, even though it had consisted mostly of his boyhood chum ranting in his ear for upward of an hour. Maybe it was the very familiarity of that situation which soothed him.

He was bone-loyal to his Chairman, there could be no question of that. But he wasn't stupid. *He* wasn't about to leave his lovely strong fortifications behind to go chasing off into a barbarian ambush the way that long-haired nitwit Selfridge had. Good drinking buddy or not, the Dallasite must have used what brains he had to fertilize all that hair.

Webbert would stall until the promised troops reached him. Then he would stall some more. He was nowhere near as smart as Dirk Posen; he knew that, had grown up with the knowledge. But he had grown up with one other bit of knowledge: exactly how to placate his mercurial master.

Posen was almost a hundred miles away, safe behind the even deeper and more impregnable defenses of Homeland. He could be dealt with until his subordinate figured out what to do about all these damned barbarians. Likely, the best would be to hunker down and keep his asshole tight and wait for them to lose interest and go away. Unlike Selfridge, he had enough stocks on hand to stay there quite a while without resupply. Outwaiting the Plains tribes was a strategy that had worked for Homeland time and again. Now that he'd had a chance to reflect, Brace Webbert felt in his bones that it would work again.

Whistling happily, he went off to dinner. It worked up a man's appetite to stand off bike trash all day. And he hadn't had a thing to eat—breakfast didn't really count, after all.

Dawn arrived at Homeland by stealthy degrees. The cloud cover was so low and comprehensive that no light spilled through from the Plains. The clouds to the east just got a little gauzy.

On the southern side of town, an open utility car bumped down a dirt track toward the razor-tape perimeter. The wire strung around the City was studded with impressive-looking concrete bunkers and towers, but Homeland's resources were much too limited to keep them manned all the time. Mobile Force and police barracks were strategically placed so that any threatened sector could hurriedly be manned. Except for sizable complements at the gates and a few lookout towers, the rulers of Homeland depended primarily on two-man patrols like this one.

The driver was cursing his luck as his helmet kept falling in his eyes. The senior member of the team thought he remembered an arroyo that crossed the perimeter near here where they had perpetual trouble with the wire tangles washing out. Smugglers might be using it as a route in and out of the City.

It was just the driver's luck to draw a hard-charging butthead for a partner—and worse, to be ranked by him. Why did he want to go looking for work? If they found a washout they would only have to repair it, which could only result in cutting the shit out of themselves with the razor tape. And who the hell *really* wanted to live in a City devoid of the kinds of things smugglers ran in despite Purity disapproval?

"It's right along here," his partner was saying, peering at the still-dark landscape. "I'm just sure it's—hey. Wait now, what's this?"

He jerked then, gasped, fell back in his seat. His eyes rolled wildly—the driver could see the whites. His right hand was flattened against his chest.

Between the fingers sprouted something long, thin, and black. "An arrow?" the driver asked aloud.

He gaped. In the gray near-light he could make out the arroyo now. It seemed to be alive with moving figures. Some were pushing . . . motorcycles?

He popped the clutch and peeled away with gravel spraying out from beneath his tires. The utility car bounced wildly. The wounded sentry flopped around in his seat, making random choking sounds. Only his belt kept him from being thrown from the vehicle.

Angela Death looked at the mohawked Merry Prankster who had feathered the first sentry. The taller woman shrugged. Both turned to watch the utility buck its way over the dawn landscape. Its progress smoothed, indicating it had found a road of sorts. A moment later the sound of frenzied acceleration reached their ears.

The Mad Thing boss looked around. Only about half her detachment had made it through the gap in the wire.

"Guess our cover's blown, ain't it?" she asked. The Prankster nodded.

"Fuck it," Angela Death said. "Use the satchel charges on the Gods-damned wire. We're Stormriders; let's show these mingy Citizens we know how to blow into town in *style*."

• • •

The explosion jolted awake the twenty-five-man Mobile Force detachment in the concrete-walled barracks half a mile from the smugglers' arroyo. Cursing and rubbing their eyes, the MoFos stumbled from their beds to see what hundreds of Citizens all over town were already aware of.

For the first time in the City's history, the Plains barbarians were loose in the streets of Homeland.

Angela Death's party was not the only one to be detected on its way through the wire. In a few places the alarm was raised in time for troops to race to their near-impregnable prepared positions. Boomer and fifteen of his Ghost Riders were killed by a particularly determined mixed force of MoFos and City police, and that attempt repulsed.

But it was too late to keep the invaders out. The nomads broke through the wire at dozens of widely separated points north, east, and south of the City. The bulk of Homeland's armed forces were a hundred miles away with Major General Webbert. Most of those who hadn't been out on the Plains all along had been bundled off in a huge convoy overnight.

Webbert and Posen—with some help from the wiles of Jamie and Jovanne—had done what generations of the High Free Folk's most daring war leaders had been unable to accomplish: weaken Homeland enough to let the nomads pour in.

Cement chips stung Tristan's cheek as a bullet whanged off the face of the old Edson Building, which housed offices of various downtown sorts. He ducked hurriedly back around the corner.

"Bunch of cops have a roadblock down there at the end of the block," reported a straw-haired young man in Nightranger colors. Tristan didn't know him—or thought he didn't anyway; his features were masked by a coating of soot and grime. He was chewing gum and clutching a Cherokee Pump shotgun to his chest. "Think they're heroes or something."

The fight for Homeland had devolved into a series of random encounters, snipings, and savage skirmishes that erupted when parties of nomads and defenders stumbled into one another. Only at a few locations were real get-down firefights being waged. Government House at the center of town was naturally one of them. It lay across the town square, on the other side of the roadblock.

Tristan had detailed tasks for all his biker bands, even the ones whose only mission was to rove around looking for Homeland patrols to get into hassles with. If the bros were busy it would put the cramp on their penchant for looting, which Tristan was all too aware was going to be a problem anyway. Jamie and her Merry Pranksters, most of whom had happily volunteered to help take Homeland down, were off running the assault on Purity House.

Jovanne had charge of the big downtown thrust toward Government House. Tristan was not here to peer over her shoulder; he knew he could trust her to get the job done. He didn't even know exactly where she was right now. He had his own agenda to attend to.

"Any white jumpsuits?" Tristan asked, risking another peek around the corner.

A snap of gum. "Yeah. At least one of the fuckards. He seems to be in charge. Least he thinks he is."

To punctuate his words he whipped his piece around the corner and fired, then hurriedly ducked back.

"Isn't the range a little long for a shotgun?" Tristan asked.

"Usin' slugs."

"Oh."

Tristan glanced around the group. Besides himself and Jeremy there were maybe a dozen Stormriders. The cops seemed to have the same number or maybe a couple more, holding down from behind two cruisers they had parked nose to nose blocking the street. None of the nomads seemed real inclined to charge into the face of the roadblock. Tristan didn't blame them.

He stepped back, and looked up at the top of the building. Yes, he remembered the place. He grinned, only partly from nostalgia. His youth hadn't really been something to get all misty over.

There were two distinct styles of building in Homeland. One was a style called Modern, which really meant post-StarFall, and which seemed to recur in vogue about every fifty years. Modern-style buildings tended to be low, squat, with windowless inward-slanting cement walls designed to shrug off the furies of the elements.

The buildings down here were mainly in the style called Classical: straight-sided, multiple-storied, bravely showing dozens of windows to wind and Front Range hail. They were what buildings used to look like before StarFall. At least, they were what people *thought* they were like.

Tristan knew these flat-topped rampart-edged roofs well. When he was doing time in the McGrory reformatory, where he had met Jeremy, he had spent plenty of time on work details sweeping off the ash from the massive volcanic eruptions many miles away in the faraway FlameLands of the Pacific Northwest.

"Anybody bring a hammer?" he asked.

31

It wasn't as off-the-wall a question as it would seem. You could never tell what kind of bizarre crap any given bunch of the High Free Folk would be toting around with them. Tools for various forms of illicit entry were actually a good bet. Even if they weren't inclined to risk the wrath of Tristan by illicit razzing, there were always dead cities to go salvage-picking in, or the locked trailers of Homeland and Dallas semis to be broken open.

No sledgehammers were available. "How about wrecking bars?" A bearded Iron Horse rider showed him a grin from which the top front teeth were missing, and produced a five-foot bar from above the exhaust pipes of his cruiser, which was blue and silver and had forks extended way out in front.

"All *right*," Tristan said, leaning the bar onto his shoulder. He pointed at four of the nomads. "You come with Jeremy and me. The rest of you keep these bozos busy."

At the count of three the nomads on the Keep the Bozos Busy detail dropped to the pavement and rolled out, or just stuck their weapons around the corner and opened fire. They did so with a happy wild exuberance; the iron ammo discipline of the Plains seldom gave them much scope for their natural desire to just hooraw things in general.

The brief bullet-storm had the desired effect of making the cops pull their heads in. Tristan whipped around the corner, with Jeremy hard behind him, and ducked into a recessed doorway. In an eye blink all half a dozen of them were crammed into the four-foot-deep alcove, breathing each other's aromas, which was probably less a trial for the others than Tristan.

"Careful here," he said, trying not to gouge an eye or whack somebody over the ear with the long bright-orange bar. The door was mostly glass. He stuck the blade in the metal frame and popped the door right open.

"Okay," he said, gesturing his men forward into the building. "Let's move like we got a purpose."

"Where we goin', Boss?" asked the Iron Horse who'd volunteered his five-foot lock pick.

Jeremy grinned. "To the roof. Where else?"

The outlaws' fire had begun to slacken after their big spasm of firing, which had passed as quickly as a spring rainsquall. The opinion of the veteran cops at the roadblock was that the nomads had lost their taste for it and given up.

"Bike trash just got no staying power," explained one, who was kneeling with his riot gun behind the nose of a patrol car, so that his gut lopped over onto one indigo-uniformed knee. He looked forbidding and important with the dark polarized visor of his helmet down before his eyes. "They're all just chickenshits at heart. They romp around a while, loot a little, loose some shots in the air, and then ride back out into the wasteland. We got nothin' to worry about; *you'll* see."

The last was directed toward the young man in the white jumpsuit of a Purity member, which meant he was theoretically in command. He was sitting in the street with his back pressed up against the door of a patrol car. He didn't look happy. He was very visibly hoping that the armored plates inside the cop car's doors were as bulletproof as they were made out to be.

What the old cop had to say was definitely what the youngster wanted to hear. A shy smile made his freckled nose crinkle, and he bobbed a head whose brick-red hair had been cropped to a peculiar pinkish fuzz.

About then the cop's uniformed head exploded. The Purity boy stared.

Around him the cops were going down, crying out as bullets punched holes through them and knocked various moist chunks of stuff out of their bodies. One of them got to a knee and turned a storm carbine toward the rooftop of an office building looming over them. Then a bullet pierced his throat, and he fell over to lie gagging and kicking on the blacktop.

The Purity boy stared a moment in horrified fascination at the spectacle of a man drowning in his own blood. His guts heaved. Vomit spewed out of him. The instinct for survival did not take time out for nausea; it forced him to his feet even as he erupted.

A bullet shattered his right shin just below the knee. He fell wailing next to the choking man.

Taken under surprise fire from above, the cops who weren't downed at once took immediately to their heels. If they were concerned to be leaving their nominal superior with his Purity white jumpsuited ass hanging well and truly in the breeze, none of them showed any signs that were visible from the rooftop.

Tristan left the four nomads on the roof to cover the intersection, and hurried down to the street with Jeremy. The Purity boy was still conscious. He was in no mood to resist their attempts at questioning, for which Tristan and Jeremy counted themselves lucky. Given the shape he was in, neither felt like grabbing him and shaking him or anything.

As Jeremy waved for the Stormriders at the far end of the block to come ahead on, Tristan knelt, not too near the boy. "Posen," he said tersely. "Where?"

"P-purity House," the boy moaned. "Please don't torture me."

"No need." Tristan stood and looked to Jeremy.

"You take over here and give Jovanne support if she needs it," he told his friend.

Jeremy raised a brow at him. "And you're . . . ?"

"Outta here."

"And you want me . . . ?"

"Out of the way." He ran back up the block to where WildFyre was parked.

After Tristan roared off on his cruiser, a disgruntled Jeremy took most of the little clump of bros forward toward the town square, where the sound of gunfire was rising like a bad prairie wind. A pair of riders stayed behind to loot the bodies.

A few minutes later they were squatting over the body of the Purity member, who lay on his belly staring with peculiar fixity at the wide dark pool of blood that had gushed out onto the blacktop from his slashed throat. They were disputing the identity of the tired but not unattractive brown-haired woman whose picture they had found in his pocket.

"I say it's his old lady," said one.

"Naw," said the other. "Lookit him. He ain't got no old lady. Still ain't had his cherry busted, I betcha."

The first nomad glanced at the boy and shrugged. "Guess he won't never get the job done now. Maybe she's his sister, y'think?"

"Bet it's his mother. These City rats commence to breedin' young. Call it their civic duty, like, to raise up little soldier boys."

The first nomad turned the picture over. "Dang. No address or nothin'."

A boot step. Both men looked up, black-nailed hands snatching for well-worn pistol grips.

Two dark figures, heavyset and shaggy-bearded, stood silhouetted against the low gray sky. "Mornin', bros," said Tramp.

"Find anything int'restin'?" asked Buzzard.

The two nomads relaxed. They were among bros. Neither man even wondered what a pair of Presidents of powerful clans were doing bumming around the street so far from the action.

The first nomad held up the picture. "Checkit out. I was figurin' we could look her up, settle our little disagreement and then maybe, y'know, *pleasure* her a spell."

Buzzard and Tramp exchanged glances. "Sounds like a plan," the Bandido Prez said. "Say, would you bros happen to know where the Maximum Lord got off to?"

"We got important stuff to discuss with him," Tramp said.

The nomad with the picture looked to his partner. "Think I heard someone say he was off somewheres called Puberty House or something."

Buzzard nodded. "Thank you kindly."

"Sure you don't wanna come along with us?" the first nomad said, waving his photo.

Tramp grinned with moist loose lips and shook his melon head. "No, but thank'ee, all the same. We'll just be moseyin' now. Y'all get back to what you was doin'. Good huntin', now, y'hear?"

The two nodded absently. Already they were engrossed in their work again.

Buzzard took two steps away from the squatting men. Then he turned, a .60-caliber Shocker revolver in his hand, and fired a single shot into each man's head.

Tramp winced and turned his head away as blood spattered his face. "Who-ee, old Thunder Dog sure do make a mess of things," he said. "You sure you had to kill 'em, Buzzard?"

The older, shorter, bigger-bellied man nodded, making his greasy ringlets dance. "Don't want 'em tellin' nobody we was askin' where Burningskull went to."

Tramp stretched his lips back in an unhappy grimace and shook his head. "Sure don't seem right, settin' out to put the whack on the Maximum Lord. I mean, his clan and ours . . ." He held up a grubby hand with fingers crossed. "We was like *that*."

"The past's dead and gone now, Tramp," Buzzard said, laying his free hand on the Sand King Prez's shoulder. Tramp did not fail to notice that he kept his Shocker in the other. "Let the dead bury the dead, son. It's him or us."

"Are you certain sure—?"

"You heard what Lonesome Dave said. Burningskull heard somebody did that hose-mouthed little greaseball Rico. He thinks we did it. He's just waiting until we finish capturing this City for him, and then *snick*."

He drew a finger across his throat for emphasis.

Tramp lowered his head and shook it unhappily. "Well," he said, "reckon a man's gotta do what a man's gotta do."

"That's the spirit, boy."

32

Purity House was nestled in the foothills south of town. Literally *in*—it was a semisubterranean structure, angling from a three-story straight-up facade down into the face of a hill. A pine balcony ran across the uppermost story.

Like the man who had built it, not all of it was exposed to view; it extended under the ground and into the hill. Not even Tristan knew exactly how far the warrens and chambers ran. He had always taken for granted that there were one or more secret escape routes hidden in the depths. Unfortunately, Black Jack Masefield had never had a chance to use his back way out. When the Purity counterrevolution hit, he and his giant Comanche bodyguard Quanah had been ambushed in his car on their way to a predawn meeting with reformist Mayor John Amos Schenk.

Tristan crouched in the scrub two hundred yards from the front of the house. Jamie was hunkered down beside him. She had a quiver of arrows slung over one shoulder and a strung bow in her hand. Her face was daubed with green and brown paint to break up its outlines.

"What's it look like?" Tristan asked.

Jamie shrugged. "Tough. Got a machine gun on the balcony, about a squad of shooters in the windows and out front. They're hard-core. Popped a couple of the Mad Things when we stuck our heads up. We tagged one or two of them, and here we sit."

Tristan rubbed his chin with a thumb. "Suggestions?"

She showed him even white teeth. "Jamie the tactician, right?"

"Hey, your plan for taking down Selfridge went down like a

semi coming off the Divide with its brakes burned out. And we're hitting on all cylinders today with what you wrenched together with Jovanne."

"No brilliant inspirations are popping into my mind, Tristan. This is a frontal-assault situation. We have no way to outflank the fuckards, unless you know a back way in?"

Tristan showed a lopsided smile and shook his head.

"Another possibility is, we bring up some of our antitank rockets and just blast our way in."

Tristan grimaced. "Maybe not."

Jamie gave him a hooded look. "The only other way I can think of is trickery. Think you can impersonate one of your old playmate's bun boys?"

"He'd never go for it. Posen's a suspicious weasel. He'd have his guards ventilate anybody who tried to get in now, even if it was one of his homeboys."

The machine gun on the balcony stuttered. Tristan and Jamie crouched a little lower.

"Tristan?"

"Yeah?"

"Your lady's in there, isn't she? What's her name—Elinor?"

"Where'd you hear that?"

"Jovanne."

"I thought you two didn't get along."

"She's okay. We talked some while we were plotting together. I think we have an understanding. She's really good, Tristan."

"I know."

"She loves you, Tristan."

"I . . . know that too."

"She thinks that, once you get your . . . ice-princess . . . back, you'll just throw her aside."

"I don't throw my friends aside, Jamie."

More shots, coming in and going out. "I don't think that's what she means."

He looked at her a moment. "Where do you stand?"

She sighed, laughed softly. "I'm your friend, Tristan. I stand by you. Not this Lord of the Plains crap—*you.*"

"Fair enough." He gathered himself to rise.

She laid a hand on his arm. "What are you going to do?"

"We tried smart, but smart didn't come up with anything." He glanced up at the house. "Now it's time to try stupid."

• • •

The canvasback two-and-a-half-ton truck came booming up the drive, straight for the front of the house. The troopers greeted it with a storm of fire. Glass exploded from the windshield. The radiator gusted steam from a dozen holes. The tires were punctured, but were designed not to go flat.

Soldiers rolled out of the vehicle's path as it bounced over the square-cut timbers that bordered the garden and slammed toward the house. A figure peeled out from behind it and roared for the door with the howl of a big V-Twin engine laid wide open.

Tristan was riding a sled borrowed from a bro who had no further use for it—he wasn't about to risk WildFyre in the stunt he was about to pull . . .

He caught a glimpse of startled faces turned toward him, pale and blank beneath helmet brims. The bike bounced up the several steps to the porch. Tristan yanked the front tire off the ground. It struck the front door and smashed it inward in a spray of splinters.

He was in the foyer, skidding on slick dark and light wood parquetry. In the spacious great room to his right two soldiers in battle dress pulled up their M52 storm carbines and wheeled away from the front window. Tristan quick-drew his Bolo, pulled the trigger before the weapon came on-line, so that the burst slashed through the troopies like a scythe.

A figure appeared in the door to the sitting room on his left, raising an M52. Tristan brought the Bolo around, fired a single shot across his body. It took the soldier in the forehead.

Tristan killed the engine and laid the bike down in the foyer. From the stairs at the end of the foyer came the rush of booted feet. Tristan slipped forward, ducked into a closet, closed the door.

As he stood breathing shallowly with the long barrel of the Bolo held up before his nose, he heard a group of soldiers clatter into the foyer, an NCO voice yelling at them to get their asses up front and take up firing positions before the damn bike scum came crawling through the windows. Boots thumped obediently away.

Cautiously Tristan pushed the door open a crack, peered out. A pair of troopies lay on their bellies amid the splinters of the door, a machine-gunner and a loader. Their attention was riveted outward. As Tristan watched, the weapon shuddered and yammered and ejected a stream of glittering brass cartridges to tinkle on the fine wood floor.

He turned and went up the stairs, quick, quiet, alert. When his head reached the level of the second floor he paused, peered. At the front of the house two soldiers crouched by the busted-out floor-to-ceiling window. They were firing regular bursts at the undeveloped grassland outside.

Tristan sprang out of the stairwell. The landing was a widened space paneled in light wood and set with a sofa, comfortable chairs, and potted plants, meant for guests or occupants to relax and converse in, or admire the view if they were of a mind. For a man of spartan inclination and iron determination and self-discipline, Masefield had had a surprisingly gracious touch for relaxation. Tristan suspected that was how he'd managed to keep his edge so long: He wasn't always cutting at what was around him. He'd known when to rest in his scabbard.

Tristan holstered his Bolo, touched the hilt of the scabbard above his right shoulder. Then he thought, *What the hell*, and drew the pistol again. He moved forward far enough to glance left and right down the cross-passage. Nothing. He would investigate later; he was going to take the building top-down. Watching the soldiers at the window, he waited for the hunching of the shoulders that indicated the soldiers were bracing for another burst, and killed them with two quick shots as they fired.

Then he was across the landing, taking a turn around the foot of the stairs up, past the huddled bodies, trying not to show too much of a flash of motion to his keen-eyed sharpshooters outside. He wasn't entirely successful; a bullet split the turned endpost of the bannister as he rabbited up the steps.

The top floor. Overhead the exposed-plank ceiling slanted down toward the back of the house from a maximum height of twenty feet. An immobile fan hung down like an upside-down wood and brass flower. The glass of the tall front window had been shot in and lay like fresh jagged hail on the floor. There were no soldiers in view. The violent sporadic thudding of the machine-gun on the balcony vibrated up through the floor.

Moving forward, cautious, to the cross-passage. Three-second looks, first left, then right. The right-hand passage was clear. To the left, though, a pair of troopies stood with slung rifles flanking a door on the hillward side of the hall.

Tristan smiled. *Dirk isn't taking any chances,* he thought. He was perhaps a tad surprised that the Purity Chairman wasn't cowering away below ground, out of reach of bullets. Of course, the walls were stout—Tristan could hear slugs thudding on them like spastic sledgehammer blows.

Tristan's recollection of the young Dirk Posen was that he had always hung back and let his goons, notably Brace Webbert and the late Halt Newsome, do his dirty work. Tristan had always had the sense that this resulted more from Posen's distaste and honest recognition of his physical limitations—Brace and Halt were strapping youths, whereas Dirk was something of a little shit—than from actual cowardice. Evidently Dirk preferred to be up here, literally on top of the action.

Tristan holstered his broomhandle. All the outbound firing came from the balcony. Shots in the corridor would instantly alert Posen and whoever was in the room with him that something was up.

He drew his sword. "Ahh!" he yelled, then gave a gut-felt groan. "Oh, *Jesus*, I'm hit, I'm hit!"

A moment, and a rattle of hurried steps. Tristan's broadsword took out the throat of the first troopie around the corner. As the soldier staggered choking to the bannister and fell backward into the stairwell, Tristan seized his partner by the front of his blouse, slammed him back up against the paneled wall, and jammed the bloody tip of the sword up under his jaw.

"Is Posen in there?" The man nodded. His jaws were trembling, his eyes rolling like the eyes of a buffalo calf being taken down by a pack of feral dogs.

"Who else?"

"The women. And two guards."

Women? What, Dirk's hosting a ladies' tea here while waiting for the barbarians?

"How many women?"

"T-two. The ice-bitch, the traitor's daughter. And—"

Tristan slammed the heavy silver pommel of his broadsword against the man's temple, let him fall. He was unwilling to just kill the poor bastard, having gotten the drop on him. The head blow might finish him off from a cerebral hemorrhage later, of course, but Tristan would go only so far for somebody whose main goal in life was almost certainly to kill *him*.

"Watch how you talk about the lady of the Lord of the Plains," he said to the slumped guard, and whipped around the corner.

He resheathed his sword, and drew his pistol. At the door he paused. The machine gun was still thundering away out on the balcony behind his back: what with that and the thick oak door, they could all have been singing inside at the top of their lungs for all Tristan could tell.

Standing to one side he tried the knob. It was unlocked. He took a deep breath, threw open the door, and threw himself into the room in a slanting dive.

The room had been a briefing chamber, windowless and well lit, with a slanting ceiling. Dirk Posen stood behind a huge table where he was studying something Tristan's gestalt flash told him was a map. Elinor stood behind him, tall, cool, and immaculate in her customary riding garb of jodhpurs and light blouse.

Two soldiers stood by the table, their weapons slung. That was slack, but then for all his ferocious rhetoric Posen had always been a candy-ass civilian with no real understanding of military matters.

Gaping in horrified shock, the soldiers fumbled to unlimber their storm carbines. Tristan shot them both. Then, holding his pistol aimed at the center of Posen's pale drawn face, he picked himself up off the floor.

"Hello, Ellie," Tristan said. "Thought I'd come and help you out. Talking with fanatics always did bore you."

She smiled. If the sudden turn of events unsettled her, it didn't show anywhere on those perfect features, in those ice-crystal eyes.

"I've managed to keep myself entertained, Tristan," she said.

While he was trying to make sense of that Tristan became aware of *presence* in the room to his left. He wheeled, cursing himself for a reckless nitwit. By and large Homeland women were trained to be helpless flowers, as unlike their nomad sisters as could be. But you didn't live to enjoy your conquest of the City that destroyed your family and betrayed you by taking that sort of thing for granted . . .

A figure, almost as tall as himself, was surrounded in a billow of brilliant yellow. The head seeming to float above the robe was shorn entirely bald. Tristan frowned. He had seen this woman twice before—and, drop-dead gorgeous as she was, bald or not, that was twice too often.

"Get over with the others," he said, gesturing with his Bolo. "Keep your hands in si . . ."

His word-stream just stopped. It was as if his tongue had suddenly gotten so thick it plugged his mouth.

Alarms jangled in his brain. He tried to press the trigger of the Bolo.

His finger refused to move.

33

Fighting toward the center of town was house to house and savage. The soldiers had grenades, though the cops did not; it could make them tough to pry out. Once the nomads managed to get in a room with them, though, the outlaw superiority in weapons and skills of hand-to-hand combat quickly settled matters. It was a slow, nasty, bloody business.

Jovanne found herself on a fourth-floor roof overlooking the town square. The squat mass of Government House bulked across the way from her. The steps and sidewalks before it were piled with sandbags, and muzzle flashes danced like festival sparklers all along it.

Hating Tristan with all her soul, she sent runners scuttling to convey orders. Yes, he was showing his faith in her by having her direct this crucial assault. But, Goddesses and Gods all damn him to the thickest-walled cell in Hell, he knew she hated this, sending brothers and sisters to pain, disfigurement, and death.

She was willing to carry the freight as Prez, to keep her clan together, to hear their problems and adjudicate their disputes, to keep them alive and fed and sheltered. But there was a reason she would not accept a directing role in combat. A reason she had been willing to live with such an insubordinate and dangerous detached asshole as John Badheart as warlord of her Jokers.

I took command before, she thought, *and I got my daughter killed.* Now Tristan had thrust her into command again, and she saw Melissa's eyes in the eyes of every sprawled rag-doll nomad corpse.

A crunch of boot-sole leather on the volcanic grit that covered the rooftop—locals tended to use it instead of gravel, since it had a tendency to get there anyway. With the wind blowing a few russet wisps of hair in her face, she turned.

A tall figure, golden-haired, lean as a whip, clad all in black, was approaching across the rooftop. The two of them were alone.

"Lonesome Dave?" she said, frowning, puzzled.

He nodded and gave her that quicksilver lady-heart-melting grin. "In the flesh, babe."

"Bit of a surprise to see you here this close to the action," she could not resist saying. She had not been about to give in to Tristan's dig against her newfound chum, but the truth was she had been wondering. The Pistolero President's actions did not seem to match his rep as a majestic hassler. For a fact, where action was hottest, there he wasn't, at least in recent days.

He shrugged. "I've been busy. Got a clan to run, and all. These are trying times."

"Yeah," she said without conviction. "Where the hell is everybody?"

"You sent them all away."

She frowned. *Did I lose track that much of what I was doing?* An ice-ball formed in the pit of her stomach. *Oh, Mother Sky, I'm fucking up already. Melissa, Melissa, I'm sorry.*

She turned away, blinking rapidly to clear her eyes of sudden moisture. "What are you doing up here anyway?" she demanded hoarsely.

"Just keeping you company, babe."

He knelt beside her, stroked her cheek with the back of his hand. Across the way the firing was picking up as a feint she had ordered opened up wildly to draw the defenders' attention and pin them down. She absentmindedly batted his hand away.

"If you really want to help," she said tersely, scanning the scene with Tristan's binoculars, "you can get ready to run a message down for me."

She lowered the binoculars and bit her lips, frowning. She was trying to get a party into the building behind Government House. If they could fight their way in, they could cross the alley and blast their way into the enemy headquarters with satchel charges. *What if it goes wrong? What if they all die? I fucked something up, I know it, I always do—*

A whip of motion before her eyes, and suddenly something tightened around her throat, cutting off her air.

• • •

The fist snapped Tristan's head around so fast his neck vertebrae squealed protest and white sparks fountained up into the back of his skull. His vision black and blurred and spinning, he staggered three steps, fetched up against a chest as wide and solid as the walls of Purity House, and slumped into massive arms.

"Y'know, Ellie," he heard himself say, "your boyfriend isn't being real . . . sophisticated, you know?"

Dirk Posen laughed. It was a taut, rusty sound, as if he didn't have much practice at it.

"This isn't subtlety," he said, "this is recreation. Play before work. Oh, I know, pleasure is dereliction of duty. But it's my privilege as Chairman—the hierarchic principle is the very foundation of Purity doctrine. At the highest levels it takes precedence over even self-denial."

The room slowed down its whirling enough so Tristan could focus his eyes, sort of. Posen's tastes still ran to beefy boys for bullies. These three were all as tall as Tristan and twice as broad. They were dressed in Purity white, not MoFo camouflage or dark cop blue. It joyed Tristan's soul to be bleeding all over all that spotless white. Well, it was a moral victory. Of sorts.

He had felt that deadly immobility, that body betrayal, before. It was a mind-trick of high-ranking Fusion adepts. He had experienced it at the final battle where he and his allies the Kobolds and the Osage had caught the Catheads and crushed them. Only this time, there was no way a fortuitous head shot from Little Teal's sniper rifle was going to break the invisible bonds.

And now they weren't needed.

The bodies had been cleared from the room, the heavy table pushed to the wall. Tristan's sword and pistol were piled neatly atop the City map Posen had been studying when he was so rudely interrupted. The Chairman himself sat in a chair with his back to the wall, with Elinor and the Acolyte standing on either side of him, like figures in an ancient morality play, allegory angels representing God knows what cosmic principles.

"That's all very interest, Dirkie," Tristan said, drooling blood. "Don't mind me. Think I'll nod off for a little nap now . . ."

An open-handed slap jarred him awake. It felt as if his skull were a brass bell, and somebody was ringing it.

"I'm going to amuse myself watching Butch, Tab, and Cliff beat you to death—almost. Meanwhile my loyal men will be whipping your savages back into the wasteland like the animals they are. *Then* comes the business part: your very public trial, conviction, and execution, which will be protracted and interesting, to improve the civic morale."

"You might not be keeping up on current events, Dirk," Tristan said, "but we're mopping the streets with your boys."

Posen laughed again. Was it the pounding Tristan had taken to the head, or was he getting better with practice?

"So you think." He glanced over his left shoulder at the Acolyte, and patted the strong brown hand she had laid on the back of his chair behind his shoulder. "My trusted special adviser here assures me differently."

The Acolyte smiled. She flowed forward with the sinuous ease of sand sliding down a dune. As she approached Tristan the goon who was holding him turned him to face her and caught Tristan's arms in a full nelson, pushing his head forward.

"It is a great day to be coming to One, is it not?" said the Acolyte.

"No day is a good day for that kind of shit."

The white-clad legbreaker shoved Tristan's head forward till his neck felt ready to split in back. "Speak politely to the lady, scooter trash."

"A major barrier to the joining together of all the Plains in blessed Fusion falls today. You should rejoice."

"I thought I got a show trial first," Tristan said. "That ought to be good for a couple days."

She smiled. Her long almond-shaped blue eyes met his. Revelation exploded in his brain like the false-light afterimages of a blow.

She leaned forward, kissed him on the forehead. "Farewell, Lord of the Plains."

She straightened. "Chairman, I must go. I have my part to play in the destruction of the invaders."

Posen smiled indulgently, waved a hand. He was playing the part of grandee to the max. Count Omohundro his fat old bald boy-loving self could have done no better.

"I will join you later for the victory celebration," he said. Elinor narrowed her eyes to death-beam slits. The Acolyte flowed from the room.

When the door shut behind her Tristan twisted in the grip. "You idiot, don't you see what she's doing?"

Posen laughed. "No." He laced his fingers together and leaned forward, all attention. "Tell me. What?"

"It's—it's a setup. She's been leading you by the dick."

Elinor scowled at that. The goon pulled an arm out and grabbed him by the brushcut hair on top, pulling his head cruelly back.

"She doesn't have any plan to wash away the Stormriders, dammit! It's us she's talking about. She's got us both where she wants us, don't you see? *She's gonna take us both out at a stroke.*"

Posen laughed and slapped his thighs. "Isn't it delightful to watch him wiggle on the hook, my dear?"

He looked back at Elinor and tried to pat her hand. She snatched it away.

"Pay no attention to his allegations, heh, heh. They're ridiculous, as you know. He'll try anything to save his miserable life."

Tristan yipped coyote laughter. "It's your ass I'm trying to save now, Posen! That bald-headed bitch is a lot bigger snake than you are. Don't you know what these Fusion fuckards *are*?"

"For the moment," Posen said, "useful allies. Tools, one might say."

"Dirk," Elinor said in a low, serious tone with none of her usual dry banter in it, "listen to him. I never trusted that bitch."

Smiling, Posen shook his head. "You disappoint me. It's so transparent, my dear. He'll say anything in order to—"

The door banged open. Posen looked toward it, his fine features hardened in a mask of irritation.

It turned to shock when he saw two burly nomads standing in the door with guns in their hands.

With horrible madman strength Lonesome Dave hauled Jovanne to her feet. She clawed at her throat, but it did no good. Her vision was already starting to fray at the edges. All she could hear was her pulse pounding in her ears.

The clawing was pure reflex, the body fighting to survive. She herself felt nothing in particular, only confusion and a sense of leaving much undone.

Coolness on her muscular thighs. Somehow the Pistolero President had gotten her fly undone and pulled her jeans halfway to her knees. She felt something rubbery-hard prodding her between the cheeks of her ass.

34

"I never thought I'd be glad to see you two," Tristan gasped.

The white-suited goon pushed him down on the floor. He took a step forward. Tramp swiveled his wide hips, fired a blast from the short-barreled Cherokee Pump riot gun he held at his hip. The whitesuit flew backward, stumbled over Tristan's legs, and sprawled across him.

The other two lunged for the door. Buzzard shot one in the belly. The man shrieked and went to his knees as the huge bullet tore through his guts.

The other caught Buzzard in a bear hug, lifting his bulk clean off the hardwood floor. He was a head taller than the squatty Bandido Prez.

But he was shorter in *mean*. Buzzard butted his forehead into the Purity goon's mouth, gashing his forehead but smashing his victim's teeth to porcelain fragments swimming in red.

The Purity enforcer squealed through his nose, let go of his man, tried to backpedal. Buzzard kneed him in the nuts. As he doubled, the biker grabbed the man by his close-cropped head and dragged his face hard into his knee.

Sobbing and retching, the man dropped to his knees. Buzzard raised a booted foot, pushed him over on his side. His raised his Shawk & McLanahan .60-caliber, took careful aim, and fired. The bullet shattered the Purity thug's head like a cantaloupe struck by a maul.

Tramp was covering Posen and Elinor with his shotgun. Elinor sidled over to stand with one hand on the table. She looked cool and unafraid.

"What'll I do with these two, Buzzard?" Tramp asked over his shoulder. "Want I should waste 'em?"

"Naw." Buzzard shook his head, swishing greasy black ringlets back and forth across his ax-handle-broad shoulders. "Don'cha see? This is gotta be the big nigger our Lord done come for. He'll make a mighty prize hostage. And that high-ass lady there—spoils of war for the conquerin' heroes, wouldn't you say?"

His head still feeling as if important parts had been shaken loose, Tristan was trying to disentangle his legs from the torso and intestines of the man Tramp had blasted. "Here now, boys. I'm grateful as hell for the rescue and all, but I have my own plans for the lady. Not to mention a prior claim . . ."

His words trailed away an Buzzard came to stand before him. He slowly raised the Shocker to aim at the bridge of Tristan's hawk's-beak nose, which by the feel of things was busted again.

"Sorry, old pal. This is the end of the Road for you." He clicked back the hammer.

"What the hell are you talking about?"

Buzzard laughed. "Lonesome Dave told us all about you. How you're fixin' to nail us 'cause Rico got washed away."

"I don't know what the fuck you're talking about." Tristan was trying to keep surreptitiously sliding himself free. It wasn't easy. Wet slippery loops of gut kept wanting to come with him. "Rico disappeared. No man knows why."

Tramp chuckled. "Yeah. So you say. You're a slippery ol' fox, Tristan, got to give you that. You'll say anything to save your ass."

"Every time I try to tell people the truth, they say I'm looking out for my ass," Tristan complained. "It's getting to be a real pisser."

"Well, anyway, old son," Buzzard said, "it don't much matter. We was gettin' fed up with your high-and-mighty ways anyhow. If we got to have ourselves a Maximum Lord, why not old Dave?

"Or . . ." A wide gold-toothed grin. "Why not Buzzard? I think I'm cut out for the job."

He squinted to aim. "Adios, motherfucker."

"Oh, thank God you're here," Elinor gasped, staring past Tramp at the door.

Tramp laughed uproariously. "You think I'm gonna fall for that old trick, skinny lady? Shoot, it's even older than you are."

Tramp was a fat boy. When he laughed his eyes got all crinkled up and tended to vanish into his cheeks. So while he was being amused with Elinor's dumb naivete—and mostly blinded in the process—Elinor snatched at the first thing to hand. It happened to be the harness of Tristan's shoulder rig. She swung it full force and cracked Tramp across the nose with the broom handle of Tristan's Bolo.

He yelped, staggered back, pawing at his broken nose. Buzzard glanced toward him.

Moving with a lot more speed than he thought he still had in him, Tristan reached out and grabbed the wrist of Buzzard's gun hand with his own right hand. He pulled Buzzard slightly toward him, to lock out the elbow proper. Then he busted Buzzard's elbow clean with a hammerblow of his left fist.

Buzzard screamed like a shot horse. Tristan surged to his knees, shifting his grip to cover Buzzard's gun hand. Tramp spun, trying to swing up his Cherokee one-handed. Tristan stuffed his forefinger through the Shocker's trigger guard over Buzzard's thick finger.

Buzzard shrieked still louder as Tristan turned the now-unmoored forearm back on itself to point the Shocker at Tramp. "No," Tramp said, dropping the shotgun. "Wait—"

Tristan pumped the trigger three times. Tramp was driven backward, bawling like a frightened child as the bullets smashed like runaway semis through his soft body. His back hit the wall and he slid down, leaving a vast smear of scarlet.

Buzzard was cussing Tristan in a voice like pieces being torn out of his lungs. Tristan pushed him away and stood. The Bandido aimed a left-handed haymaker at Tristan. Tristan weaved back out of the way, kicked him in the gut.

Buzzard doubled, the breath exploding out of him. Head down, he lunged for Tristan, hoping to use his greater bulk and raw strength to power down his injured overlord.

Tristan pivoted like a matador out of harm's way. He seized Buzzard's long hair and helped him forward. The Bandido hit the heavy table with his head, cracking it, and went down in a heap.

He came up blowing like a horse that had been for a roll in a stream. Tristan landed on his back. Roaring, Buzzard tried to rise. Tristan grabbed his head, cracked it sharply twice against the wall.

Buzzard groaned, sagged. Tristan got a grip around his great shaggy head. Buzzard grabbed his arms, tried to bull them free.

A gigantic heave, a sound like the Shocker going off. Buzzard collapsed, his bull neck snapped.

Tristan stood, turned—and found himself staring down the enormous barrel of the Shocker.

"That's enough," Dirk Posen breathed. His thins nostrils were flared; spots of color burned on his cheeks. His eyes were sunken and intense. "Highly impressive, but enough."

"Give me the gun," Tristan said, stepping forward.

Posen backed up before him. "Don't come any closer! I'll shoot!"

"We don't have *time* for this bullshit. The Acolyte is just giving herself time to get clear, then this building's gonna blow. I'm surprised we aren't all sitting on Jesus' lap already."

Tristan was backing the Chairman steadily toward the door. "Stay back, I tell you!" Posen screamed. "Aren't you afraid of me?"

"I'll never be afraid of you. I *am* afraid of the Acolyte."

"I have a gun! Are you afraid of my gun?" He bumped against the wall next to the door.

Tristan laughed. "You were always a big gun-control freak, weren't you? You were hot for control of any kind."

"What's that got to do with anything?"

The Lord of the Plains was almost in his face. "It means that, like most folks who hate guns, you don't know jack about them."

"Oh, yes?" Posen's face twisted in a maniacal leer. He stuck the heavy revolver against Tristan's nose and pulled the trigger. *Click.*

In echoing silence Tristan reached out and plucked the Shocker away. "A Shocker just has five chambers in the cylinder," he said softly.

With a strange whistling scream Posen snatched open the door and vanished into the hall.

Lonesome Dave's attempted rape-in-progress cut through the fog of disassociation and uncovered emotion: Jovanne was *really pissed off*!

Do I have to put up *with this?* she thought. Her left hand grappled down behind her bare ass. Dave's pubic bush rasped her knuckles, and then her fingers found something soft and dangly. And *squeezed.*

Lonesome Dave screamed like a woman. The killing pressure on Jovanne's throat slackened.

She reached her right hand over her shoulder, grabbed Lonesome Dave by his glorious gold hair. Then she jackknifed her body forward, hauling with all her might.

Lonesome Dave sailed right over. Over her body, over her shoulder, and finally, over the parapet. He hollered nicely on his way to the street.

Jovanne stood there staring down at him spread-eagled down there, black and gold and red. Made a pretty picture, she thought.

"Dave," she said softly, "you have a hell of a way with the ladies."

With difficulty she got the thing around her neck unknotted, and pulled it off. It was a silk stocking, such as a City lady might wear with a garter belt.

"I'll be damned," she said. "He was the Strangler."

"Uh—Jovanne?"

She turned. A young Nightranger was standing there staring at her with eyes about twice the size of his head.

"What the fuck are *you* staring at?" she demanded.

The rustling of the breeze in her own pubic hair, and its cool kiss on the cheeks of her bare ass reminded her. "Oh," she said, and pulled up her pants.

She glared at the boy till he shut his mouth. "What?" she demanded. "Haven't you ever seen a twat before? Don't just stand there, boy, you're wasting my time."

"Aren't you going to chase him?" Elinor asked. She was breathing heavily, and her face was flushed. Tristan was gratified to note that she had human frailties after all. He hadn't seen much evidence of those in the past.

"No," he said, snatching his sword harness from the wreckage of the table and bending to scoop up his shoulder rig. "We need to *move*. Thanks for saving me back there, by the way."

"I decided I preferred your company to that of your friends."

"I'm flattered." He slipped an arm around her, kissed her any which way on the nose. "And Dirk?"

"He seems to be out of the picture."

Tristan laughed. It only had a touch of undercurrent to it. "Come on."

He urged her along, out of the room, into the room opposite.

The French doors to the balcony stood open. A firefight seemed to be rising toward a crescendo outside.

Elinor hung back. "What about the soldiers?" she said. "What about the shooting?"

"We'll worry about that if we're still alive when we hit the ground."

"When we hit—" she started to say. But he was sweeping her irresistibly forward again.

They blew out onto the balcony. Soldiers raised startled faces from behind their weapons.

"If I were you boys," Tristan said, leaping up onto the square-cut beam railing, "I'd haul ass out here."

Before anyone could react he had hauled Elinor up by the arm, taking her in his arms, and stepped forward into space.

At his back the house erupted in orange flame.

PART FOUR

THE LAST MILE

EPILOGUE

The rotunda of the former Government House still showed evidence of the fury of its capture: the walls pitted with bullet holes, the marble floors splashed with dark stains that would take quite a while to scrub out.

Right now it echoed with murmured voices and the rustling of footsteps as preparations for the triumph were rushed to completion. Jammer was helping Tristan into a splendid and ridiculous red tunic with huge gold epaulettes that he had designed himself and kept an army of seamstresses up all night cobbling together.

"Ouch," Tristan said. "Do I have to put this damned thing on? I feel like an idiot. What's wrong with a black leather jacket?"

"Any biker trash can put on a leather jacket. You gonna be a conqueror, boy, by Brother Wind you gonna *look* like a conqueror."

Tristan puffed his chest out and posed for a full-length mirror Pony held up for him. Then he laughed. Then he grimaced.

"I guess every circus needs a clown," he said, "and we're the biggest circus on wheels. Jesus, that hurts."

"When I make up the songs about this day," Jammer said, "I'll be sure to leave out how the Maximum Lord of the Plains and the City was held together mostly by tape and bandages when he made his victory march through Homeland. *And* how he bellowed like a City-cattle calf at the branding when we stuck his hip back in its socket."

He finished a last-minute adjustment to Tristan's amazing coat and straightened. "Damn fool thing, to go jumping out a third-story window, boy."

"Would you've preferred it if I took the stairs and got blown to pieces?"

"Naw. Songs go over better if they got a happy ending."

"Not always, old friend."

Jammer clapped him on the arm and grinned. "*This* time, old friend."

Tristan walked over to where Jovanne and Jamie stood watching. Jovanne wore her usual black T and slinky jeans, and Jamie was in her elf suit.

Jovanne turned her face away when Tristan approached, and eluded him when he reached to embrace her.

"What's wrong, babe?" he asked in a soft voice.

She shook her head. "Nothing."

"Remember, we still got Brace Webbert's boys out on the Plains to deal with. Though they're going to have a hell of a time breaking back *into* the City now that we've got a hold of it."

"I'll stand behind you, Tristan," she said in a stiff voice. "Whatever happens."

He stood blinking after her, then turned to his boyhood friend. To his surprise her piquant face was wet with tears.

"You too?" he asked. "This is supposed to be a happy occasion."

She shook her head. "You just don't get it, do you?"

His eyes answered her. She threw her arms around his neck, hugged him fiercely, and ran out into the overcast morning.

He stood a moment looking after the two women. Then he shook his head.

"Is the Lady Elinor ready?" he asked a nearby rider in Burningskull colors.

The woman nodded her head. Her mohawk was a little extreme even by the standards of the High Free Folk, but Tristan thought he could get used to it. Some of the Merry Pranksters had decided they preferred the High Free Life—and vice versa.

"She's getting pretty damned impatient too," the former horse barbarian said, and went to get her.

A moment while Tristan stood there feeling, for no discernible reason, like a teenager on his first date. And then Elinor appeared, in a long, sheer ice-blue gown that matched her eyes and set off the diamond tiara in her hair.

She gave him a blinding smile, flowed in his arms, hugged him. "I feel as big a fool as you look," she whispered in his ear.

He laughed. "Then we're a perfectly matched set. Come, my lady."

He offered her his hand. She took it. He led her to WildFyre, parked in her glory in the center of the rotunda, and helped her sidesaddle onto the pillion seat. Then he mounted before her, and kicked the sled to life with his immaculately polished boot. Her engine echoed within the dome as if it would never stop.

He put her in gear and rolled forward through the foyer. Burningskulls held the front doors—now just frames, with the glass blown out—wide for their Lord and his lady.

The clouds broke open. A ray of sunlight lanced down, and brought WildFyre to radiant flame that proved her worthiness of her name. And so he and she and the wonderful bike rode forth, into the screaming crowd and into legend.